*A long time ago in a galaxy
far, far away . . . .*

MEDSTAR II:
JEDI HEALER
A Clone Wars Novel

Michael Reaves and Steve Perry

BALLANTINE BOOKS • NEW YORK

Star Wars: MedStar II: Jedi Healer is a work of fiction. Names, places, and incidents either are products of the authors' imagination or are used fictitiously.

A Del Rey® Book
Published by The Random House Publishing Group

www.starwars.com
www.delreydigital.com

ISBN 0-345-46311-0

Manufactured in the United States of America

First Edition: October 2004

OPM 9 8 7 6 5 4 3 2 1

For my son Alexander:
"The Force will be with you—always."—M. R.

For Dianne—S. P.

CLONE WARS
TIMELINE

With the Battle of Geonosis (EP II), the Republic is plunged into an emerging, galaxywide conflict. On one side is the Confederacy of Independent Systems (the Separatists), led by the charismatic Count Dooku who is backed by a number of powerful trade organizations and their droid armies.

On the other side is the Republic loyalists and their newly created clone army, led by the Jedi. It is a war fought on a thousand fronts, with heroism and sacrifices on both sides. Below is a partial list of some of the important events of the Clone Wars and a guide to where these events are chronicled.

MONTHS
(after *Attack of the Clones*)

0	**THE BATTLE OF GEONOSIS** *Star Wars:* Episode II *Attack of the Clones* (LFL, May '02)
0	**REPUBLIC COMMANDO** *Star Wars:* Republic Commando (LEC, Fall '04)
0	**THE SEARCH FOR COUNT DOOKU** Boba Fett #1: *The Fight to Survive* (SB, April '02)
+1	**THE DARK REAPER PROJECT** The Clone Wars (LEC, October '02)
+1	**THE BATTLE OF RAXUS PRIME** Boba Fett #2: *Crossfire* (SB, November '02)
+1.5	**CONSPIRACY ON AARGAU** Boba Fett #3: *Maze of Deception* (SB, April '03)
+2	**THE BATTLE OF KAMINO** Clone Wars I: *The Defense of Kamino* (DH, June '03)
+2	**DURGE VS. BOBA FETT** Boba Fett #4: *Hunted* (SB, October '03)
+2.5	**THE DEFENSE OF NABOO** Clone Wars II: *Victories and Sacrifices* (DH, September '03)
+3	**MISSION ON QIILURA** Republic Commando: *Hard Contact* (DR, November '04)
+6	**THE DEVARON RUSE** Clone Wars IV: *Target Jedi* (DH, May '04)

CLONE WARS
TIMELINE

MONTHS
(after *Attack of the Clones*)

+6	**THE HARUUN KAL CRISIS**	*Shatterpoint* (DR, June '03)
+6	**ASSASSINATION ON NULL**	*Legacy of the Jedi* #1 (SB, August '03)
+12	**THE BIO-DROID THREAT**	*The Cestus Deception* (DR, June '04)
+15	**THE BATTLE OF JABIIM**	Clone Wars III: *Last Stand on Jabiim* (DH, February '04)
+16	**ESCAPE FROM RATTATAK**	Clone Wars V: *The Best Blades* (DH, November '04)
+24	**THE CASUALTIES OF DRONGAR**	MedStar Duology: *Battle Surgeons* (DR, July '04) *Jedi Healer* (DR, October '04)
+29	**ATTACK ON AZURE**	*Jedi Quest Special Edition* (SB, March '05)
+30	**THE PRAESITLYN CONQUEST**	*Jedi Trial* (DR, November '04)
+30	**LURE AT DJUN**	*Yoda: Dark Rendezvous* (DR, December '04)
+31	**THE XAGOBAH CITADEL**	Boba Fett #5: *A New Threat* (SB, April '04) Boba Fett #6: *Pursuit* (SB, December '04)
+33	**THE HUNT FOR DARTH SIDIOUS**	*Labyrinth of Evil* (DR, February '05)
+36	**ANAKIN TURNS TO THE DARK SIDE**	*Star Wars:* Episode III (LFL, May '05)

KEY:

DH = *Dark Horse Comics, graphic novels*
www.darkhorse.com
DR = *Del Rey, hardcover & paperback books*
www.delreydigital.com
LEC = *LucasArts Games, games for XBox, GameCube, PS2, & PC platforms* www.lucasarts.com
LFL = *Lucasfilm Ltd., motion pictures* www.starwars.com
SB = *Scholastic Books, juvenile fiction* www.scholastic.com/starwars

1

In the moment, there was little time for thought. No real space to let the conscious mind judge action and reaction, no time for decisions about form and flow. The mind was far too slow to defend her in this life-or-death situation. She had to trust muscle memory, had to let go of any connection to past or future concerns. She had to be totally and completely in the *now*, if she was to survive this battle.

Even these thoughts passed in the space of no more than a heartbeat.

Barriss Offee cut and slashed with her lightsaber, whirling and twirling it, her movements weaving a shield of luminous energy before her, stopping blaster bolts, arrows, swords, even a few slung rocks, without reflecting any directly back toward the attackers. That was of vital importance, and the hardest part of the battle—*don't kill any of them*. Master Kenobi had been adamant on that. Do not lop off arms or legs or heads; do not thrust through the bodies of their attackers. Not those of the Borokii, nor those of the Januul.

It was much harder to fight and disarm or wound than

to maim or kill. It was always harder to do the right thing.

Barriss fought—

Next to her, Anakin Skywalker was displaying a fair skill with his lightsaber, though his technique was still somewhat rough. He had come into training much later than had most Jedi Padawans, but he was managing quite well. She sensed through the Force that he wanted to do more, that he wanted to strike them all down, but he held himself in check. She could feel the difficulty he was having in doing so, however. And that slight smile on his face as he wove a defensive energy web before him bothered her just a bit. He seemed to be enjoying this far too much.

To her left, Master Kenobi's buzzing energy blade stitched an ozone-scented tapestry of blurred light, knocking blaster bolts into the ground, blocking incoming arrows, and shattering durasteel blades almost too fast for the eye to follow. His expression was set, grim.

Moving with that incredibly supple grace that was her hallmark, Master Unduli danced her defense, deflecting the attacks with ease. Barriss stood beside her tutor, her blue blade moving in perfect synchronization with the pale green shimmer of her Master's lightsaber. Separately, each was an opponent to be reckoned with; together, merged by and in the Force, they were a fighting unit far stronger and faster than the sum of its two parts. So thoroughly and completely did they complement each other's feints, parries, and blocks that many of the wild Ansionian plainsfolk stared in disbelief even as they pressed their attack.

When the howlpack had first advanced despite her practiced skill, Barriss had felt a surge of fear; there were so many of them, and to control without killing was much, much harder. But now, as she leapt and parried and swung her weapon, the Force guiding her every move, the initial panic was gone. With the four of them together this way, she had never felt the Force flow as strongly as it did now. She was with Anakin and Master Kenobi, nearly as completely as she was with Master Unduli. It was an unbelievably powerful, heady sensation, intoxicating, overriding, filling her with confidence: *We can do it—we can defeat* both *armies—!*

Rationally, she knew this could not be, but the conviction was a thing of the heart, not the mind. They were invincible. They batted death from the air: full-power particle beams, needle-tipped arrows, swords sharp enough to shave the Ansionians' long manes . . .

It seemed to go on for a long time—hours, at least—but when it was at last done, Barriss realized that the entire encounter had taken perhaps ten minutes or less. Dozens of shattered weapons lay at their feet, and the surprised combatants surrounded them, plainly in awe of the fighting skills of the Jedi.

As well they should be . . .

Barriss smiled at the memory of the encounter on Ansion. She had felt the Force many times, before and since, but never had it been that . . . *compelling.* Even when they had demonstrated their "spirit" for the Alwari—she with her compass dance, Anakin with his singing, Master Obi-Wan Kenobi with his storytelling, and Master Luminara Unduli with her Force-sculpture of whirling sand—she had not felt so alive as during the battle, fighting alongside her Master and the others. Fighting alone was one thing, but fighting in tandem or in a group? That was much, much more.

But that was the past, and if she had learned nothing

else from her years in the Jedi Temple, she had learned that the past could be revisited, but not relived. She was no longer on Ansion now, but on Drongar, that humid hothouse of a world, and even though her mission to find the thief who had been stealing the valuable bota crop grown here was over, she had yet to hear from her Master as to the next step in her training.

Even as she felt frustration rising again within her, her desktop comm unit warbled. She activated it, and a small holoproj image of her teacher shimmered into view in the warm air. The comm unit was small, and it seemed to have a slight malfunction; aside from the usual blinking and ghosting common when communicating across many parsecs, some element in the power amplifier seemed to be emitting a too-warm-circuit smell, so subtle that she was uncertain if she was actually sensing it or simply imagining it. It was a not-unpleasant odor that re-minded Barriss of roasted klee-klee nuts.

Master Unduli was lightyears away now, back on Cor-uscant, albeit her image was close enough to touch. The three-dimensional likeness was insubstantial, though, and it would be like trying to touch a ghost.

Barriss sighed, feeling tension loosen within her. Here on Drongar she had felt the separation from her instruc-tor keenly. Just the sight of Master Unduli, even in a flick-ering, low-res holocast, was enough to help center her. And she badly needed centering. What with the Rimsoo's recent forced relocation, some fifty-odd kilometers to the south to avoid being destroyed by Separatist battle droids, along with Zan Yant's death and the nonstop batches of incoming wounded, she felt badly in need of the calming, centering influence that her teacher always brought with her.

After a mutual greeting, Barriss said, "So, I suppose my mission here on Drongar is finished."

Master Unduli cocked her head. "And why would you suppose that?"

Barriss regarded the image, suddenly uncertain. "Well . . . I was sent here to find out who was stealing bota. The ones responsible for that, the Hutt Filba and Admiral Bleyd, are no longer doing so, being dead. The military has dispatched a new admiral to command Med-Star and the Rimsoo facilities planetside—he should be here shortly, and I expect he's been selected for his honesty, given the value of the bota crop."

"That was only part of your mission, Padawan. You are also a healer, and there are still people there in need of that, are there not?"

Barriss blinked. "Yes, Master, but—"

There was a pause as her teacher regarded her. "But you don't think that sufficient reason, do you?"

"With all due respect, I seem to be making very little difference here. It's like trying to move a beach full of sand one grain at a time. I could be replaced easily by any competent physician."

"And you think that your talents would be better utilized elsewhere." It was not a question.

"Yes, my Master. I do."

Master Unduli smiled. Even in the flickering projection Barriss could see those intensely blue eyes twinkle. "Of course you do. You are young, and your desire to be a shining force for good has blinded you somewhat to things all around you that still need attention. But I sense that you are not done there yet, my impatient Padawan. There are still lessons to be learned. Spirits require healing, too, as much or more than do bodies sometimes. I will contact you when I think it is time for you to leave Drongar."

Master Unduli's image winked out.

Barriss sat on her cot for a time. She reached for calmness of spirit and found it difficult to acquire. Her Master's purpose in keeping her here eluded her. Yes, she was a healer, and yes, she had saved a few lives, but she could do that anywhere. There seemed little on this fecund planet that would help her become a fully fledged Jedi Knight. It seemed to her that her Master should be looking for some place to properly test her, to challenge all her skills, and not just those of a healer.

But instead, Master Unduli had decided to leave her on this soggy dirtball, where battles were fought as they had seldom been fought in the last thousand years—on the ground, between armies fielded to wage war cautiously to avoid damaging the valuable bota plant that grew thicker here than anywhere in the known galaxy. Bota—a miraculous adaptogenic growth from which a variety of wondrous drugs could be made—was easily prone to damage, and even a mild concussion from an explosion too close could kill an entire field of it. Sometimes even the thunder from a nearby lightning strike—of which there were plenty, this being a young and volatile world—could damage the fragile plant. Neither the Republic nor the Confederacy wanted that, so the weapons and tactics of the war here were primitive in the extreme. Battle droids fought clone troopers mostly within hand-blaster range, in small numbers, and without much in the way of artillery or large power beams. When the plant over which both sides battled for control was worth its weight in precious gems, nobody wanted to shock it to death or set it on fire—which was all too easy to do in the high-oxygen environment, despite the swampy territory.

While it was true that both sides had on occasion fielded heavier weaponry—witness the recent Separatist attack that had required moving the entire base—for the most part the infantries fought, and bled, for each precious centimeter of ground, all because of the kid-glove approach that bota required. Not for the first time Barriss wondered how an indigenous plant that was so fragile had managed to cling to its ecological niche for so long on such a tempestuous world.

Such questions did not matter now. All that mattered was that the bota thief was dead—and yet, Master Unduli still bade her stay. Why? What was the point?

She shook off the thoughts. Clarity of mind did not come with too much thinking—quite the opposite, in fact. She needed to empty herself, to allow the Force to provide the calm and serenity it always did—when she could reach it.

Some days, it was a lot harder than others.

2

Lying on his bed, Jos Vondar glared at the young man in the lieutenant's uniform standing in the doorway to his kiosk. Hardly more than a boy, really; he looked like he was about fourteen standard years old.

"What?"

"Captain Vondar? I'm Lieutenant Kornell Divini."

"That's nice. And you're standing there in the open doorway, letting the heat into my humble home, because . . . ?"

The boy looked slightly uncomfortable. "I've been assigned here, sir."

"I don't need a houseboy," Jos said.

The boy grinned unexpectedly. "No, sir, I don't expect you do—seeing how neat and clean your kiosk is."

Jos didn't reply to that. It was true that things had gotten a little . . . disorganized of late. He glanced around the small living space. His last two changes of clothes were hanging on the back of a formplast chair, the drink chiller was dilapidated enough to make even a slythmonger think twice about imbibing, and the mold creeping up the walls was as thick as Kashyyyk wood-moss. Candidly, Joss had to admit that a marsh pig probably wouldn't live in a sty as dirty and cluttered as this place.

Of the two of them, Zan had always been neater. He

would never have let it get this out of control. Jos could almost hear the Zabrak's voice: *Look, Vondar, I've seen garbage scows more aseptic than this. What're you trying to do, max out your immune system?*

But Zan wasn't here. Zan was dead.

The boy was speaking again. Jos tuned back in: ". . . been assigned to Rimsoo Seven as a surgeon, sir."

Jos sat up on his cot and stared. Was he hearing right? This—this *child* was a doctor?

Impossible.

His disbelief must have shown, because the boy said, somewhat stiffly, "Coruscant Medical, sir. Graduated two years ago, then did a year of internship and a year of residency at Big Zoo."

That did bring a smile from Jos. Big Zoo was the unofficial name of Galactic Polysapient, the multi-sentient-species medcenter on Alderaan, at which he himself had interned. It boasted no fewer than seventy-three separate environment zones and ORs, and treatment protocols for every known carbon-based sentient species in the inhabited galaxy, as well as most of the silicon- and halogen-based forms. If it was alive and reasonably conscious, sooner or later you'd see it at Big Zoo.

Jos gave the boy a closer, more appraising look. He was human—either Corellian like Jos or some other close variant—towheaded, with cheeks that looked like they had yet to experience depil cream. "You should have had three years of residency before they drafted you," Jos said.

"Yes, sir. Apparently they were running short on doctors in the field."

The vestige of Jos's smile vanished. Zan had been dead only a week. And this boy was supposed to be his replacement? The Republic was getting desperate if it was snatching babies from their cradles this way.

Besides, nobody could replace Zan. Nobody.

"Look, Lieutenant . . . Divini, was it?"

"Uli."

Jos blinked. "I beg your pardon?"

"Everyone calls me Uli, sir. I'm from Tatooine, near the Dune Sea. It's short for Uli-ah, the word for Sand People children. How I got the nickname is kind of an interesting—"

"Lieutenant Divini, far be it from me to question the wisdom of the Republic—I don't think anybody really could, since they don't *have* any wisdom to question—so, fine, welcome to the war. You check in with the unit commander yet?"

"Colonel Vaetes, yes, sir. He sent me here."

Jos sighed. "All right, I guess we'd better find you a place to stay." He rose from his cot.

Young Divini looked uncomfortable. "The colonel said I was to bunk with you, sir."

"Stop calling me sir. I'm not your father, even though I feel old enough for that these days. Call me Jos . . . Vaetes sent you to stay *here*?"

"Yes, sir. Uh, I mean, yes, Jos."

Jos felt his bottom teeth settle firmly against his upper jaw. "Stay right here."

"Okay."

Vaetes was waiting for him when Jos arrived at his office. Before he could say a word, the colonel said, "That's right, I sent the boy to your cube. He's been assigned here as a general surgeon and I'm not going to have the construction droids drop everything and build a new kiosk when you have an empty bed in yours." He raised a hand to forestall Jos's comments. "This isn't a debate class, Captain, it's the army. You're the chief surgeon in this unit. Show him the drill, get him set up. You don't have to like it, but you have to do it. Dismissed."

Jos stared at Vaetes. "What's the matter with you, D'Arc? Someone split your head open and drop a regular army brain in? You sound like a character in a bad holovee. Have you taken a look outside recently? We're not even totally relocated yet, only one bacta tank's on-line, and we lost an entire case of cryogen during the move. Meanwhile, nobody told the enemy we're having problems, so they just keep shooting our guys and we have to keep patching them up somehow. I *don't* have the time to wet-nurse some rimkin kid!"

Vaetes looked at him mildly, as if they'd been discussing the weather. "Feel better now? Good. The exit's behind you. Just turn around, take a couple steps to trip the sensor. And you might want to hurry along, because—"

"I hear them," Jos said in disgust. At least two medlifters were approaching. "But we're not done with this, D'Arc."

"Hey, drop by anytime. My door's always open. Well, except when it's closed. Which you can see to on the way out."

Jos stalked out of the colonel's office into the wet and smothering Drongaran afternoon.

This is just what I need, he thought. A youngling more naive than a freshly decanted clone. The kid might think he was ready for fieldwork, but those were long odds, in Jos's opinion. True, things could get intense in any big medcenter, but he'd seen hardened veterans with years of experience in all the myriad ways that sentients could die have to bolt from a Rimsoo OT to keep from upchucking in their masks.

"Mimn'yet surgery," they called it, after a meat dish of

questionable origin popular with the bloodthirsty reptiloids of Barab I. It was a vivid metaphor, illustrating the fast and furious patchwork pace that they had to follow. Stop the bleeding, slap a synthflesh patch or spray a splint, and move on. No time for niceties like regen-stim; if someone wound up with a livid streak of shiny scar tissue across the face, it didn't really matter—as long as he or she could still shoot.

There were times when Jos was on his feet twenty hours straight, his arms coated with red, with barely any time between patients. It was primitive, it was barbaric, it was brutal.

It was war.

And this was the sterile hell into which Vaetes had just plunged a kid who didn't look old enough to legally pilot a landspeeder.

Jos shook his head. Lieutenant Kornell "Uli" Divini was in for a rude awakening, and Jos did not envy him it.

On the other hand, there was one possible positive aspect to the situation: Tolk would probably love the kid.

Thinking of her did bring a genuine smile to his lips. His relationship with the Lorrdian nurse was the one good thing that had come out of this war. The *only* good thing, as far as Jos was concerned.

Den Dhur was on a mission.

It was a mission that had little to do with the war between the Confederacy and the Republic, except in rather abstract terms. And, even though he was a freelance field correspondent, it was not something he was likely to file a story on. No, this quest was to aid a friend—someone whom he'd become acquainted with during his stay at Rimsoo Seven, and whom he'd come to consider a kindred spirit.

Those who knew the hard-bitten Sullustan of old would no doubt find it hard to believe that Den would profess friendship for any living thing. Which meant that their opinions of him could remain intact, since the being Den was undertaking this favor for wasn't a living one—not in the traditional sense, anyway.

Which made it all the more challenging.

Den was sitting with his comrade in the base cantina. He was nursing a particularly potent concoction of spice-brew, Sullustan gin, and Old Janx Spirit called a Sonic Servodriver; no one appeared to know why the drink was named that, and, after the first one or two had been imbibed, very few cared. His companion, as usual, was drinking nothing. This wasn't surprising, since he had no mouth or throat, and he'd managed to convince Den earlier that pouring alcohol into his vocabulator was probably not a good idea.

Den focused his large eyes blearily upon I-5YQ. The droid had an annoying tendency—exacerbated by the polarized droptac lenses the Sullustan wore—to separate into multiple images. Other than that, all seemed normal enough. "We *gotta* get you drunk," he told I-Five.

"And this is such an imperative because . . . ?"

" 'S'not fair," Den told him. "Ev'rybody else can get blasted outta their craniums—"

"Which they do with alarming frequency, I've noticed."

"Ev'ryone 'cept you. 'S'no good. Gotta fix that."

"Assuming for a moment that intoxication is a state to which I aspire," the droid said, "I see a number of problems that must be solved. Not the least of which is, I have no metabolism to process ethanol."

"Right, right." Den nodded. "Gotta work aroun' that. Don' worry, I'll think of somethin' . . ."

"At this point you'd be hard-pressed to think of your

own name. No offense, but I wouldn't trust you to rewire a mouse droid's circuits right now. Maybe later, when you've—"

The Sullustan suddenly fluttered his dewflaps in excitement. "Got it! 'S' *perfect*!"

"What?" The droid's tone was wary.

Den knocked back the rest of his drink, then had to hang on to the edge of the table for a moment until the entire cantina, which had suddenly and unaccountably launched itself into hyperspace, steadied. "W'do a partial power-down on your core. Scramble th' sensory inputs a li'l bit, loosen up those logic circuits."

"Sorry. Multiple redundancy backups. They're hard-wired—I could no more voluntarily interfere with them than you could stop breathing."

Den frowned at his empty mug. "Blast." He brightened. "Okay, how 'bout we realign the circuitry directly? Jus' temporarily, o'course . . ."

"That might work—if you had the picodroid engineers needed to do the realignment. Which are only available at Cybot Galactica repair centers or their authorized representatives. I believe the nearest one is approximately twelve parsecs from here."

Den belched and shrugged. "Well, we'll figure som'thin' out. Don' worry—Den Dhur's no quitter. I'm on it, buddy." His head dropped to the table with an audible *thud*, and a moment later he began to snore.

I-Five stared at the unconscious reporter, then sighed. "Something about this," the droid murmured, "feels *so* familiar."

3

Jos wouldn't have started the kid off this way, had there been any choice, but the operating theater was full of wounded clone troopers, the drone of the medlifters bringing in new injuries seemed as constant as a heat exchanger as they arrived, and anybody who could lift a vibroscalpel was needed. *Now.*

He didn't have time to watch the kid—he was up to his elbows in the chest cavity of a clone full of shrapnel. Count Dooku's weapons research group had come up with a new fragmentation bomb, called a weed-cutter—a smart bomb that, when launched, arced up and over any and all defensive grids, came down in the middle of a trooper force, and exploded at thoracic level above the ground, sleeting tiny, smart, razor-sharp durasteel flechettes in a circular pattern. The weed-cutter was deadly for two hundred meters against soft targets, and the clone trooper armor didn't stop much, if any, of it.

Whoever had designed and produced the clone armor had much to answer for, in Jos's opinion. The Kaminoans might be geniuses when it came to designing and sculpting soft tissue, but the armor was, as far as he could see, practically useless. The nonclone field troops referred to the full-body suits as "body buckets." It was an aptly descriptive term.

He started to ask for the pressor field to be stepped up a notch, but Tolk beat him to it: "Plus six on the field," she said to the 2-1B droid managing the unit.

Tolk le Trene was a Lorrdian; her kind had an uncanny ability to read most species' microexpressions and to somehow sense emotions, to the extent that it almost seemed like telepathy. She was also the best surgical nurse in the Rimsoo. And more, she was beautiful, compassionate, and Jos's sweetheart, despite her being ekster—non-*permes,* an outsider, not of his homeworld clan—which meant there wasn't supposed to be any future for their relationship. The Vandars were enster, and that meant marriage had to be with someone from one's own system, preferably one's homeworld. There were no exceptions.

Temporary alliances with eksters were allowed, with a wink and a nod about sowing-one's-wild-grains and all, but you didn't bring a non-*permes* girlfriend home to meet your kinfolk, not unless you were willing to give up your clan and be permanently ostracized. Not to mention the infamy such an act would offer your family: *He married an* ekster! *Can you imagine? His parents keeled over dead from shame!*

Jos glanced at Uli, and then at Tolk, who said, "Uli seems to be doing okay. The orderly droids just wheeled his first patient out and they weren't heading toward the morgue. He's a cute kid."

Jos shook his head. "Yeah. Cute."

He risked a quick look around. They were still two doctors and three FX-7 surgical droids short of a full unit, and that was going to cost them today—

Even as he thought his, he saw a masked-and-gowned figure step up to one of the empty tables. The sterile field kicked on, and the figure gave a *bring-'em* gesture to the orderly droids.

"I don't know who that is," Tolk said as Jos was about to ask.

After months of work in this tropical pesthole, the OT doctors could recognize each other even when faces and heads were covered with surgical masks and caps. Which meant this was a new player. And that raised the question: why hadn't anybody told him, Captain Vondar, the chief surgeon, that they had a new guy?

A fresh bleeder opened up, sprayed blood in a fan, and Jos suddenly had other things to worry about.

Nine patients later, Jos caught an easy one, a simple lacerated lung he was able to glue-stat shut in a few minutes. Tolk began to close, and Jos looked around. They didn't have a new patient prepped. Things had slowed down, finally. He looked at the triage droid—it was I-Five today—and the droid held up that many digits, indicating the number of minutes before they would have another one ready.

Jos stripped off his sterile thinskin gloves and slipped on a fresh pair, thankful for the moment's breather.

"I could use a hand over here," the new surgeon said, "if you don't have anything pressing."

The voice was deep, and it sounded older than he'd usually heard in this operating theater, where most of the surgeons and doctors were the age equivalent of humans twenty to twenty-five standard years. Jos moved over three tables, squeezing past Leemoth, who was working on a Quaran Aqualish who had deserted from the Separatists. He looked at the procedure the new surgeon had in progress on a clone trooper.

"Heart–lung transplant?" he asked.

"Yep. Took a sonic pulse, blew out myocardium and alveoli all over the place."

Jos looked at the new organs, fresh from the clone banks. The dissolving staples holding the arteries and veins together were X-style—he hadn't seen those since medical school. This guy *was* older—they must be scraping the bottom of the recycler for doctors now. *First a kid, now somebody's grandfather*, he thought. *Who's next—med students*?

"You want to do those nerve anastomoses distally there?"

"Sure." Jos regloved, took the adapto-pressor suturing tool offered by the nurse, and began the microsutures.

"Thanks. *Ohleyz Sumteh Kersos Vingdah,* Doctor."

If the man had slapped him across the face, Jos wouldn't have been more surprised. That was a clan-greeting! This man was from Corellia, his homeworld, and more, he was claiming *kinship* on his mother's side. Amazing!

"Lose your manners, son?"

"Uh, sorry. *Sumteh Vondar Ohleyz,*" Jos said. "I'm, uh, Jos Vondar."

"I know who you are, son. I'm Erel Kersos. *Admiral* Kersos—and your new commander."

And here was another whack across the face. Erel Kersos was his mother's uncle. They had never met, but Jos knew about him, of course. He had left the homeworld as a young man, and never returned . . . because he had . . .

Jos tried not to let his shock show. This was astonishing, flat-out unbelievable. Of all the Rimsoos on all the worlds in all the galaxy, what were the chances of running into Great-Uncle Erel in this one?

"Maybe we might have a chance to talk later—if you feel that's proper," Kersos said.

"Uh, yeah. Right. I'd like that. Sir."

Amazingly, his hands did not shake as he finished the suturing. His great-uncle, clan-shunned for sixty years, here on Drongar. And running the show.

What were the odds?

Kaird of the Nediji watched the Jedi healer working on the wounded trooper. The cloned soldier had just come from the OT into postop, and the marks of the laser suturing stood out against his bronze skin. The healer was performing a laying on of hands; no doubt something to do with the Force. Kaird knew little about such things, and cared less. He had no doubt that the Force was real, but since Jedi did not normally concern him, neither did their mysterious power source. As an agent of Black Sun, his primary focus was on more practical matters.

Still, it was interesting to observe her work. And he was in a position to observe it quite well, since he was standing near enough to touch her in the postop chamber. Hidden, as it were, in plain sight.

Normally, Kaird would stick out in just about any crowd of sapients, for those of his species were not well known in the galaxy; Nedij was one of the more outlying worlds, and quite insular. Only those who had forsworn the fellowship of the Nest tended to wander the spaceways. His sharp face, stubby beak, violet eyes, and skin covered with pale azure down would definitely draw stares, were he dressed in his usual garb. But now he was effectively invisible, having chosen for this assignment a perfect disguise for a medical facility.

The siblinghood known as The Silent were ubiquitous

throughout the galaxy. They never spoke, they usually kept their features and bodies hidden inside flowing, cowled robes, and for the most part they did nothing except stand and *be*. They believed that their meditative presence in the vicinity of illness or injury somehow aided in the recovery of afflicted patients. And the amazing thing about it—the thing that reputable scientists and doctors were at a loss to explain—was that The Silent were right. Statistical studies showed without question that sick and wounded people recovered faster and more often when the shrouded figures were around than when they were not. Apparently it had nothing to do with the Force, either; the order's adherents came from all species and social strata, and exhibited none of the biological markers that sometimes indicated an affinity with the mystical energy field. Nor could the phenomenon be totally attributed to the placebo effect, because patients who had never heard of the order benefited just as much. It was a truly inexplicable marvel.

Kaird didn't know how such a thing could be, and didn't particularly care, although he did sometimes wonder if his presence was having the same palliative effect, since the thoughts usually passing through his mind were about as far from the serenity of a Silent as Drongar was from the Galactic Core. No matter. He was pretending to be one of the siblinghood because it let him become part of the background in a way no other role in this Republic Mobile Surgical Unit—"Rimsoo"—could. He had earlier ingested an herbal concoction brought from his homeworld, which effectively masked his distinctive scent from most species' senses. Together with the shrouded robes, his anonymity was thus assured—quite necessary for an agent of Black Sun, whose business here had nothing to do with either the war or the treatment of those injured in it.

Kaird was here because of the bota, pure and simple. The rare plant would be a heavyweight addition to any physician's armamentarium; it could be an antibiotic, a narcotic, a soporific—all manner of things, in fact, depending on the species using it. It was a more effective curative than cambylictus leaves or bacta fluid for the Abyssin, a more potent psychotropic than Santherian tenho-root if you were a Falleen, and an anabolic steroid that could help Whiphids attain their personal bests. Black Sun could make a fortune moving as much bota as they could get their hands on—it was a product with true universal appeal.

Ironically, use of the wonder plant here in the Rimsoos on Drongar had been interdicted. The official word claimed it was in order to discourage black marketeering, but it was generally felt that the real reason was economics—the farther one traveled from Drongar, the more valuable bota became. Why waste it at the source on clone troopers? After all, it wasn't like they were going to run out of them anytime soon . . .

A number of the physicians here were petitioning to get the interdiction reversed. And a few, Kaird had heard, simply ignored the law and found ways to treat their patients with it anyway. As an individual and a warrior, Kaird applauded their courage and dedication. As a member of Black Sun, however, he might have to do something about it if and when the ordinance was changed.

Up until recently, the crime cartel had been able to obtain fair amounts of carbonite-encased bota, which could be smuggled without detection or damage, from a pair of black marketeers in the local Republic forces. Alas, both of these suppliers were no longer among the living—one appeared to have deleted the other, and Kaird himself had killed the survivor. Thus, Black Sun needed another local contact, and until he developed one, the vigos had decreed that he would remain here.

Black Sun did have a contact onplanet—in this very Rimsoo, in fact—but unfortunately, it couldn't utilize this op, who was a double agent, working also for Count Dooku's breakaway factions. The spy would not risk discovery by becoming active as a procurer, and Kaird could understand that. Furthermore, Lens's current task of leaking information about both sides to the criminal organization was far too valuable to them.

He shifted uncomfortably, feeling the robes sticking to his skin. The air coolers on the base operated only sporadically, and the osmotic fields kept some, but not all, of the heat and humidity at bay. Drongar's pestilential environment was completely unlike the clean, thin air in which the avian Nediji had evolved. Their wings were long gone, their soft, feathery hair but a pale shadow of the plumage sported by their distant ancestors, but the Nediji still preferred the cool heights, the crags of mountains drifted deep with snow, to the lowlands.

Ah, if he could but be there now . . .

Kaird smiled to himself, his expression hidden inside the cowl. Might as well wish for a crèche of females and a hillside full of rath-scurriers, the Nediji's traditional prey, while he was at it. And maybe a little vintage thwill-wine to complement the hedonistic fantasy.

The smile became a frown as he watched Padawan Offee moving the palms of her hands slowly over the clone's bare chest. He wondered if this Jedi might be potential trouble. Her presence on this world struck him as very odd. To be sure, she was a healer, but the Jedi were spread very thin these days. It seemed a waste to send one here, even if that one was a Padawan still not fully fledged. As a Black Sun operative, Kaird suspected everybody and everything he could not immediately explain. There were old ops and there were careless ops in his position, but no old and careless ops. One stayed alive by constant vigilance, by always being one swoop ahead of a potential enemy.

This woman wasn't a danger to him directly, even though her connection to the Force granted her considerable mind-probing abilities. His thoughtshield techniques were far above average, however—his training had been the finest his vigo could afford. A mere Padawan, even a healer, would sense nothing about him that he did not allow to be sensed. Still, it was worrisome. Whomever he wound up installing as the supply agent would need to be able to avoid giving her- or himself away with an errant thought or feeling. It would not do to have the Jedi woman nose out the new agent—then Black Sun would have to start all over again, and that would be . . . troublesome.

Perhaps he should kill her. He allowed it some thought. It would be easy enough, and the immediate worry would be assuaged. Perhaps . . . ?

No. Few things were certain in this galaxy, but one of them was: kill a Jedi somewhere, anywhere, and other Jedi *always* came to investigate. He could take out this Padawan easily, but the next one might be a Jedi Knight or even a Master, and thus more trouble to deal with. Better the *d'javl* you knew than the *d'javl* you didn't, as the old saying went.

The Padawan finished her healing ritual. The trooper's eyelids flickered. Through the cowl's mesh, Kaird could see the man's chest rising and falling regularly and gently, and his eyes moving beneath their lids in healing, dream-filled sleep. Whatever she had done, it had been effective.

As she passed him, she nodded—a gesture of respect and gratitude from one healer to another. Kaird nodded back, keeping his thoughts blank until he judged that she had left the building. Then he smiled.

For now, he decided, it made the most sense for him to concentrate his energy on finding and developing a new partner for Black Sun. Then, once the flow of bota began anew, he could deal with whatever other problems might arise. Black Sun was, after all, nothing if not adaptable.

4

Being a spy in an enemy encampment was not easy. There was nothing particularly original or surprising in this observation—the truth seldom has those attributes. But that didn't make it any less difficult. To work undercover in an enemy military base, one had to have more eyes than a Gran and be as vigilant as a male H'nemthe. One had to be ever mindful of the fact that a spy was an outsider, an interloper; one could never relax one's guard, even for a second.

Not that anyone had reason to suspect the spy—less so, now that the Hutt and the former admiral had been shown to be something other than they had appeared; not to mention both of them dying. But this was war, and spies were summarily executed when caught. And they *were* caught—many of them—in places far less likely than a Rimsoo on some lonely planet way out on the tail end of the galaxy.

Complicating matters further was the fact that there had been deaths. Deaths for which the spy, who served two masters under two aliases—Column to Count Dooku's Separatist forces and Lens to Black Sun—had been at least partly responsible. Did it matter to the dead that the one known as Column or Lens was responsible? No. Did it matter to one of the two sub rosa personas if the other was found out and executed? That was worth a rueful smile.

Column—the first sobriquet was the one with which the spy tended to identify, having been recruited by the Separatists before Black Sun—liked many of these people. The recent death of one of the doctors had been surprisingly painful, though it was not the result of an undercover operation. Column had thought often about the perils of living submerged amid the enemy. Even if one dwelled among a tribe of murderers, one could develop certain attachments to some of them. And none of the doctors and nurses and staff here were killers—they were healers, all, and if an enemy fell and was brought before them, they tended to the wounded with the same skill and dedication as one of their own. It was their duty to save lives, not to judge them.

That made it hard, too, when, as either Column or Lens, the spy had to offer them harm, as had sometimes become necessary. It was true that the long-anticipated end would come from righteous justification—still painful after decades—but sometimes the goal seemed impossibly far off, hidden in a fog as thick as the vapors that wafted from the endless swamps, and the little details of day-to-day life—as well as friendships, concerns, alliances—tended to get in the way.

Column sighed. One could not build wooden houses without chopping down trees, but that didn't make it any more pleasant when a giant bluewood fell on those who considered one a friend and colleague. Yet there was no avoiding it—as painful as it was sometimes, it was duty, and it had to be done. There was no help for that part of it. None.

Column stood before the window of the cubicle, looking out at the base. Rimsoo Seven had been mostly rebuilt by now; the move from the lowlands to the highlands had been accomplished with relatively few problems. The admin center, supply buildings, and, most importantly, the medical and surgical structures had been put up by the construction droids in less than two of the local day cycles, a Drongarian day being just over twenty-three standard hours. The cantina and the chow hall had been completed before nightfall of the third day. On the surface, at least, things seemed to be back to normal.

But not without cost.

The move, made under heavy Separatist fire, had incurred the loss of three patients—all from trauma associated with relocation—the wounding of fifteen, and the death of one doctor: Zan Yant.

A great pity, that. Yant had been not only an excellent doctor, but also a superlative musician, at times holding the entire base spellbound through the magic of his quetarra. He could make that instrument sing, truly; melodies so hauntingly beautiful that they seemed capable of calling dying troopers back from the threshold of eternity.

But there were no compositions, no fugues, no rhapsodies, that could call Zan Yant back.

Column turned away from the window, toward the desk that took up most of one wall. The Separatists were waiting to hear the latest, and it was necessary to work up one of the complex coded messages and send it to Dooku's forces. The process was unwieldy and complicated: once the cumbersome code had been used to encrypt the message, the security protocol required transmitting it via sublight waves through a hyperspace wormhole connection rather than the usual subspatial carrier pulse. A complex and boring exercise, all in all, but necessary—failure to decode such messages in a timely matter might be fatal. The warning of the attack that had killed Dr. Yant had been carried in just such a message, and, had Column decoded it quicker, Yant's life might have been prolonged for a short while longer. That was a lesson to remember. However laborious and time-consuming the process might be, Column needed Dooku's resources and help to defeat the Republic, and some things had to be suffered for that.

Best get to it, then. It wasn't going to get any easier . . .

Den had to hand it to Klo Merit—the Equani therapist had not so much as twitched a whisker in surprise when the reporter had shown up in place of Jos Vondar. In fact, of the two, the counselor was probably much more comfortable with the situation than was Den, this being the first time he had ever so much as set foot inside a minder's office.

It had been a last-minute decision, he told Merit nervously. He didn't feel that he needed to unburden his troubles, not on the Equani's broad shoulders or on anyone else's—at least, not until a few high-octane Bantha Blasters had loosened his frontal lobes enough to set him talking. Den was firmly of the opinion that pubtenders made the best therapists, and he told Merit so.

Merit nodded and said, "Sometimes they do. Believe it or not, some of my best sessions—impromptu, but memorable nonetheless—have taken place in similar circumstances. And, by the way, I usually frown on patient substitutions, particularly last-minute ones. But I'm letting that slide this time." He leaned forward. "So—what brings Den Dhur to my inner sanctum?"

Den chewed his bulbous lower lip. Blast, but this was a lot harder than it had looked to be. He'd never thought he'd be this uncomfortable just talking . . .

"Jos said I should take his time," he said finally. "He's up to his hairline in wounded troops currently."

Merit made no response to this at first. Then he leaned back and said, "And . . . ?"

Den could already tell this was going to be no fun at all. "Uh, well . . . he said I needed it more than him."

Merit looked slightly surprised. "Did he? Well, it being against the tenets of my profession to reveal anything about a patient's private sessions, I'll just say that that's a surprising statement, coming from Doctor Vondar."

"I know," Den said, relieved at being able to discuss Jos's woes instead of his own, if only for a moment. "Doctor Yant's death really hit him hard. I mean, he deals with death all the time in the OT, but this is different—Zan was his friend. And it was pointless. So pointless . . . but what death in a war isn't?"

Merit nodded. Den realized he was feeling much more relaxed already—maybe it had something to do with the Equani's empathic abilities. Whatever it was, it made the minder very easy to talk to. On the whole, however, Den still preferred alcohol.

"And how did his death hit you?" Merit asked.

"Hard," Den admitted, "but not as hard as it hit Jos. I don't think it hit anyone as hard as it hit Jos. I mean, I really didn't know Zan all that well . . . he'd show up for the sabacc games, and he played a mean quetarra, but . . ."

Merit leaned back in his chair. "But it's not his death you want to talk about, is it?"

Den stared at the minder in surprise. "Oh, you're good," he said. "You're *very* good."

"That's why I make the big credits."

Den squirmed in the formchair, despite how comfortable it was. "Well, it's just that—recently I came across some more intel about the men that Phow Ji killed—you remember, he died in his one-man assault."

Merit didn't move, but something about him warmly invited the reporter to continue. "The twirl pundits managed to sell him as a hero—no one wanted to touch *my* story with a ten-meter force pike. Ji was a killer, cold as vacuum, when he was alive. Now he's a milking hero.

"Thing is, he just might really be one."

"How do you mean?"

Den fluttered his dewflaps. "He took out a whole contingent of Salissian mercs and a super battle droid. Never seen anything like it. Padawan Offee said he just went berserk—killing mindlessly. But he knew he was going to do it—he had himself holoed, and sent the 'cron to me.

"And, according to my source, he didn't pick those mercs at random. They were an elite combat team on a training mission, sent here because of the extreme conditions. Supposedly, they were a strike force being prepared for a major covert attack."

"So you're led to what you feel is an inescapable conclusion: that Phow Ji, instead of just indulging in an orgy of mindless murder, gave his life in a heroic action that may have had large-scale benefits for the Republic."

"I'm not entirely dismissing the mindless-murder-orgy element," Den said. "But basically—yeah." He paused. "When I heard this, I was stunned. *Stunned*. I felt like Ji himself had kicked me in the gut. I thought I had his number: he was crazy as a dyslexic Givin, and he couldn't stand being humiliated—so he thought—by a Jedi Padawan. He defeated a Jedi Knight in a match once, you know. So he heads for the front lines and goes out in a blaze of glory. Simple."

"Indeed. And it lets you feel a satisfying righteous outrage when he's painted as a champion."

Den sighed. "I'm nearly twenty standard years a reporter, Doc, and if *anyone* knows the galaxy isn't black and white, it's me. But now I feel like some wet-between-the-dewflaps cublet who's just learned his system's Senator takes graft. I feel . . . betrayed." He snorted, shook his head, and looked at Merit. "Why?"

"I have a theory. So do you. Let's hear yours first."

Den looked skeptical. "Why not yours first?"

"It's my office."

Merit smiled slightly, and Den couldn't help grinning back. *A minder, a Jedi, and a Silent in the same camp,* he thought. *No wonder the psychic energy around here's thicker than swamp gas.*

He pursed his lips, then shrugged. "Padawan Offee told me I had the 'aura' of a hero," he said.

"You certainly proved that when you rescued Zan's quetarra for him."

"Lotta good it did him. Nobody to play it at his funeral. Look, I don't want to be a hero, Doc. Heroes may get medals, but mostly they get dead, in my experience."

"No one's insisting you be a hero, Den."

"Good, 'cause they'll be disappointed. But I don't want some rabid nexu idolized as one, either. I just want people to know the truth."

"Your truth," Merit said. "*Your* version of events. And you want them to do more than know—you want them to *believe*."

Den frowned at him. "You sound disapproving."

"I neither approve nor disapprove. This is just the view from here. But," Merit added, "in all modesty, it's a view that's backed by considerable expertise in reading people."

Den was suddenly feeling very uncomfortable. He didn't want to hear Merit's theory; he wasn't interested in spacing down the lane the minder was going. He stood and turned toward the door. "Look, I gotta go. It's nearly dark and I haven't had one drink yet. Don't want to fall behind."

"You can hide from this behind a mug for a while, Den," Klo Merit said. "If you do, two things can happen. One: the mug will have to get bigger and bigger, to keep shielding you from whatever it is you don't want to look at. Eventually, you'll fall in."

"And the other thing?"

Merit shrugged. "You look. And you deal with what you see."

"Terrific," Den said. He activated the portal and stepped out into the glare of the setting sun. "You'd make a lousy pubtender, Doc."

5

Drongar's tropical twilight had begun when Jos finally left the OT. He saw Uli sitting on a bench under a broadleaf tree. The kid had dumped his gown into the recycler and was wearing a Republic army one-piece that looked too large for him. A small cloud of fire gnats buzzed about him, but he was evidently too tired to even wave them away.

Jos ambled over. He pulled a chunk of spicetack from a pocket and held it out. "Here. You look like you could use this."

The kid hesitated. "Go ahead," Jos told him. "It's safe enough. A mild rejuvenant. You'll still feel like you've been dragged through a thorn-needle bush—just not backward."

Uli took the spicetack and wadded it into his mouth. "Are you kidding?" he asked around his chewing. "I lived on this stuff during my residency. Like everyone else I knew."

Jos sat down. "Yep. I remember it well," he said with a sigh. "Stimcaf and spicetack—the diet of champions." He nodded toward the OT. "You handled yourself pretty well in there. Better than I thought you would, frankly."

Uli rubbed his eyes. Jos noticed that his hands were

trembling slightly. "Is it *always* like this? And please don't say, *No, usually it's worse.*"

"Okay. But it is."

The youth glanced at him with eyes far too old for so young a face. "The first one I worked on had been hit by an agonizer."

Jos nodded grimly. The agonizer was new, an experimental hand weapon that targeted the limbic system with a high-collimation microsonic beam that somehow stimulated runaway prostaglandin formation. The result was intense pain without any physical trauma. It couldn't be blocked by somaprin or other heavy soporifics, and it was often so intense that the patient died from sensory overload. The only way to override it was to sever the nociceptor synapses in the thalamic cortex. This required a delicate neurolaser procedure—just the sort of operation ill suited for quick-and-dirty mimn'yet surgery.

"I think I did pretty well, all things considered," Uli said, his voice hollow. "Stopped the pain. Of course, he'll have severe dyskinesia and motor ataxia for the rest of his life . . ."

Jos grimaced in sympathy. Neither spoke for a moment. Then Uli said, "I heard about what happened to Doctor Yant. I'm sorry, Jos. I can see how you wouldn't want a new kiosk mate just now."

Jos said, "Sometimes I feel like finding whoever started this rankweed war and performing a pneumonectomy with my bare hands."

"Really."

"For starters, yeah."

Uli chuckled. He glanced at Jos, and Jos, after a moment, grinned. Then, suddenly, they were both laughing, hard gusts and whoops that were not about mirth so much as about anger, loss, frustration . . .

After a minute they subsided—although neither was really laughing anymore.

"I know how you feel," Uli said, wiping his eyes. "I lost a good friend, nearly two years ago, in Mos Espa on Tatooine. There was some battle going on between a couple of bounty hunters and she was too close to it." He hesitated. "It never goes away, does it?"

"No," Jos said. "No, it doesn't. But it does get easier to bear."

"I can't do anything about it," Uli said.

"That's right. And you need to understand that you can't. Blaming yourself because you couldn't save your friend, or stop this war, is a waste of effort and energy. It isn't your fault, Uli. None of it is your fault."

Jos stopped, realizing that he was speaking more to himself than to the boy. He shook his head again. Easy to say that. Harder to believe.

But maybe, just maybe, easier with time.

Kaird was again uncomfortable. The robes disguising him as a Silent had been bad enough in this weather, but this new masquerade was worse, since he was now wearing a flex-mask as well. Such precautions were necessary, however. One of the reasons he was successful as a Black Sun operative, despite being someone who tended to stand out in a crowd, was his skill at camouflage. He had hidden his distinctive features and form behind a number of different identities in his years of service, all to good degrees of success. He had even worn a "Hutt suit" once, a plastoid frame with synthflesh skin and face. By the Egg, *that* had been a chore. Compared to that, this Kubaz flex-mask and robes weren't all that bad.

His choice of species to impersonate was somewhat limited, due to the shape of his own features. The truncated trunk of a Kubaz nose hid his own beaklike mouth very well, however, and the goggles that the bug-eaters wore in bright sunlight covered his violet eyes. No one glanced twice at him at the spaceport; Kubaz were ubiquitous throughout the galaxy.

Kaird was waiting for the latest transport to land. Along with the supplies and matériel it was delivering, it was also bringing a team who had been highly recommended to him. One was an Umbaran, the other a Falleen. According to Lens they were not cheap antenna-breakers, but possessed subtlety and skill. They were opportunists, con artists who made their way along the space lanes from world to world by virtue of various scams. Like most grifters, Lens had said, they had had periods of solvency, even wealth, and periods of desperation. The latter was their current lot in life.

Which meant that they might be useful to Kaird.

The transport lowered on repulsor beams down through the crimson and copper spore clouds, was admitted through the force-dome's interrupt, then settled on its pad. Droids and binary loadlifters began unloading the cargo. Kaird watched the disembarkation ramp. There were only a few passengers on this trip: a Kaminoan there for some sort of biological inspection, and a trio of human officers to discuss the bota plant shipment quotas with Colonel Vaetes. Some droids, and his two potential employees, rounded out the list.

His two prospects were the last to debark, followed by an RC-101 "redcap" droid carrying their luggage. Neither seemed disturbed by the hot, soupy air, even though the spores were particularly bad today. Kaird appraised the prospects. They appeared as different as it was possible for two carbon-based humanoids to be, so dissimilar as to be almost ludicrous. The Umbaran was short, perhaps one and a quarter meters, bald and pallid. The Falleen, on the other hand, was more than a head taller and wore her hair gathered in a topknot. She walked proudly, like a warrior. She carried no weapons, but from the fluid play of her muscles under the tight synthcloth one-piece, Kaird judged that she would be dangerous even unarmed.

In contrast, the Umbaran looked like a strong wind would send him sailing away over the poptrees, particularly with that voluminous cloak enveloping him from neck to feet. Kaird had done his research on both species, and knew that the garment was called a shadowcloak. To most humanoid species it appeared as chalk-white as the Umbaran's skin, but not to other Umbarans, since their vision range was primarily in the ultraviolet wavelength, below three hundred nanometers.

Nor did it appear that way to Kaird. The winged raptors that were his ancestors had had access to a visual palette wider than the narrow slit of radiation available to most eyes. Though hundreds of thousands of generations removed, the Nediji eye could still see deep into both ends of the visible spectrum. To him the cloak was a churning riot of colors for which few languages beside his own had names: berl, crynor, nusp, onsible . . .

It really was beautiful. As the Umbaran walked, the cloak's designs seemed to eddy and swirl into ever-new shades and hues, a constant, kaleidoscopic play of light and shadow. A magnificent garment, Kaird thought. He had seen rulers of worlds who were content to wear far less.

He stepped forward and greeted them, the vocoder chip in the mask imitating a harsh Kubindi accent. "Hunandin of Apiida Clan, at your service. I have been di-

rected by our mutual friend to welcome you to Drongar."
The "mutual friend" was, of course, the spy, Lens. "How
may I be of use to you?"

The two regarded him. Kaird felt a definite tug of
something—yearning? charisma?—toward the Falleen.
He knew the probable cause of this. The reptiloids could
give off pheromones with a broad chemosignal base that
subtly—or not so subtly—influenced many different sentients. He wondered if she was releasing the pheromones
on purpose or as a reflex action. It didn't matter—as long
as he was aware of them, his mind was disciplined
enough to cope.

Then he was shocked when the Umbaran spoke. "Fly
free, fly straight," he said, "Brother of the Air."

The Nest Blessing, spoken with the proper laryngeal
inflection! How? How did they know? His disguise was
good enough to fool everyone in the camp, even other
Kubaz. There was no way—

Wait. He recalled now another fact about Umbarans:
they were reported to have paramental abilities, to be
able to see and even influence others' thoughts. *Wonderful. Yet another mindplayer in Rimsoo Seven. A miracle
all our heads don't explode.*

Evidently he wasn't the only one who had done research. Few non-Nediji knew any of the language of The
Flock. Lens did, and now these two . . .

He said in a low voice, glancing about to make sure no
one was within earshot: "I congratulate you on your per-
spicacity, but let me assure you it is to our mutual benefit
to maintain the illusion of—"

"Of course," the Falleen said. The Umbaran's voice
had been little more than a husky whisper; in contrast,
hers was rich and full of life. "Your secret identity is safe
with us, *Hunandin.*" There was a slight twist of sarcasm

when she spoke the name. "And excuse our poor manners; we have yet to introduce ourselves." She drew herself up, and Kaird realized that she was slightly taller than he was. "My name is Thula." She gestured to the Umbaran. "This is my associate, Squa Tront."

"Delighted," the Umbaran whispered dryly. "Might there be some place on this forsaken world where one can get a drink?"

Inside his mask, Kaird smiled. "Certainly. Come with me; we have much to talk about."

6

Perhaps half a dozen meters behind Barriss's kiosk was a small clearing bounded on three sides by thick and verdant waxy-leaved croaker bushes—so called because of the odd sound the leaves made when rustling in a breeze. The thick plants were half again her height, and it was here Barriss came to practice various fighting techniques with her lightsaber. Such training wasn't something Jedi ordinarily did in public, but this place was as private as she could find. The only way somebody would see her was if they happened to pass by the open end of the little clearing. Since the local swamp started a dozen meters past that, it was unlikely anyone would be walking around in the ooze for their health.

The heat lay upon the small open space like a sodden blanket. Under it, and under the loose brown robes she wore, she sweated, the perspiration soaking hair and skin, hardly evaporating at all in the high humidity. Unpleasant, but a fact of life on Drongar. She'd gotten used to carrying a hydropak with her at all times; to do otherwise was to risk dehydration.

As she had done countless times before, Barriss ran through the basic arm- and shoulder-limbering exercises, cutting and slashing the fetid tropical air in simple two- and three-combination moves, switching her weapon from hand to hand. The martial movements she danced were primarily those of Form III, one of the seven fighting systems that the Jedi had developed over the ages. Master Unduli favored Form III over the others, even though it was disparaged by some as primarily a defensive discipline. It was true that it had been developed originally as a response to blasterfire and other projectile weapons, but over the centuries it had developed into much more. "Of all the seven forms," her Master had told her, "Form Three, with its emphasis on anticipating and blocking lightspeed energy blasts, requires the greatest connection to the Force. The road is long, but it is worth the journey, for a true master of Form Three is invincible."

The lightsaber's power hum was a comforting drone, the hard-edged energy beam as familiar to her as her own arm. She could not remember a time when she had not wielded a lightsaber. As a child, there had been the low-powered practice models, with which she and other young Padawans had dueled. They were strong enough to deliver a powerful jolt; when one of them stung you, you knew it.

Pain was a most tasking instructor.

When she turned sixteen she had built her own fully powered unit, choosing a blue crystal as her beam's signature hue. It had been hooked to her belt ever since—she knew every part of it as well as she knew her own fingers. As part of her training, she had taken it apart and reassembled it using only the Force. It was more than a weapon—it was an extension of her body, an almost organic part of her . . .

She smiled as she stepped forward, spinning the lightsaber rapidly before her, creating what seemed a solid shield of light. *Thinking too much again. Concentrate on the moment.*

At that instant, there came a blast of cold air, as if someone had opened a freezer door just behind her, shocking in its intensity. It was gone almost before she knew what it was, but the combination of her drifting thoughts and the frigid breeze startled her. She knew immediately that the lightsaber, now moving across her lower body and headed up and around, was—too low.

She heard rather than felt the tip of the pulsing blade slice through the top of her boot. The boot was spun-plast orthotic, pliable yet extremely tough. When she'd bought the boots, they'd come with a guarantee—wear them out and the manufacturer would replace them, free, for as long as the original owner lived. Spun-plast would turn the edge of a sharp durasteel blade, or even a vibroknife.

There were few material objects proof against a lightsaber, however, and tough as it was, spun-plast wasn't among those.

Barriss quickly extinguished the lightsaber. She looked down and saw blood welling in the surgically neat slice across the top of her boot.

She was astonished—not by the wound, but by the error that had resulted in the accident. How many times had she done this form? Five thousand? Ten? This was a beginner's mistake, a blunder that would be inexcusable in a Padawan child nowhere near her skill level.

Had she imagined it? It was tempting to think so, but when the moving air had rustled the croaker bushes, she had distinctly heard their unmistakable, mournful sound. The breeze had been real.

She hung the lightsaber on her belt, lifted her foot, and pulled the boot off, balancing easily on the other foot.

The cut was narrow and not too deep, maybe three centimeters long, and a couple of centimeters above her second and third toes. The epidermal edges were burned, but the cut was still bleeding freely; evidently the spun-plast had absorbed just enough of the blade's energy to prevent complete cauterization of the wound. Barriss stood there, still balanced on one leg, staring at the injury. She shook her head.

She reached for the Force, felt it flowing through her, and concentrated on the cut. There was no danger of her bleeding to death from it, but she certainly didn't fancy hopping back to the base for treatment, leaving a trail of blood behind her.

The steady flow ebbed, then stopped. She could feel the pain beginning to throb, now; she breathed deeply, made space for it, shunted it into that space. She mentally applied the Force to the wound again. The edges seemed to draw together a bit, but then gaped again.

"Better let me take a look at that," came a voice from one side. She looked up, surprised. It was Lieutenant Divini, the new surgeon.

"I can manage it," she said.

The boy—Uli, she remembered—whose issue coverall was clotted with swamp mud to midthighs, stepped forward and peered at her foot. "Looks as if you nicked a couple of tendons. They'll need to be synostatted, plus you're going to need three or four staples and a dermaseal, at the least. Lot of nasty little microorganisms swarming around this place." He waved his hand to encompass the entire planet. "Better patched and sealed than infected and sorry, don't you think?"

He was right, of course. Barriss nodded. "And how do you propose to do this?"

He grinned. "No problem—I'm packing." He patted a small pouch on his belt. "Got my trusty kit right here." He gestured at a relatively dry spot of ground. "Be seated, m'lady."

Barriss sat, restraining a smile, and Uli squatted next to her in that relaxed, rear-on-heels position available only to those with flexible ankles. He opened the medpac, laid the sterile sheet out and triggered it, then slipped into a pair of thinskin gloves while she positioned her foot. The field tickled as she extended her leg through it.

He used a flash-sterilizer on the wound, the bright strobe of actinic blue and the accompanying *zap!* indicating that the injury had been cleansed of bacteria and germs, then reached for a sprayer of nullicaine.

"I won't need that," she said.

"Right. I forgot."

He put the anesthetic back in the kit. He lubed a resector with synostat, and used a hemostat to spread the cut wide. Bending close, Barriss could see that the tendons leading from her toes had small cuts in the sheaths, revealing a pair of paler, pearly white ellipses.

She concentrated on keeping the pain at bay.

Uli dabbed synostat onto the cuts and waited. In five seconds the cuts changed color to match the uncut tendon sheaths.

"You forgot what?" she asked.

"I did my internship at Big Zoo, on Alderaan," he said, reaching for the biostapler. "I treated an injured Jedi once. *Great* body control—the ability to stop minor bleeding, shut off pain—very useful."

He inserted the tip of the stapler into the wound and triggered it. The staple—which, Barriss knew, was made of a biodegradable memory-plastic—formed a tiny loop. It would hold for a week or so, then be absorbed by her body. By then the wound would be healed.

"How did that happen?" she asked, referring to his story. "The Jedi have their own healers on most of the

Core worlds, including Alderaan. They don't usually see outside doctors."

He dialed another staple into the applicator's tip. "One fine evening, a bunch of drunken hootyboos decided to take apart a cantina in downtown Aldara. Started a riot that boiled out into the street. The Republic Senator was passing by, and her flitter got caught in the melee. She had a Jedi protecting her. There were thirty, thirty-five rioters who took it upon themselves to turn her flitter onto its back. The Jedi—a Cerean, as I recall—ah . . . *objected* to this action. The mob decided to teach the Jedi a lesson."

"What happened?"

He laughed as he triggered the third staple shut. Barriss looked at his face, thought, *Someday, when he's old enough to have laugh lines, he'll be stunningly handsome.*

"What happened was, four surgical interns—including me—and two residents spent the rest of the night reattaching hands, feet, arms, and legs to the rioters. Lightsabers leave neat, surgical cuts. Every bacta tank in the place was fired up. The Senator wasn't hurt, but they brought her in to check, of course, and her bodyguard came along. He had a vibroknife wound on one arm, good-sized laceration, all the way to the ulna. Wasn't bleeding, though, and it didn't seem to be bothering him. I cleaned and stapled it for him."

Barriss smiled. She wondered who the Jedi had been. Ki-Adi-Mundi was the only Cerean Jedi she knew, and the talents of a Jedi Master would not be squandered on a bodyguarding assignment these days, even for a Senator. *Probably one of the many who died at Geonosis,* she thought. *We are so few now, so few . . .*

Uli put four staples inside, then looked at the external

wound edges. "Even with a dermaseal, I'm thinking a couple of extra staples to close the skin," he said.

She nodded. That would keep the strain off the edges of the healing cut when she walked.

He began the external repair, his movements very neat and precise.

"You do nice work, Doctor Divini."

"Call me Uli," he said. "Doctor Divini is my father. Also my grandfather. And my great-grandfather. All of them still in practice together."

"Disappointed them when you didn't go into the theater, did you?"

He laughed. "A Jedi with a sense of humor. Will wonders never cease."

After he finished, she thanked him. He stood and gave a grandiose bow. "Glad to be of service," he said. "It's what I do." He watched her with a speculative frown as she put her boot back on. "Now, an ordinary human or humanoid, it'd take five, six days to heal. With you . . . what? Three?"

"Two. Two and a half, at the most."

Uli shook his head. "Wish we could bottle that."

The unsettling image of beings dying in the OT arose unbidden in her mind, and she could see by his expression that it had in his as well. She changed the subject.

"You spend much of your time slogging around in the swamp?"

He smiled, and once again he looked about fourteen. "My mother collects Alderaanian flare-wings," he said. "Some of the bugs on this world look very similar; might be panspermic relatives. Thought I'd bag a few for her."

Suddenly his name sounded a chord of recognition. "I saw a display once, in the Coruscant Xenozoology Museum. The most extensive collection of flare-wings in the known galaxy. Filled up three of the biggest rooms in the building. Presented by the renowned mudopterist, Elana Divini. Any relation?"

"Mother never does things halfway." He looked at his chrono. "Gotta run. I'm back on duty in ten minutes."

"Thanks again for the stitchery."

"Thanks for the opportunity."

After he was gone, Barriss walked around the clearing. Her foot was fine, and it would heal quickly. But that sudden cold wind she had felt was nowhere to be found now. She'd been on this hothouse world for so long she'd almost forgotten what cold air felt like. How could a cold breeze possibly be produced anywhere on Drongar, without mechanical aid? And inside a force-dome? It was human body-heat temperature out here within moments of sunrise, and it never got much cooler than that, even at night.

More importantly, even if a chill breeze had touched her, how could she have allowed her concentration to lapse to the extent that she had *cut herself with her lightsaber*? The last time that had happened, she had been nine years old—and it had been a nick on her wrist, nothing nearly as bad as this.

No two ways about it—she had reacted like a rank amateur.

Barriss started back to her kiosk. This was a bad sign. The longer she stayed on Drongar, the more she seemed to be moving away, not toward, her goal of becoming a Jedi Knight.

She shivered. For a moment it seemed that she could feel that chill breeze again—not on her skin this time, but in her heart.

7

The cantina was fairly busy, it being one of the rare times when the spore-ridden skies were not full of medlifters, themselves full of wounded clone troopers. At their usual table sat Den Dhur, Klo Merit, Tolk le Trene, Jos Vondar, I-Five, and Barriss Offee. These were the regulars for the twice-weekly sabacc game. Occasionally others, like Leemoth, would sit in, but for the most part it was the same six. The game was a way of relaxing, of rebuilding themselves for the next onslaught of blood and pain. They could never forget about the war, but for an hour or two it would not be uppermost in their minds.

The air coolers were working fairly well, which was also unusual—the filters in the refrigerating units were especially susceptible to spore-rot, and, because all the other Rimsoos on Drongar had the same problem, replacement parts were on constant back order. Even though spores couldn't penetrate the force-dome when it was lit, there were pass-throughs for incoming and outgoing vessels, plus all the local flora and fauna that were already there when the dome was first triggered. Consequently, most of the time, rooms filled with cool, clean, and dry air were few and far between.

In addition to the heavenly coolness, the cantina had recently acquired a few other luxuries, either by accidental consignment or through the efforts of the new quartermaster, a Twi'lek named Nars Dojah. One was a dejarik game, complete with holocreature generator, which was being played at one table now between two human female nurses. Another was a new autochiller for drinks. But the most impressive was a perky TDL-501 unipod waitress droid, whom Den had promptly nicknamed Teedle, and who scooted adroitly around the crowded room on one wheel while balancing trays of drinks.

Teedle pulled to a quick stop in front of the sabacc table and placed drinks before Jos, Tolk, Klo, and Den. "One Coruscant Cooler, one Bantha Blaster, one Alderaanian ale, and a Johrian whiskey," she said briskly. "Seventeen credits, folks."

Den waved one hand in dismissal. "On the tab."

"*Whose* tab, hon? Your bill's higher'n a skyhook already." A static *pop* accompanied every sentence, sounding almost like a wad of dreamgum cracking.

Den turned slowly and looked at Teedle. "I beg your pardon?"

Teedle jerked a durasteel thumb toward the bar. "Mohris says he can't float you anymore. So you either pay up or bring a repulsor next time."

Jos saw that the other patrons of the table, with the exception of I-Five, were having just as much trouble holding laughter back as he was. "Put his on my tab," he told Teedle. "He's covered for tonight."

"You got it, Cap'n," the waitress droid answered, and zipped away.

Den gave her a sour parting look, then said to Jos, "Thanks. It's hard to program good help these days."

Jos was about to respond when he noticed I-Five staring after Teedle. The others had noticed it as well. "Anything wrong, I-Five?" Klo Merit asked.

"She's *beautiful*," I-Five said reverently.

Everyone stared. Jos put his cooler down so hard it splashed onto his pile of chips. "I-Five . . . are you saying you're *attracted* to Teedle?"

The droid continued to look at Teedle—then abruptly turned back to study his cards. "No," he said lightly. He glanced up, and Jos would have sworn that those immobile features had somehow contrived to look sly. "Had you wondering for a second, though, did I not?"

The others burst into laughter. Jos grinned. "Why, you chrome-plated water heater—I oughtta—"

"You ought to shut up and play," Tolk interrupted good-naturedly. She looked around. "Where's that CardShark?"

The cantina's other new droid—and as far as Jos was concerned, the jury was still out on how much of an actual improvement this constituted—was an automated sabacc dealer, an RH7-D CardShark. A smaller, mobile version of the big casino automata, the droid now floated down from the ceiling to hover over the table via repulsorlifts. It shuffled the deck in a blur of motion, then slapped the cards on the table. "Cut," it said to Jos, its electronic voice raspy.

Repressing his annoyance at the droid's tone, Jos cut the cards. The CardShark quickly dealt two rounds with its manipulator appendages. "Bespin Standard," it announced. "First hand. Place your bets, gentlesirs."

"Hey," Tolk said sharply, looking up at it. "Clean your photoreceptor and try again."

"Your pardon, madam," the CardShark said crisply. "Bets, please, gentlebeings."

"Not much improvement," Tolk grumbled as she checked her cards.

They had been talking about the newest addition to the

surgical team. "One problem with the new guy that's obvious from the start," Den observed as he tossed a cred chip in the pot. "He's too young to come into the cantina. So I guess he won't be playing sabacc anytime soon."

"He's not *that* young," Barriss said. "And he's a long way from home." She added her bet to the hand pot, then noticed Jos, Tolk, Den, and Klo grinning at her. "What?"

"For shame," Den said with mock severity. "And you a Jedi."

"I'm shocked," Jos added. His grin grew wider at the blush that spread over her cheeks. It contrasted nicely with her facial tattoos.

"I didn't mean—" she started, then glared at Den. "Mind in the gutter, Dhur," she said. "Again."

The reporter shrugged. "Hard not to be when the whole planet's a gutter."

"I just meant," Barriss continued, "that we should do our best to include him in things like this. Make him feel welcome."

"She's right, of course," the Equani said. "Adolescence—particularly human adolescence—is hard to endure without support."

"Just how old is he?" I-Five asked. "I confess that estimating age differences isn't something I'm extensively programmed for."

"You'd make a terrible nanny droid," Tolk told him.

"For which I thank the maker devoutly."

"He's nineteen standard years," Klo Merit said. "Something of a prodigy, I'm told. Aced all his courses, graduated with the highest honors. Interned at—"

"Big Zoo," Jos finished. "Hey, most of us have seen Wonder Boy work. He's very good."

"I can vouch for that," Barriss said. "I fold."

"Please shift hands, ladies," the CardShark said.

Everyone stared at the hovering droid. "Sweet Sookie," Jos said, shaking his head. "Whoever dumped this one on Nars saw him coming."

Den looked around. "Maybe the new droids will earn their keep," he said. "More people in here now than I've seen in a while. And some of 'em I don't even know." He indicated a corner table, where three beings were engaged in intense discussion.

Klo Merit looked, and frowned. "I recognize two of the species, though not the individuals. The Kubaz, of course, and the Umbaran. But the other I'm not familiar with."

"She's a Falleen," Jos said. "They tend to be insular; outside of some high mucky-mucks on Coruscant, you don't see a lot of them offworld. Wonder what she's doing here."

"Just don't get too close to her," Tolk warned him with a grin.

Den looked puzzled. "Falleen exude pheromones," Jos explained. "Strong stuff, crosses most species boundaries. Usually signaled by cromatophoric changes in pigmentation. It's said that they can mix precursors and influence endocrine levels."

"Thanks. It's all clear as swamp water now."

"They can manipulate how you feel by what they sweat," Tolk told him.

Den blinked. "They must be *real* charismatic in this weather."

I-Five dropped a chip in the sabacc pot. "Raise."

Jos looked at his cards, frowned. "I think you're bluffing, tin man."

"And I think you're sweating, puny human."

"Who isn't? I call."

The players spread their cards. Jos grinned. He was

holding a Commander of coins, a Mistress of sabers, and an Endurance of staves. He put the hand into the interference field broadcast by the CardShark, freezing it. "Anyone closer? No? That's what I—"

"Unless my math module has suffered severe damage," I-Five said, "I believe my hand beats yours."

Jos looked down. His jaw dropped. The droid's hand consisted of an Idiot, a three of staves, and a two of sabers. An idiot's array. The one hand that beat all others, even pure sabacc.

"That's not fair," Jos said mournfully as I-Five gathered in his winnings. "What does a droid need with credits anyway?"

"Didn't I tell you?" the droid replied. "I'm off to see the Sorcerer of Tund to buy a heart and brain."

Jos didn't reply. The remark had suddenly put him in mind of CT-914, the clone trooper whose life he had saved in the OT, only to learn later that the vat-grown soldier had been lost, along with his entire garrison, in a surprise Separatist attack. It had been Nine-one-four and, to a lesser degree, I-Five, who had raised Jos's consciousness to a level including the awareness that clones, and even, under certain circumstances, droids and other artificial intelligences, should be considered self-aware sentients, and thus deserving of the same rights.

This was something he had known all along, but he'd unconsciously kept it at a lower level, not really considering all its moral implications. Clones were created to fight wars; the desire for little else was encoded in their genetic programming. They had no fear of death, a sense of fulfillment and contentment when engaged in battle, and just enough pain receptors to warn them away from actions that could result in injury or death.

Until Jos had gotten to know Nine-one-four, he'd also

assumed clones were incapable of forming close bonds, either with each other or with beings of other species. But CT-914 had felt a sense of brotherly affection for his vat-mate CT-915, and when the latter had been killed, Jos had watched the clone grieve.

Similarly, I-Five, with his enhanced cognitive module functions and deactivated creativity dampers, had impressed them all repeatedly with his "humanity." Though initially his world had been turned upside down by all this, Jos now was grateful, because this wider definition of what was human had led directly to his being able to embrace—literally and figuratively—Tolk as a potential life mate, even though she was a non-*permes* esker.

He loved Tolk, he now knew. No matter the consequences of espousing an outworlder, he was determined to follow his heart in this matter. But he could not help but wonder what the new commander, Great-Uncle Erel, would think of this.

It wasn't long before he found out. As the casino droid set up for another game, a Bothan corporal approached the table. "Admiral Kersos requests your presence, Captain Vondar. Please come with me."

8

"*Ohleyz Sumteh Kersos Vingdah,*" the admiral said. "*Than donya sinyin.*"

"*Sumteh Vondar Ohleyz . . . dohn donya,*" Jos responded, hesitating just a bit. It had been well over a standard decade since he had spoken in the High Tongue. Everyone spoke Basic nowadays. As a boy, he'd only spoken the older, ceremonial language during Purging Days.

His great-uncle looked tired. His face was about half a day shy of depilation, and his uniform had one of the front tunic flaps unbuttoned. Without the man's surgical mask, Jos could see a distinct family resemblance. Somewhere during his boyhood, he and a cousin had discovered in the family archives fragments of broken holograms—shattered images of, among others, the young man who had thrown away his heritage and been disowned by the family he chose to abandon. They'd peered through the fragments as if they were windows open on the past, providing glimpses of that young man, who was also apparent in this older man's features.

By all that was strict and proper, Jos knew he ought not to be speaking to Erel Kersos at all, save as a military subordinate replying to a superior officer. Great-Uncle Erel was still non-*permes*—the social and personal invisibility did not diminish with time, or even with death. But then again, given Jos's current status with an esker female and his determination to keep it that way, the prohibition against speaking to a shunned relative didn't seem quite such a major infraction.

Plus, there was nobody from the homeworld around to see it. And the reason Erel Kersos had been expunged from the clans was of compelling interest to Jos: the man had married an esker.

They were in Vaetes's office, just the two of them. Jos had a hundred questions he wanted to ask his great-uncle, and at the top of his list was one in particular. Standing there uncomfortably, wondering if he should be the first to speak, he suddenly remembered the first time his father had talked to him about outsiders . . .

At six years of age, Jos had never been offworld, and the only sightings of aliens he'd had were at a distance. So when the subject of outlanders came up in the school rec-dome, it had been puzzling to him. He had asked his father about it, on one of the rare evenings when his father had been home and not working at the clinic.

It had taken him some time to work up the courage to approach him. His father was never violent, and Jos had no doubt that the man loved him. But he was *big;* when he stood, he towered over Jos. And he could be loud, very loud, though never when he was talking to his son.

In retrospect, it was clear that his father had not been ready for this conversation. What Jos recalled of the time was that, once he had approached and told him about his schoolmates' talk, his father had stopped whatever he was doing—reading the evening newsdisc was what Jos remembered—and looked at his son in mild surprise. "Well, son, aside from being of different stock—that's like the difference between a blethyline and a tarkaline; they look similar, but they're different colors and sizes—

aside from that, they don't have the same beliefs that we do. They are—" He searched for an appropriate term, and finally came up with one. "—less *pure*. They mix things together that we don't mix together, and that includes who they, um, marry."

Jos had nodded, not understanding what his father was getting at, but aware that the subject was making the man uncomfortable. "Uh-huh."

"They aren't . . . *bad* people," his father had said then. "Just . . . *different*."

"*How*, Da?"

His father had frowned. "You know how you like saltnut butter on bread?"

"Yeah!" The kind fresh from the farm, the nuts just cracked. Spread it on thick, it was the best!

"And how you also like bluefruit jam on bread?"

"Yeah . . ." It wasn't as good as saltnut butter, but it was still a treat.

"But how if you mix saltnut butter and bluefruit jam on the same bread, you don't like it?"

"Uh-huh." It was true. The two tastes, individually wonderful, when eaten together would gag a sand cat. That had always seemed very unfair.

"Well," his father had said, "that's how ensters and eksters are. They just don't mix together."

"But, Da, people aren't all the same, like saltnut butter and bluefruit jam, are they—"

His father cut him off: "You'll understand this when you're older, Jos. Don't worry about it now."

Now, sitting with his shunned great-uncle decades later, Jos now had a much better idea of what his father meant. At home, this attitude was normal. But to outsiders, it was called xenophobia, speciesism, or worse. For years he had shrugged that off. Outsiders didn't understand the complexities of *permes,* so they spoke from ignorance. They were to be pitied more than feared or scorned. Even after his rotations on Coruscant and Alderaan, during which dozens of sentients had been laid open before him, even though he no longer spoke the High Tongue or observed the Purging Days—even then, though he fancied himself fairly galactopolitan, the interdiction, the barrier between his kind and all others, had worked for him on a deep level, so deep he hadn't even realized its power.

But then he'd fallen in love with Tolk—a Lorrdian nurse who was not of his planet or even his system, a fact that was supposed to be the death knell for any possible long-term relationship. In the words of many older and infirm beings he'd treated, he'd fallen and he couldn't get up.

And he wasn't sure he wanted to.

"Go ahead," his great-uncle and admiral said then. His voice was strong—a voice that knew how to give an order—but kind as well. "Go ahead. Ask."

Jos looked straight at him. "Was it worth it?"

Silence for a long moment, the two of them looking straight at each other—and the older man gave him a small smile. "Yes. And no." He sat down with a sigh in Vaetes's chair. "For six glorious years, I was sure it was."

Jos raised an eyebrow. His uncle gestured for him to sit as well, which he did.

"Feleema—my spouse—died in a mag-lev accident on Coruscant six years after we married. So did four hundred others. It was quick—a superconductor failed, the safeties malfunctioned, and the train left the rail at three hundred kilometers per hour and rammed into a row of deserted industrial buildings in the southern hemisphere. No survivors in any of the cars."

"I'm sorry."

His great-uncle nodded. "Thank you. It's been more than thirty years. No one from the family has ever said that to me. Or anything else."

Jos was quiet, touched by the man's sense of loss.

"So, there I was," Erel Kersos continued. "A fresh lieutenant in the service of the Republic, my wife gone, and my family and culture no longer available to me. We had no children. I couldn't go home. So I applied myself to my work, I made a career for myself in the military." He smiled, and Jos thought there was a slight bitterness in it. "Which is how I wound up here, nearly forty years later."

"You could have recanted."

"I would have had to deny my dead wife to do that. I could not do so. And could not abide a family that would have demanded it."

There was another silence—not one that was particularly comfortable to Jos. Then Erel Kersos looked him square in the eyes and made it worse. He said, "Jos, you need to think about all this, very seriously."

Jos blinked. Was the old man a mind reader? Didn't they have enough of them here already?

"I found out you were on this world before I applied for this duty. I . . . inquired about you. I know why you are willing to talk to me. I know about you and the Lorrdian nurse."

Jos felt his temper rise abruptly. Kersos must have sensed it; he shook his head. "Don't blow a major vessel, son. I'm not telling you what you should or should not do. I'm only offering my experience. When I elected to marry Feleema, I never looked back. I was young, brave, and she was, in my mind, worth all of my disapproving family put together. I had her—I didn't need them.

"Then, suddenly I didn't have her—and I didn't have them, either." He paused. "Family is sometimes more important than we think. Especially when they are still there, but denied to you. Things happen. People change, they separate, for all kinds of reasons. And they die. The woman you love today might turn into somebody you can't stand five or ten or fifteen years from now. Or she might not be here at all. There are no guarantees."

Jos nodded. "I know. Just tell me this: if you had it to do over again, knowing what you know now—would you do the same thing?"

His great-uncle smiled, and it was not a happy expression. "I'm not you, Jos. My mistakes were mine—yours will be your own."

"Not a responsive answer."

The older man shrugged. "Maybe not. But it's true." He paused. "There are times when there is no question in my mind—yes, I'd have done it exactly the same. Six years with Feleema was better than six hundred years of my family.

"But there have been other times when I wonder: what would it have been like, to see my brother's or sister's children grow up? The nephews and nieces I never met, never saw, never even knew were born? I couldn't go home for my father's funeral. My mother is still alive— I've kept track through the census data banks—but I am dead to her. The choice I made was simple—as simple as it was irrevocable. But it wasn't easy. And it never got any easier. There's an old saying, Jos, maybe you've heard it: there's no easy way to shave a Wookiee."

Jos sighed. Just what he needed to hear.

9

After Jos had left the table, the remaining players discussed the new commanding officer, Erel Kersos, for a few minutes. "I hear he's much more hands-on than Admiral Bleyd was," Barriss said.

"A Bespin cloud creature is more hands-on than that brain case was," Den said. "They never did find his assassin, you know. There's a thought to keep you nice and cozy at night."

The CardShark began to deal cards again. Den held up a hand. "We're done. Just finishing our drinks."

The casino droid paid no attention. "Dantooine double-hand," it said. "Place your bets, pplleeeaaass—"

The CardShark's voice suddenly droned off as its arms drooped. It slowly spiraled to a resting place on a nearby empty table. The players looked at each other in puzzlement. Then, as one, they turned to look at I-Five.

"What did you do?" Barriss demanded.

If droids could shrug, I-Five would have done so. "I shut it down. It was hardly the most sparkling of conversationalists."

"You weren't anywhere near it," Den said.

"True. It wasn't necessary. I simply aimed a microwave beam at one of its EM receptors and overloaded a capacitor. I knew it would go into emergency shutdown mode."

"Maybe trying to get you drunk isn't such a good idea," Den mused. "You're dangerous enough as it is."

The other three looked at the Sullustan and the droid skeptically. "Why would you want to get a droid drunk?" the Padawan asked.

"Not just any droid." Den stood and threw an arm around I-Five's shoulders, an accomplishment made possible only by the fact that the droid remained seated. "I-Five needs to let his dewflaps dangle a little."

"Thanks for that," I-Five said. "It's a thoughtful gesture, but I think we've already decided that it's impossi—"

"You might be able to accomplish it," Klo Merit broke in, "by varying the oscillator signal so that the phase harmonics shift into a multipulse instead of a standard pulse configuration."

Everyone turned and stared at the minder. Merit spread wide, four-fingered hands, the short fur on their backs shading to dark leathery palms. "What? I can't have more than one skill?"

"It might work," I-Five said thoughtfully. "The nonlinear feedback pattern established could create a new heuristic response."

"Your synaptic grid processor would have to be in electron depletion mode," the Equani pointed out.

"Of course. That goes without saying. Perhaps programming could be devised . . ."

Den cocked a suspicious eye at Merit. "Where did you pick up all this esoterica? And don't lie to a reporter—we always know."

Merit smiled. "I've had a number of jobs before I settled into minding. Including six months working as a boson wrangler for Industrial Automaton."

Den shrugged. "Who knew?" He turned back to I-Five. "What say we give it a try? And just to make sure you're not flying solo, I'll be your copilot." He gestured to the serving droid, who swerved her single wheel and headed in their direction. "Hey, Teedle, bring me a Pan-Galactic Gar—"

"Quiet!" Tolk had her head cocked in a listening pose—a pose they all knew all too well. In the sudden buzzing quiet a sound slowly became audible—a sound they also all knew too well.

"Lifters!" Tolk headed out of the cantina at a fast trot, followed by Barriss. Mcrit, moving his bulk with surprising ease and speed, left as well.

"Looks like we'll have to temporarily forgo pushing back the boundaries of science," I-Five said to Den as he started for the door. "Hold that thought."

Others at nearby tables were also leaving, heading for their various stations. Only the three sentients in the corner—the Kubaz, the Umbaran, and the Falleen—stayed put.

Den shrugged, and settled back to wait for his drink.

They sat in the cantina, in the middle of the midday meal crowd, hidden, as Kaird liked to think, in plain sight.

Kaird, still in his Kubaz disguise—thank the Egg for a working air cooler, finally—leaned back and looked at his two potential employees. They returned his gaze, both faces noncommittal, as far as he could tell; he'd always had trouble reading those fleshy blobs and gashes that served as faces for most humanoids. There was no question as to whether they would take the job, however—if you were an outlaw and Black Sun made you an offer, it was not in your best interests to refuse.

Whether they could do the job was the question.

They ordered drinks, and then, before Kaird could say a word, the Falleen female said, "Okay. We'll do it. What would our end be?"

"Just like that?" Kaird said, vaguely disappointed. He'd expected some pretense at haggling, at least.

"You're Black Sun," Thula said. "Do we look stupid?"

"How? How will you manage it?"

As Kaird watched the Falleen, her pale green skin began to change color, shading into a warmer, reddish orange tone. And almost immediately, he felt a powerful sense of desire stirring in him. An attraction to her so strong it was all he could do to resist it.

It was the same attraction he'd sensed earlier, but multiplied a hundredfold. He knew what was causing it. Pheromones. Airborne chemicals released solely to cause emotional reactions in others. A number of different species used them, he knew; some for communication, some to mark territory—and some to enhance sexual attraction.

Thula smiled. She knew exactly how her pheromones were affecting him. "*That's* how," she said. "The military hires civilians now and again, especially those with appropriate credentials. It just so happens that Squa and I have excellent documentation—the best that credits can buy—attesting to our expertise in a number of disciplines. Shipping dispatch and systems controls are among them. With a . . . *patron* who is attracted to me, I am sure we can get work somewhere in the shipping system."

"What if the person in charge of hiring is female? Or some other sex entirely?" Kaird asked. "Like the Triparates of Saloth, out in the Minos Cluster. Ever hear of them?"

The two exchanged a calm look. Then Squa Tront said, "No, we haven't. And neither has anyone else, because you just invented them."

Kaird laughed, and his mask made the snorting, gurgling noises that to the Kubaz indicated mirth. These two seemed to be unflappable, an essential quality for smugglers.

Thula gestured to her partner. "In any event, should we run afoul of the fair sex, Squa has certain talents in that area. His methods differ from mine, but the result is the same." The Falleen grinned. "Though you'd never think so to look at him."

"I resent that," Squa said. "Among my species, I am considered well above average in looks."

"Not much to brag about." But Thula smiled as she said it, and Squa smiled in return.

Kaird detected a warmth in the Falleen's voice and expression, mirrored by that of her companion. An odd couple, indeed.

"Once hired," Thula said, "we'll be in a position to influence those with direct access to the product. A piece of easy. But—how much is it worth to Black Sun?"

Ah, now came the fun part. He had a lot of leeway in transactions like these. Two percent was standard, but he could go as high as 4. He would start by offering 1 percent of the net, which he could sweeten with a small advance, five thousand creds or so . . .

"Let's not dicker like a couple of Toydarians," Squa said in his dry, papery voice. "What say, we get . . . four percent? And a small advance, oh . . . five thousand credits?"

Kaird shook his head, and mentally cursed himself. It was hard to bargain with somebody who had empathic or telepathic abilities. He had a pretty good thought-shield defense when he concentrated on it, but he had relaxed and let it slip. A good lesson in that.

There was something charming about the two—something aside from their hormone- and mind-manipulating abilities. They were a pair of likable rogues. This was to be prized. Emotions, thoughts, even the senses could be fooled in various ways, but spontaneous charisma was always in short supply.

"Done," he said. "But since you can see things you ought not to be able to see, you know what will happen if there are any problems. If, for instance, you suddenly decided to abscond with a hundred kilos of bota to set up shop on your own? See what my thoughts about *that* are."

Squa grew slightly paler, if that were possible. He swallowed dryly. "We'd never dream of such a thing," he said.

Thula, her skin faded back to its normal pale green, added, "We aren't stupid, *or* greedy—which is why we're here, alive. You don't need to be a Republic armorer to know a big gun when you see it. We do the job, we make money, you make money, everybody gets happy. And maybe someday, Black Sun will want to throw some more work our way."

Kaird smiled behind the mask, which, after a heartbeat, translated it into the Kubaz equivalent—the short proboscis curling up and over itself. "Always a pleasure doing business with professionals," he said. "I'll stay on-planet until you get things set up and running, then it's all yours."

He held up one hand, palm-down, in the traditional Kubaz sign for agreement.

Both Thula and Squa Tront mirrored his gesture.

Excellent! A few days, a week or two, and Kaird could be on his way, leaving behind a new operation up and running, while he spaced back to more interesting places and things.

He headed back to his quarters to change his disguise, and an odd thing happened: a cool breeze touched him as he walked across the compound. He could just feel it through the heavy and hot disguise, and it lasted but an instant, so short a time that he wasn't sure he hadn't imagined it. He stopped and looked around, but there was nothing to be seen, nobody even close to him.

He scowled—the mask turned it into a Kubaz frown, curling the short facial trunk up and under, tucking it close to the chin. Kaird didn't notice. A blast of air cold enough to feel even through all he was wearing? Coming, apparently, from nowhere? This was unnatural. And Black Sun operatives did not live to a ripe old age by ignoring the unnatural.

On a hunch, he looked up. The sky wore its usual bands of colors: pale green, yellow, a bit of blue and red. The spores were thick outside the force-dome, and there were some small clouds of the stuff floating around inside the energy shield, up high, but nowhere near enough to cause a health hazard.

Could the blast have come from *outside* the dome, somehow? He shook his head. That made no sense—if anything, it was hotter outside, not colder.

Kaird slowly continued on his way. Something strange had just happened and its cause was unknown—now.

But he would make it his business to know it. Soon.

10

The announcement came over the hypersound speakers, sounding as if a quiet voice were speaking privately to each sentient being in the base. The announcer, however, was an Ugnaught, and his thick, Basic-mangling accent made it hard to decipher the words.

"Att'ntion. In t'ree local days Hol'Net 'N'tainmen', in, uh, collab—collab'ration wit' da R'public Mil'tary Ben'-fit As—so—ciation, brings you Jasod Revoc and His G'lactic Revue, you bet. Wit' Epoh Trebor, Lili Renalem, Annloc Yerj, Eyar Marath, an' Figrin D'an an' da Modal Nodes, yar."

Uli, who was examining a cephaloscan readout on his handheld, frowned and looked at Jos. "What did he say?"

"He said the carnival is coming to town. The troops are going to be entertained—and so are we, theoretically. Unless, of course, we're in here playing mix-and-match with various viscera." Jos gestured to the FX-7 on duty to take over the resectioning of the trooper on the gurney before him. It had taken him nearly forty-five minutes to remove all the shrapnel that had been embedded in the clone's mediastinum. Shrapnel extraction was the cause of nearly all the invasive work done in the Rimsoo—far more than slugthrower fire, sonic disruption trauma, vibroblades, or anything else from the murderous catalog that was ground war in a jungle. He figured he'd probably pulled a good ten kilos of twisted, seared metal from the insides of various troopers. The damage was always horrific. A chunk of durasteel traveling at near-sonic speed hit a body's midsection like a hunger-maddened reek, and chewed it up even worse.

"I don't know about you," he continued, "but I am sorely in need of some laughs. Revoc's people perform pretty well, I hear." He grinned at Uli. "Of course, the kind of music they play might seem a little stodgy for your taste . . ."

"I'm always up for a good band," Uli said. "Leap-jump, like that. My big goal now is to find a date—preferably carbon-based, humanoid, and female, though after three weeks here I'm learning not to be so picky."

Jos nodded thoughtfully as he stripped off his gloves and gown in the postop chamber. Had it really been three weeks since Uli had arrived? He realized that he hadn't thought of Zan lately, and felt a pang of self-reproach. *Why?* he asked himself. *Any good physician knows that loss heals eventually—grief is a process.* Zan would have wanted it that way. Still, he felt obscure guilt. The truth was that Uli, despite his youth, made a pretty good cube mate. He was neat, and his tidiness had inspired Jos to be a bit more mindful of the immediate environment as well, so that the walls were no longer furry to the touch, at least. He certainly had a different perspective on a lot of things than Jos, but, unlike most people his age, he wasn't at all dogmatic in his beliefs. The two had had interesting conversations about everything from galactic politics to favorite Coruscant restaurants; Jos preferred the elegant—and expensive—Zothique, while Uli was partial to a greasy spoon called

Dex's Diner. No doubt about it, the new had helped ease the passing of the old.

Three weeks. It had been nearly that long since Admiral Kersos had taken over. His great-uncle had yet to meet Tolk, save briefly in the OT—various administrative duties had kept Kersos orbitside in the MedStar frigate for much of that time—and Jos had been making efforts to keep them apart. Even though Kersos had been guilty of the same sin Jos was contemplating, Jos was afraid that his uncle would not like her—or that Tolk might not like him. He was honestly not sure which eventuality would be worse.

Well, the two would undoubtedly encounter each other socially at the HoloNet Entertainment show. And he wasn't at all sure he wanted to be there—or anywhere on the same hemisphere—when they did.

Column stared at the decoded message on the flatscreen, feeling somewhat queasy at the content. As much as the spy hated the idea, the powers-that-be had ordained a course of upcoming action that would involve violence.

Extreme violence.

The Separatists wanted this world and its valuable bota. They intended to try to swing the precarious balance of power their way, and the manner in which they planned to accomplish this was, in a word, despicable.

Just the thought of the consequences of this action was enough to cause nausea. It would not fall entirely to Column to implement this sabotage; still, the spy would have to instigate a vital element of the plan at the appropriate moment. And as a result, some of the Republic's forces were certain to die—perhaps many of them, and among their number would be quite a few noncombatants. Yes, they were mostly military personnel, but this was largely by virtue of conscription—Column had met very few medics who elected to join the army or navy by choice. While there were always those who thought military service was a valid idea, helping the wounded and sick, by and large surgeons, medical doctors, nurses, and techs were draftees. They had no choice in the matter—it was be inducted or be imprisoned. Some made the latter choice, though they were in the minority. Eventually, the war would be over, win or lose, and if they survived, the conscripts would go home, back to their lives. But electing to go to prison in lieu of the military could follow a person for a lifetime. It was not an easy choice. Before this war had begun, before there was an agent with the alias of Column or Lens, the bearer of both names had known moralistic objectors in other wars who had taken stances against the concept. Some could withstand the onus; some broke beneath the weight of that choice, crushed like a wingstinger under a heavy boot.

Column sighed. In times like these, only the distant goal could remain clear. The objects and people near to hand were fuzzy, and, like the tiniest parts of matter, did not bear close examination. To peer too closely at them while knowing what was inevitably going to happen was to court madness. How could a being smile at those close by, interact with them, share their hopes, dreams, and frustrations, while simultaneously taking part in a plot that would end in the deaths of at least some of them?

No, the immediate ugliness had to be ignored. When all this was done, when the Republic had been roundly defeated and old-but-not-faded wrongs had been righted— then there would be time enough to grieve.

Often clichés contain more than a grain of truth—

which is why they become clichés. In this case, sometimes the ends really did justify the means, no matter how heinous they seemed in the moment.

That's how one had to look at it. To see it any other way would cause paralysis. And, whatever else might happen, the Republic had to lose this war.

It *had* to lose.

Tolk sat on the end of Jos's cot and blotted her wet hair with a syncloth towel.

"Your 'fresher's sonic dryer is broken again," she said.

Lying on the bed and watching her, Jos smiled. "Do tell? I'll have the butler droid give the mechanic droid a call straightaway," he said, affecting a posh upper-class East Quadrant Coruscant accent. "I do hope you haven't suffered too much in these dreadful and barbaric circumstances, my dear."

She smiled back, finished blotting her hair, and threw the damp towel at him. It hit him in the face before he could get a hand up to block. He laughed, and her smile broadened.

Then, abruptly, it faded.

"What?"

"Nothing." She started to get up; he reached, gently pulled her back. "You aren't the only person who pays attention to faces around here, you know. Now, tell Doctor Vondar."

She nibbled at her lower lip. "I've been contacted by the director of Surgical Nursing Services on MedStar."

"And . . . ?"

"And they want me to rotate up for a Continuing Medical Education short course in decubitus care. Six hours, lecture and lab."

He snorted. "A CME class on *bedsores*? What idiot

came up with that one? We don't have patients here long enough to develop decubitus ulcers! Anyway, with the massage fields it's not a—"

"I know. The order came directly from the admiral's office."

Jos frowned. "I see . . . anything else?"

"According to an old friend in SNS, as of this morning I am the only surgical nurse onplanet who has been ordered to take the class. What do you think that means?"

The answer was fairly obvious. Why would the admiral's office order a single nurse to attend a course that was, given the nature of the Rimsoo treatments here, pretty much useless?

"Great-Uncle Erel," Jos said, his voice tight. "He wants to check you out—and he doesn't want me around when he does it."

She nodded. "That's how I figure it."

Jos sat up. "I can tell MedStar we can't spare you right now," he said.

She shook her head. "No. I'll have to talk to him sooner or later. Might as well be now. I've been holding my breath ever since you told me who he was."

"Tolk—you don't have to—"

She leaned over and put her hand over his mouth. "Shush. I'm a big girl. I won't melt if your uncle looks at me crooked. If he is going to be family—" She stopped. "Are you having second thoughts?"

He put one hand on her cheek. "Never."

She smiled. "All right. Then I'll go see Uncle Admiral and we'll find out what's what. It'll be fine."

"Are you sure?"

"I'm a face reader, Jos. At least we'll know where we really stand with him."

He was still worried, and obviously she could see it in his expression. She grinned, took his hand from her cheek, and kissed his palm—and worrying about his uncle suddenly fell off the top of his to-do list.

11

The MedStar frigates were the acme of the Republic medical corps' fleet. Equipped with state-of-the-art xeno- and biomedical facilities that would rival those of many planetside hospitals, *MedStar*-class vessels were designed to accept Rimsoo-stabilized ill or injured patients and, when necessary, continue their treatment. Such ships were extremely expensive, and there were but a handful of them presently in active service. Given the nature and length of the war, others were being built as quickly as Kuat Drive Yards could turn them out.

In war, the roads to victory—or defeat—always wound through mountains of bodies.

Column, seated in the transport headed for MedStar, gazed through the small, thick porthole at the verdant landscape rapidly dwindling below. The ship's A-Grav field ensured that the crew and passengers remained at a comfortable planetary constant, but, judging by the quickness with which Drongar fell away from them, the spy estimated that the transport had to be pulling at least five g's. The reason for the swift ascent was to pass quickly through the spore strata. Column watched as colonies of the single-celled proto-animalcules splashed against the transparisteel port like insectoids against a windscreen. Smears of color, most of them various shades of red or green, were turned into liquid streaks by the transport's speed.

Drongaran life was both mutagenic and adaptogenic, and its rate of evolution seemed to be constant, rather than punctuated, as well as extremely rapid. Studies had found that the species on this world possessed DNA that granted undedifferentiation properties to virtually every cell of the organism, allowing it to adapt to environmental threats in an astoundingly short time. The swift mutability posed a real threat to the aliens who had come here to harvest bota. Spores, bacteria, viruses, RNA-ersatz, and no doubt millions of other tiny life-forms yet undiscovered roiled through and clogged everything on Drongar. A ship traveling through the spore clouds had to hurry; tarry too long, and the teeming protolife attacked and overcame the seals, sometimes digesting material as quickly as might a strong caustic. It could do much the same—and frequently did—to alien biological systems such as lungs, livers, kidneys, gutsacs, spiracles, and so forth. Fortunately, the most damaging concentrations of spore swarms stayed just above the treetops, high enough to allow people relative safety at ground level. No one was sure why. It might, Column mused, have something to do with wind patterns. Or perhaps it was the heat. Whatever the reason, everyone was grateful that the myriadfold of Drongaran life was not more inimical to offworlders.

Column sighed, knowing that this rumination on the local fauna and flora was simply a way to put off thinking about the job to come. The stroke of a finger on the holoproj control changed the image from an aerial view of Drongar to the magnified image of MedStar, waiting above in geosync orbit. What had to be done was an unpleasant agenda, no two ways about it. A spy was, at times, not simply a gatherer of information. There sometimes came a crux when a more active role was required. Sometimes one had to cross into the territory of saboteur. It was part of the business—hard, but unavoidable.

Column reflected upon this unhappy, but necessary fact for . . . what? the thousandth time? Reflection did not change things, however. It was war. People died in war, some deserving, some not, and, wishes to the contrary, spies and saboteurs in the enemy's camp had to bear responsibility for violent acts. If not Column, somebody else would be here. Perhaps, Column liked to think, that agent would have fewer qualms about death and destruction.

Not that Column could be considered scrupulous; there had been actions for which the spy had been directly responsible over the past few months that had claimed both lives and property. Actions that were, as the ancient Ithorian revolutionary Andar Suquand had said, "Casting sand in the gears of the machine." Such an action wasn't going to stop the war, but it would slow things down a bit.

Sometimes, that was all one could hope to do.

This coming action would be more akin to throwing pebbles than sand, at least locally. After Column was finished, gears would metaphorically grind to a stop, camshafts would break, and the repairs would cost time, money, and valuable labor—all of which would be a drain on the Republic's war chest. Not a big drain, to be sure; in fact, given the length and breadth and depth of the Clone Wars, as the aggregate battles were beginning to be called, it would hardly be noticed. But wars were often won, not with a few major breaches, but with many tiny punctures. Even pinholes, were there enough of them, would empty the largest container.

Column glanced again at the holoproj built into the

next row's seat back. MedStar slowly grew in size, all alone against the backdrop of space, as the transport approached. Column sighed again. What had to be done would be done. Such was the nature of war.

Jos came out of a series of simple and dull procedures, routine stitchery that any first-year resident could do. But simple or not, they were time-consuming when piled on half a dozen or more deep.

As he tossed his dirty surgical gown into the recycle hopper, Uli emerged from the OT, looking as if he had just had ten hours of restful sleep, a sonic shower, and a cup of hot bajjah.

Truly, youth was wasted on the young.

"Hey, Jos," the kid said. "They just kept 'em coming today, didn't they?"

"Yeah, they do that sometimes. Too many times. How'd it go?"

"Great. Two bowel resections, a cardiac transplant, a liver repair. All still alive, no sweat."

Jos smiled and shook his head. None of those procedures was cut-by-the-numbers, even back in the real galaxy. This kid shrugged off stuff that would have had Jos sweating transponder battery acid when he'd been a *third*-year surgical resident. He had a platinum vibroscalpel, Uli did, no question. The uncertainty Jos had seen on the boy's first day had quickly been replaced by confidence verging on cockiness. Jos knew that, even though Uli had spent the day snatching lives back from the brink of eternity, death was still an abstract concept to someone that young.

"You holding up okay?"

Slightly startled by the question, Jos looked at the younger man. "Sure. Why wouldn't I be?"

"Well, you know. Tolk being gone and all . . ."

"She's not the only surgical nurse on the rotation."

"True. But she's the only one you're, uh, *involved* with."

Jos raised an eyebrow. "What makes you say that?"

Uli grinned, just like the big kid he was. "Come *on*, Jos. We share a cube. It's not that big, and a couple of plastoid panels down the middle doesn't exactly make it soundproof."

Jos felt uncomfortable. "I thought we were pretty circumspect."

"Not really. Besides, it's obvious even to people who don't live in the same clutch with you. She okay?"

"She's fine. She had to go up to MedStar for a CME class. She'll be back in a day or two."

"You miss her."

It wasn't a question, and Jos supposed he could have slapped the kid down for it, but it sounded like a sympathetic comment, not a smarmy one. "Yeah. I miss her."

There was an awkward pause. "I think I'll go get a bite to eat," Jos said. "Join me?"

"Maybe later. I need to check on a patient first."

Barriss had been practicing with her lightsaber diligently since the accident in which she had cut herself. There had been a little hesitation at first, a concern that had slowed her moves, but that had gradually faded, and now she was back up to speed. Whatever the problem was, it had not come back, and so her confidence had risen, even though she still could not imagine what had caused the slip. A move she had made ten thousand times was not one about which she would normally think—in fact, she shouldn't have to think about it. Thought was far too slow.

She also had no idea what had created the sudden blast of cold air. She'd checked with others in the area, as well as some of the techs. No one else had experienced it, and no one had any explanation for what might have caused it.

It was tempting to believe it had been her imagination. But she knew it hadn't. In addition to the croaker bushes, she had felt energy of some sort rippling through the Force.

She trusted in the Force; had done so since the first time it had surged to life within her and she'd understood what it was. She had also learned quickly what it was not. It was not, first and foremost, a protector, or a weapon, or a mentor—though it could, at times, manifest aspects of all those things. The Force was what it was, no more, no less. Errors in wielding it belonged to the user.

She had just finished the section of Form III in which she danced against four imaginary opponents, all of whom were using blasters. The greatest Jedi who ever lived could not stop four bolts fired from different angles at the same moment, but that wasn't the point. Jedi combat principles were founded in the concept of constantly reaching for perfection. A Jedi began the battle with the idea of facing multiple attackers, who would be armed, and skilled. If you trained for combat believing that you would always be outnumbered and outgunned and that you could still prevail, you stood a much better chance than if you allowed in the idea of defeat because the odds were against you.

Someone approached Barriss from behind. She reached out with the Force . . .

Uli.

"Hey," came his voice.

Barriss turned, pleased that she had identified him before he spoke, and amused at herself for taking pride in such a trivial thing. "Hey, yourself."

"How's the foot? No residual impairment?"

"No, it's fine. Completely healed." As he smiled in rueful admiration of her healing abilities, she asked, "Are you going off to hunt for flare-wings again?"

He shook his head. "Just finished my shift in the OT, and I needed to move around a little." He looked at her, not quite meeting her eyes. "May I ask you something?"

Barriss extinguished her lightsaber. "Sure."

"How can you be a healer and use that lightsaber like you do?"

"Practice. Lots and lots of practice."

Uli smiled and shook his head, but before he could reply, Barriss said, "You really mean *why*, not *how*, right?"

He nodded. "Right."

A wingstinger buzzed past, looking for prey smaller than the two people standing in the hot sun. Barriss pointed to the hard shade of a nearby broadleaf tree, and they walked to it.

"Since these wars, the Jedi have become primarily warriors," she said. "Made more powerful by their abilities to use the Force. Throughout history, as guardians, we have always sought to use our powers for the good of the galaxy—thus, for defense, rather than aggression. Even so, a warrior must know how to fight at levels from full-out battles to one-on-one personal combat. And part of that is taking responsibility for our actions.

"We believe that, if you must slay someone, if you must snuff out a life, then you must be willing to look that being straight in the eyes while you do it. The killing of a fellow sentient, even one who richly deserves it, is not a thing to be done lightly. Nor should it be a thing done easily. You should be close enough to see what it takes, to understand the pain and fear that enemies suffer when you dispatch them. You must feel some of their death."

"So that's why the lightsaber," he said.

"That's why the lightsaber. Because it puts you next to an enemy, face to face, not at some far remove. You can use a holoscoped blaster to put a bolt through your opponent a kilometer away—it's more efficient, and there's much less risk to you in so doing. But you don't hear the death rattle, you don't smell the fear, you don't have to wipe your enemy's blood from your face. If you must kill, then you need to know how great the cost is—to your opponent, and to you."

"Okay, I understand that part. But—"

"How can I be a healer and a warrior at the same time?"

He nodded.

"They are but opposite sides of the same coin. Take a life, spare a life—there's always a balance. Most cultures teach that people are a mix of good and evil—seldom all of one or the other. In most folk, there is an innate decency. They live lives that are more virtuous than not, but there's always an option to choose bad over good.

"I can't create life, Uli, but I can restore it. Being a healer helps me keep in balance the fact that I have—and no doubt will again—taken lives. Sometimes, an opponent doesn't deserve the ultimate penalty. If I amputate a hand or an arm, I will have accomplished what needed to be done. Allowing this enemy to die, then, is wrong. Being able to repair what damage I've caused can thus be of value."

"But not all Jedi are healers," Uli pointed out.

"True. But all Jedi are taught basic medical skills and first-aid techniques. And sometimes, of course, we are called upon to heal our friends—and our own—as well as our enemies."

He nodded again. "Yes, I can see that."

"Then why the question?"

He looked at the ground, as if his boots had suddenly become fascinating. Then he looked back at her. "I'm a surgeon. It runs in my family, but it's also what I've wanted to do ever since I can remember. Fix patients, cure them, make them well. And yet . . ."

He was quiet, thinking. Barriss waited. She already knew what he was going to admit—the Force had told her, loud and clear—but it was important that he say it himself.

"And yet," Uli said, "there's a part of me that wants to kill. To hunt down the people who set this war in motion and exterminate them, by any and all means. I can feel it—that killing anger. I'm . . . that's not how I want to see myself."

Barriss smiled, a small and sad expression. "Of course not. Decent folk don't want to travel that path. Good people, people who love and care, would rather not have those feelings."

"So how do I get rid of them?"

"You don't. You acknowledge them, but you don't allow them to control you. Feelings don't come with 'right' or 'wrong' labels, Uli. You feel how you feel. You are only responsible for how you act.

"That's where choice comes in. Even the Force, a great power for good, can be used for ill."

"That's the 'dark side' I've heard mentioned?"

Barriss frowned. "Jedi refer to the 'light side' and the 'dark side,' but really, these are only words, and the Force is beyond words. It is not evil, just as it isn't good— it simply is what it is. Power alone doesn't corrupt—but it can feed corruption that already exists. A Jedi must constantly choose one path or the other.

"Tell me, if you actually had a chance to meet Count Dooku, face to face, and you had it within your power to kill him—would you?"

He reflected on that for what seemed a long time. Barriss could hear the *rhurp-rhurp* of the nearby croaker bushes, the high, thin buzzing of fire gnats swarming around her, the leathery slap of an Ishi Tib's bare feet striding through a nearby mud puddle.

"Probably not," Uli said.

"There you are."

"But I'm not *certain* I wouldn't. After all, he's been directly or indirectly responsible for planetary genocide, the destruction of things like the Museum of Light on Tandis Four . . ."

"This is true. On the other hand . . . are you familiar with the Vissëncant Variations, by Bann Shoosha?"

He nodded. "Less than two years old, and already considered one of the great musical works of the millennium."

"They were a great favorite of Zan Yant's. The music was written to celebrate the Shoosha family's escape from Brentaal. Had that battle not taken place," Barriss said, "the Variations might never have existed."

Uli looked troubled. "But is any work of art worth thousands of lives?"

"Probably not. I'm not saying it is—I'm just saying things aren't simple. That's really what it's all about, isn't it? Making choices and living with the consequences?"

"I guess . . ." He still sounded doubtful.

Barriss relit her lightsaber. "Well," she said to Uli, as she resumed her practice, "that's all we've got."

12

Seated near the top row of the hastily constructed bleachers, Jos, Den, and Uli, along with several others of the trauma team, watched as various species filled the rest of the seats rapidly. It was evening, and the short tropical twilight was rapidly darkening into night. The area was lit, brilliantly but without glare or shadows, by powerful full-spectrum LEDs. Doctors, nurses, assistants, techs, workers, and other Rimsoo staff personnel had one set of staggered plasticast row seating for themselves, while the troopers and other enlisted personnel occupied two others.

Uli watched as the clones filled the rows, dozens of identical faces and forms. "It's one thing to see them one at a time on repulsor gurneys," he commented to Jos. "But all lined up like that . . . well, it's pretty remarkable. Like they came out of a holoduplicator."

Jos nodded without comment. He, too, was watching the clones. They sat next to each other, laughing, chatting, some boisterous and outgoing, others quieter, more preoccupied. He could see no real difference in their behavior from that of a group of soldiers anywhere in the galaxy who were anticipating being entertained for a couple of hours. True, many were eerily alike in their mannerisms and gestures, and they also had little reti-

cence in sharing drinks or bags of cracknuts, but such behavior, he knew, was common among monozygotic
twins as well. Still, identical whorls of DNA did not necessarily mean identical personalities, even if those personalities had been geared toward certain similarities
since birth—or decanting, in the clones' case.

Jos bit his lip thoughtfully. He knew now that he had
come to think of the troopers as being interchangeable
mostly because their organs were—because transplanta-
tion could be performed without the need to pump them
full of immunosuppressants to prevent rejection syn-
drome. Klo Merit had been right: his training as a surgeon, however benevolent its intention, had conditioned
him to look upon the vat-born as less than human. Now
that he knew the truth, he wondered how he ever could
have seen them any other way.

The bleachers were full now, with some latecomers sitting on the ground. There was no structure on the base
big enough to hold the troupe of entertainers, so a half-
rotunda stage had been set up in the large center compound. Now, abruptly, the white-noise audience sounds
were stilled by the announcer's voice: "Gentlebeings of
all species, please welcome your host, Epoh Trebor."

On one side of the stage, the Modal Nodes, with their
leader Figrin D'an, struck up the well-known theme music for Trebor, a Bith composition that translated into Basic as "Appreciated Reminiscences." Trebor, a human,
was one of the HoloNet's most enduring entertainers. Revoc was the current younger and popular holovid star
whom HoloNet Entertainment had insisted have top
billing, but Trebor had been doing this in various venues
for decades. Since the beginning of the current conflict,
he had been one of the driving forces behind these tours
to various battle fronts to entertain the troops and, as he

put it, "the other unsung heroes of the war." Jos had never particularly cared for Trebor's brand of humor; he found it overly sentimental and a bit too party line. But there was no denying his popularity, judging by the applause.

"Good evening, fellow sentients—and a special greeting to our troops." This brought renewed applause and cheers from the troopers. "Y'know, I hear the Kaminoans feel that the entire clone army project has been so successful, they're thinking of branching out into other areas. They're planning on cloning Falleens as marriage counselors . . . Zeolosians for farm and gardening aid . . . and Gungans to teach elocution."

The laughter and applause continued as Trebor delivered his opening monologue. Most of his quips were somewhat funny, but Jos's mood continued to be somber. He wished Tolk were here with him, instead of high overhead on MedStar enduring some ridiculous and unnecessary tutoring—and possibly well-meant but equally unnecessary interrogation by Admiral Great-Uncle. He found it difficult to get into the festive spirit with her circumstances weighing on his mind.

He wondered how long this war was going to continue, and what their lives together would be like afterward— always assuming that there would be an afterward. Like Erel Kersos, if Jos espoused an ekster he could never go home again. He had no worries about making a living— with his skill as a surgeon he could find work just about anywhere there was a medcenter, as could Tolk. They could even have children, since Lorrdians and Corellians were both basically human.

But to never see his homeworld, his friends, his family, again . . .

That would be hard. Brutally hard.

Erel Kersos had lived the life of an exile, and Jos could read the regret in the lines of the man's face. He felt his mood growing darker. He wished Merit were here so that he could unburden himself to him, but the minder was also away from the Rimsoo on some errand. No, he would have to deal with these sorrows himself.

And the only reliable way he knew to do that was, of course, to drown them.

The cantina was probably close to deserted, but Teedle would be on duty, and his mood would be best served by drinking in solitude anyway. Thank the stars he didn't have to worry about becoming addicted to alcohol—five hundred milligrams of a new drug called Sinthenol before the first drink prevented the potent concoctions from having long-lasting effects on the brain. It also sometimes helped alleviate hangovers, and the times that it didn't he could always go to I-Five. The droid had recently discovered in himself the ability to soothe headaches and other postparty symptoms with sonic tones.

"Two clones walk into a cantina . . ."

Jos felt suddenly impatient. The show seemed to him pointless, or worse: a classic case of whistling past the pyre. The chances of it being interrupted by more incoming patients were even higher than usual, since the Separatists were currently aggressively extending their front lines. Abruptly he stood, made his way to the steps, and left.

Den and Uli watched Jos leave the bleachers. Uli scratched his head. "I thought he was looking forward to this."

"Probably so did he. After you've been here a little longer, you'll realize that our good captain, while not exactly bipolar, can sometimes be a little . . . moody."

"I think he misses Tolk."

"Of course. But he's also been waxing existential of late about the whole war effort. I get the feeling Jos was pretty much apolitical when he was conscripted, maybe even leaning toward war a bit. But I'd say his sensibilities have taken a sharp turn away from the party line since he's been on Drongar."

Uli snorted. "Show me one person who hasn't made that turn."

"I could have, but he's dead now. Went out in a blaze of glory, mowing down Separatists and probably, it looks now, preventing an assassination attempt that might have cost the Republic dearly." Den shrugged. "But he was definitely in the minority. Around here, in fact, he pretty much *was* the minority."

"Phow Ji," Uli said. "The Martyr of Drongar, they're calling him. HoloNet News is doing a documentary."

"Of course they are." For a moment, Den thought about joining Jos in the cantina, for that was surely where the captain was headed. But then Epoh Trebor introduced Eyar Marath, a most comely Sullustan singer and dancer, and he decided to stay for a while longer. Nothing wrong with watching a good-looking fem wearing next to nothing, was there?

Nevertheless, it was hard not to brood on the cosmic injustice of it all. True, Ji was dead and thus unable to enjoy his brief notoriety. But that only deepened the irony as far as Den was concerned.

Ah, well—all fame is fleeting. He watched Eyar Marath prance about the stage, belting out the lyrics of one of the songs that had recently made it onto the Galactic Top 40,000. She was beautiful, of course. She was hot plasma now, but where would she be in ten years? And the band backing her up—what were they called? The Modal Nodes?—were also rocketing high now, but if, twenty years later, they wound up playing for pouch change in a dingy spaceport bar somewhere, he wouldn't be at all surprised. It was the nature of the business. No matter how bright the spotlight on you, sooner or later it went out.

At that point *all* the lights in the camp went out.

A surge of panic enveloped the crowd. Den heard cries of shock and surprise, and the uneasy babble of questions. Both he and Uli were small enough to hunker down and roll under the bench, and he was about to tell the young human to be ready to do so if the crowd around them panicked. Better an uncomfortable squeeze than being trampled.

But before he could open his mouth, the emergency generators kicked on, washing away the darkness. Den could see Trebor, Marath, and some other members of the troupe looking about in puzzlement and apprehension.

The collective stir of fear ebbed with the light. But then things got really interesting. Den felt a cold draft touch the back of his neck. Then, in the somewhat-dimmer-but-still-sufficient-to-see lighting, fat white flakes began to drift down upon the gathering. One of them landed on Den's hand. He stared at it, watched it melt.

Snow.

Holy milking Sith! *Snow?*

13

Jos had just settled himself at a table in the cantina—he had plenty from which to choose, since nobody else was in the place except the serving droid Teedle—when the lights blinked off. The emergency generators rumbled online and quickly replaced the darkness with a slightly dimmer, more hard-edged lighting.

Now what? he wondered.

Teedle rolled up on her gyroscopic single-wheel platform. "Hey, Doc. What'll it be? The usual?"

"Sure. Keep 'em coming and—" He stopped, staring at one of the windows. Outside the transparisteel there was some kind of chaff falling. Spores? No, these were too big, and there were too many of them. Anyway, they didn't look like spore colonies . . . these were white and flaky, like ash or like . . .

"Snow?"

Teedle said, "That's what it looks like, don't it? And my sensors tell me that the temperature in here is going down faster than an off-duty Ugnaught."

At her words, Jos noticed it himself. Son-of-a-raitch, it was getting colder. A *lot* colder.

He stood and headed for the door, Teedle rolling along just behind him.

Outside, he looked up. The force-dome, high overhead,

was usually transparent, though sometimes a slight crescent of pale bluish ionization was visible after dark. Not this time, though. Instead, the camp glow reflected back from what looked like low, thick clouds.

Sometimes, on a particularly hot and humid day, they would get some condensation under the dome, but nothing like this. The osmotic exchangers were fairly efficient, letting in air and even rain, while keeping out a lot of less desirable things. But for it to be snowing, the temperature differential had to be far outside normal limits. Short of parking a battery of refrigeration units on null-grav sleds up there, he had no idea how it could happen.

Zan would have known. Zan had worked for a relative on force-domes when he'd been young.

"Never saw anything like this before," Teedle said, adding that gum-popping sound her vocabulator sometimes made. "Of course, I've only been operational for six weeks, so it's not like I've seen all that much."

Jos walked away from the cantina, toward the OT. The cold was increasing, and the snow continued to drift down. The ground and most of the other exposed surfaces were still too warm to allow it to pile up, but if the temperature kept dropping like this, it wouldn't be long, he estimated, before they would have to start shoveling the stuff.

He remembered hearing or reading somewhere that the dome was in fact a spherical bubble, rather than a hemisphere, with half of it underground. He wondered if that would have any effect on the soil temperature.

Jos shivered. He needed a jacket. Had he even brought one to Drongar? Had anybody? The sticky wet heat that had hit him like a personal insult the moment he'd stepped off the transport had never stopped—it had remained body heat and hotter during the days, maybe three-quarters that at night, and a humidity factor of less than 90 percent was big news.

Even so, the current ambient temperature, in defiance of all the laws of thermodynamics, was fast approaching freezing. He needed a coat, at the very least. A heavy-weather parka would be even better . . .

"Attention, all personnel," came Vaetes's voice over the public address system. "There has been a heat-exchange malfunction of the camp's osmotic force-dome. There is no cause for alarm—the shielding aspect of the dome remains in effect. Technicians are working on the problem and will have it repaired shortly. Until they do, you are advised to don warm clothing or to remain indoors."

Jos stared around him. The flakes were turning to slush and mud upon contact with the still-warm ground—even so, the sight was pretty unbelievable. He'd seen this place in the lowlands practically every day for the past year and a half, and it had looked no different after the move here. Yet it now seemed completely transformed. He wondered what it would look like with the buildings covered with snow, with it piled up in drifts on the roads and against the sides of structures.

Jos couldn't help but smile. Zan would have *loved* this. *Almost a pity things'll be back to normal before it has a chance to accumulate*, he thought. *I'd like to get in one good snowball fight with someone . . .*

"Hey, look at that," he murmured aloud. There'd been less residual heat than he would have thought—the snow was starting to pile up already.

He might get his wish after all.

Barriss stood in the falling snow, which was coming down quite heavily now. It lay piled at least finger-length deep, turning the camp into a glistening white tableau that was quite beautiful. She'd always loved the sight of a snowy landscape. It transformed even the ugly durasteel and plasticast structures of the Rimsoo into something fresh and clean and new. The temperature was near freezing, cold enough for the stuff to keep falling, and, somewhat to her surprise, the ground was now cold enough for it to stick.

Along with her appreciation of the snow, Barriss also felt vindication. That cold draft she had felt, the impossible chilly breeze that had contributed to her accident, had been real. And, she knew, if the force-dome's power had fluctuated at just the right frequency, the resulting pulse could have affected the crystal of her lightsaber.

Such events were rare, but the crystals that powered the center of a force-dome were similar to those at the heart of a lightsaber—though much larger, of course. The energies involved were more powerful, and the arc wave was focused differently to produce a dome instead of a blade. Thus, Barriss reasoned, it was just possible that a warble in the force-dome's more powerful field harmonics generator might have resonated with her weapon's focusing crystals, causing a sympathetic reverberation, just as thunder could sometimes cause the strings of a musical instrument to vibrate. Normally, the shielding in a lightsaber was proof against such interference—enemies had tried to short-circuit Jedi weapons before. But perhaps one of the dome's crystals had a hidden flaw in it, impossible to spot in a normal inspection, but sufficient to cause the field to pulse just enough to shrink the blade a hair. Or to grow just a hair longer . . .

Barriss felt a relaxation of a tension she hadn't realized she'd been holding. Perhaps it was not so, but that at least made more sense than the idea that she had cut her own foot doing a move she should be able to do in her sleep.

The snow continued to fall, and she smiled into it. The colonel had said that this anomaly wouldn't last long, so she planned to enjoy it while it was here.

Sometimes the now was easier to dwell in than other times. This was definitely one of those times.

Robed as one of The Silent, Kaird the Nediji gloried in the cold outside the Recovery Room, watching with something akin to joy as the snow continued to fall lazily upon the camp, adding thickness to the white shroud that now blanketed everything exposed to it. His career in Black Sun had been long and successful. He was respected, adept, and eventually, did he stay with the organization long enough, could look forward to becoming at least a subvigo, perhaps a full vigo. But when he was on worlds where the cold held sway, the call to return home was always strong. He hadn't felt it here on this tropical pesthole, which had been entirely—until an hour ago—hot, humid, and almost malignantly verdant. But now . . .

It really was amazing. Outside the malfunctioning dome, jungle and swamp still ruled—you could see it just beyond the arc where the dome touched the ground. But here, for the moment at least, the air was crisp and clear, reminding him of the eyrie in which he had been born and raised.

Maybe it was time to go home. He had enough credits stashed away so that he could retire to Nedij and live comfortably, if not opulently, for the rest of his days. Find a few nubile females, build a nest, while away his time as patriarch of a new brood. Build his own family and forget the past that had driven him to leave Nedij in the first place. His flock considered him not of the Nest, but Nedij was a big world. There was room enough for him there somewhere.

The cold and the snow called strongly to Kaird. He had spent decades as an operative of the organization, and his masters would not like him to leave, but it could be allowed under the proper circumstances. He knew where too many bodies were buried—corpses that he had created on the orders of his superiors. Should he die suddenly, under suspicious circumstances, he had seen to it that certain information would come to light, and so it was in the best interests of his employers to make sure that he lived a long and healthy life.

The thrill of the hunt, the taking of dangerous prey— yes, he would miss that. But sooner or later, those thrills would be the end of him. Not today, perhaps not for years, but eventually he would be a half step too slow, a heartbeat off in his calculations, and a faster, hungrier opponent would walk away from the field instead of Kaird. He had, on some level, never believed it, but on another, he knew it must be so.

The unexpected snow here was some kind of sign. True, it was caused by a malfunctioning machine, but even so, it *meant* something. Kaird was sure of it.

Abruptly, he made a decision. Yes, by the Cosmic Egg! After he completed this assignment, which should not take much longer, he would return to Black Sun and figure out a way to tender his resignation. A sufficiently large gift would make his vigo disposed to wave him along. He could go back to his homeworld and enjoy a different kind of life, one in which he tickled downy fledglings and cooed sweet words to his wives instead of killing people and engineering disasters.

It was no less than he deserved.

The beings who had gathered in the cantina were a motley bunch. Jos, unable to find anything remotely resembling a coat, had found a blanket and cut a hole through which he'd put his head—it was makeshift, but it worked reasonably well to keep the cold out. Uli had, of all things, a paraglider jacket, with full seals and gloves. He was the subject of many envious glares. Den Dhur, who had spaced long enough to be prepared for any weather, had a shiny thermal polyfab windbreaker that kept much of his body heat in, and he received his share of glares as well. Barriss wore her usual Jedi robes and looked as if she was enjoying the change from tropical to frigid. I-Five, was, of course, unaffected by the chilly air, which was cold enough even in the cantina to allow breath-fog, but still considerably warmer than it was outside.

The cantina was the warmest public building in the camp, due to the place having been double-walled to contain the sounds a typical cantina would produce on a crowded night. That, combined with the body heat the warm-blooded species within gave off, made the temperature within survivable, if not comfortable.

Many members of the traveling show had also found their way here, and, while they mostly kept to themselves, they seemed friendly enough, particularly after the first few rounds of drinks.

"What did Vaetes say?" Den asked Jos. He took another gulp of some fiery red liquor that he claimed was guaranteed to kick an imbiber's internal thermostat up a notch. Jos was tempted, but the liquid gave off a rank odor that reminded him of a full and long-forgotten laundry hamper.

"He said there should be spare parts on MedStar, and as soon as somebody up there can find them—they seem to have been misplaced—they'll get the regulator reharmonized and things will go back to normal. Or whatever passes for normal around here."

"Never thought I'd say it, but the heat wasn't so bad," Uli said.

"Me, I prefer caves," Den said. "Constant eighteen to twenty degrees, plenty of mushrooms, no loud noises. Don't see why everyone doesn't live in 'em."

"Words like *dark, gloomy*, and *depressing* come to mind," Jos said.

Teedle rolled silently up. "How ya doin', sentients? Everybody okay on libations? Anything little old me can do for you?"

Everyone in the small group allowed as how they were fine, and Teedle wheeled away to check on the show people.

"Another funny droid. Place is getting thick with them," Den mused.

I-Five said, "I'll let you in on a little secret. *All* droids have a sense of humor. Which is more than I can say for a lot of bio-sentients."

"The snow was kind of pretty when it first started falling," Den said, looking out the window and ignoring I-Five. "But once it got waist-deep—that's knee-deep for you overgrown breeds—it stopped being fun. I never heard of this kind of dome malfunction happening before."

"Of course not," Jos said. "When it comes to original disasters, we set the bar."

"I understand somebody in Central Supply has figured out a way to make battery-powered heaters out of food zip-paks. They produce enough heat to keep a kiosk relatively warm." This from Uli.

" 'Relatively warm'?" Den said.

"Might keep you from freezing solid in your sleep," Barriss said.

"Of course, without food you'll eventually starve," I-Five said.

"Let me guess," Jos said. "And afterward you and Teedle repopulate the planet."

Den shook his head. "Won't be easy."

"*E chu ta,*" I-Five muttered.

"Whoa," Uli said. "Touched a circuit, did he?"

The droid was about to reply, when he suddenly stiffened and cocked his head somewhat. It was a posture Jos had seen before.

"Oh, no," Jos said softly.

"I hear it too," Den said. In another moment, the others picked it up as well—the faint drone of faraway medlifters.

"Kark," Jos said. He finished his drink in one swallow. The others hurried to finish theirs as well.

Just then a comm-tech came running into the cantina, obviously very agitated. He slammed into and nearly knocked over one of the crew members of the troupe, a big and burly Trandoshan. The reptiloid's drink sloshed all over him. He ripped out a curse in Dosh that Jos was glad he couldn't understand, grabbed the comm-tech and lifted him off the floor with one hand.

Several people charged over to stop the impending slaughter, but before anything could happen—

"There's been an explosion on MedStar!" the comm-tech shouted. "Half the flight decks and most of a storage level just got blown to vac!"

Fear stabbed Jos.

Tolk—!

14

There were a few matters that needed to be taken care of before Kaird could begin planning his triumphant return to his homeworld. Foremost among these was making sure that the rogues Thula and Squa Tront were established securely in the linkage that ran from the bota fields ultimately to the cargo holds of the Black Sun freighters. This meant, among other things, that they insinuate themselves into the good graces of Nars Dojah the quartermaster, an old and irascible Twi'lek. Fortunately, Twi'leks were one of the many species that could be easily affected by Falleen pheromones. Unfortunately, Dojah was aware of this, and as a result was enormously suspicious of Thula. During the interview he had gone so far as to insist on wearing a filter-equipped rebreather. All of this Thula related later to Kaird—or, as far as anyone passing by their cantina table could see, to Hunandin the Kubaz—with great amusement.

"You seem to find this funny," Kaird said in annoyance. "If Dojah does not hire you because of this prejudice, I assure you, my employers will not be smiling, and neither will I."

"Oh, you'll be smiling in a minute," the Falleen assured him. "I haven't finished my story."

Kaird leaned back. "Amuse me, then."

"Dojah's researches into Falleen body chemistry are incomplete. I also shed protein analogs, which work through skin contact rather than the olfactory organs."

Kaird smiled, and the mask's sensors once again translated it into the Kubaz equivalent, rolling the pendulous snout up like a proboscis. "So—even though he could not smell your scent, you nonetheless had an effect."

"Just so." The Falleen quaffed the rest of her Dark Side Daiquiri. She leaned back, muscles shifting lithely under her finely scaled skin. Kaird could feel his own libido stirring slightly. Amazing—he was probably about as genetically compatible with the reptiloid as he was with bota DNA, but even so . . .

He saw her watching him and smiling slightly. Obviously, she didn't need her partner's mind-reading abilities to know what he was thinking. Kaird cleared his throat and turned to the Umbaran. "And you?"

"Not to worry," Tront said in his whispery voice. "I am firmly ensconced as a shipping data processor. The diversion of small amounts of bota looks to be no problem."

"Glad to hear it. Unfortunately, there will be a problem meeting the quota Black Sun requires for this week. The explosion on the MedStar blew out one of the storage compartments that had been consigned for our purpose, and we lost a sizable shipment of carbon-frozen contraband. In addition, as you are both no doubt aware, the extreme temperature fluctuation has decimated much of the local crop base. We will need another two hundred kilograms of processed material in the next three days. Fortunately, the harvests from Rimsoos Six, Nine, and Fourteen are usually routed through here for shipment."

Tront's eyes widened slightly. "This is a considerable amount to be shifted without notice, particularly so early in the game." He gestured at the window and the steadily falling snow. "This bizarre dome malfunction makes things even more difficult."

"Agreed," Kaird said. "Nevertheless, such is our state of affairs. What with the assassination of the last agent sent here, and the current aggressive Separatist tactics to advance and encompass the fields, my superiors are growing nervous. This is a volatile situation, and I've been told to make every effort to maximize profits while still possible."

Tront frowned. "Do you know the fable of the Crystalline Kåhlyt, Hunandin?"

Kaird shook his head.

"A popular parable on M'haeli. A farmer comes across a kåhlyt—an inoffensive oviparous creature—that has the miraculous ability to lay rubat crystals in the form of eggs, once every moon cycle. The farmer sells the crystals and begins to accumulate wealth. But his wife is impatient. She doesn't want to wait for riches, so she kills the kåhlyt and cuts it open to remove all the crystals at once."

Kaird made an impatient gesture. "And . . . ?"

"And she finds only the innards of an ordinary kåhlyt—no crystals at all." Tront delicately sipped his drink. "Perhaps your superiors have not heard this tale, friend Hunandin. It is not a wise thing to kill the kåhlyt that lays the rubat crystals."

"Perhaps not," Kaird replied. "But it is also not particularly wise to yank on a nexu's tail, which is tantamount to telling the new underlord 'No.' "

Thula shifted uncomfortably. "I have heard stories of the underlord's temperament." She glanced at Tront, then shrugged. "Squa and I will make it happen."

"Excellent." Kaird rose, dropped a couple of credits on the table, and left the cantina.

He strode across the snow-blanketed compound, thinking. For their sake, Thula and Tront had better meet the smuggling quota. Now that Kaird had determined to quit Black Sun and return to Nedij, he was impatient with anything that smacked of hesitation or obstruction. The sooner he raised ship and left Drongar behind forever, the better.

And may the Cosmic Egg crack for anyone who got in his way.

I-Five had managed to rig enough of the battery-powered heaters in the operating theater so that at least the patients' blood wasn't freezing anymore. A small AG droid had been reprogrammed and dispatched to the roof, to plane the snow down to a level where it wouldn't cave in the thin structure and bury everybody. The droid had been instructed to leave a few centimeters of the white stuff in place, to act, oddly enough, as insulation.

Jos cut and stapled and glued wounded troopers, but it was as mechanical as the droid above shoveling snow from the roof. Tolk had not commed him, and his gut was twisted in fear.

Vaetes had come in himself, to relay as much as he knew about the explosion on MedStar—which wasn't much. Nothing was certain, but the colonel passed along what news there was in a terse recital as Jos operated:

"A seal blew on one of the external ports—possibly a micrometeor impact, though how it got through the shields is unknown. The blowout caused a short-circuit in the ship's electrical system. The system monitor shut down the power grid, but somehow a container of volatile chemical spilled, and the vapor from that ignited, setting off other flammable material in the supply hold. There was a secondary explosion, which blew the integrity. Automatics sealed off the section, but there are at least a dozen dead."

Jos's throat was dry. "Tolk?"

Vaetes had shaken his head. "I don't know, Jos. The ship's comm is on emergency status, they aren't letting any calls in or out until they lock things down. I got the mortality figure from the pilot of a transport—that's how many bodies he counted in space outside the hull rupture. No report of the onboard casualties yet. As soon as I hear anything more . . ."

"Yeah. Thanks."

The sterile field had a heater, almost never used on this world, but the surgical droid assisting Jos had cranked the field up to maximum, so at least his hands were warm.

The chill he felt over the rest of his body, however, was nothing compared to the cold in his soul.

Tolk . . .

She *couldn't* be dead. No cosmos could be so cruel as to allow such a travesty. After he had worked so hard for so long, healing so many wounds, saving so many lives, it was inconceivable that the one life that meant the most to him could be lost.

Do you really believe that?

I have to, Jos told himself. *I have to.*

Uli stepped up next to him. "I'm caught up," he said. "Need a hand?"

Jos let the nurse wipe his brow, then shook his head. "I'm good." He couldn't recall telling a bigger lie in his entire life, but there was nothing the boy could do to help him—not on any level. He just had to keep working. He excised and debrided burns, amputated and reattached limbs, stanched bleeding, drained wounds, ligated bleeders . . .

The sufferers passed beneath his healing hands, and Jos kept working, hoping that their injuries would be his anodyne.

In the cantina, Den Dhur worked the room. He pulled in every favor he had built up since he'd stepped off the transport months ago. All the drinks he'd bought for techs and grunts, all the unauthorized uses of his private comm to let people call their families, crèches, litters, and so on back home, the creds he had lent until payday . . . he begged, cajoled, wheedled, shamelessly. This was a big story, and he needed access to it.

Bits and pieces began to drift in, and eventually to coalesce. Den tallied them.

From an Ugnaught shuttle mechanic, he heard that one of the supply sections that had spewed its contents into vac had been the electronics small-parts storage. Which, according to the mech, meant that those replacement harmonizers and crystal stabilizers the dome-dinks were waiting on to stop the mopakky snow? They were gonna be part of the meteor shower lighting up the sky soon as they hit atmosphere, blood, y'know?

Talk about your vaporware . . .

From a comm droid that had been on duty when the accident happened, before the emergency status shutdown had hit, Den heard that there had been 186 people stationed on the affected decks. Some of them had made it past the blowout doors before they'd automatically sealed. Some had not. There were probably pockets of air in the affected section, rooms that could be shut and seals rigged, but with life support off, it was going to get milking cold in there real fast, and until the blowout was patched, no heat or air would be forthcoming.

There were emergency suits in disaster lockers, of

course, mostly thinvac suits with limited air supplies, but no way to tell how many people could get to those.

From a Kubaz transport shuttle pilot, Den got an updated body count. At least twenty-six frozen corpses were pinwheeling through space in the vicinity of MedStar. "It been one *major* 'plosion t' 'ject dat many, you bet," the pilot said, his trunk curling up and down in horror.

And that was pretty much all he could get that was of substance. There were a few people from this Rimsoo up there, card-playing friends like Tolk and Merit, and for all Den knew they could be two of the many trapped—or worse, twisted and ruptured ice sculptures orbiting the damaged ship. Den was a reporter; he'd seen friends and acquaintances killed in brush wars all over the galaxy, but that never made it any easier. He had to shift into his objective mode, turn off his personal feelings, if he was to do his job. But of late, that had been getting harder and harder to do. When Zan Yant died, it had *hurt*, more than he'd thought possible. It was one thing to play the cynic for the people around him, to shrug it all off with a *what-can-you-do?* attitude, but when it was just him, alone, with nobody watching, it wasn't as easy as it had been back when he'd been young and full of himself and going to live forever.

Den sat and tossed down Bantha Blasters like there was no tomorrow, wondering how many people he knew for whom that was literally true. Despite the latest influx of wounded, the cantina was full of people who had nowhere else to be, waiting to hear news, be it good or bad.

Teedle rolled up. "Need a refill, sweets?"

"No. I'm good."

As the little droid rolled away, Den stared at his mug.

Good—that was a word he was finding less and less useful and fitting when talking about himself.

Maybe it was time to get out of the field. Just find a nice quiet planet somewhere, work the local news beat, and leave the war zones to the young ones who still thought it glorious and exciting. Yeah, the big stories could be found, even on worlds like Drongar, supposedly far from the "main action," but more and more they were all starting to sound the same: war. Lots of beings dead, maimed, injured, all for the greater glory of the Republic. Details in the full 'cast, coming up . . .

He raised a hand, signaled Teedle. Maybe he did need another shot. *At least these shots you can walk away from. Well, up to a point . . .*

Barriss entered, brushing snow from her robe, and saw Den sitting alone at a table, staring into his empty mug. She moved toward him. "Mind some company?"

He smiled tipsily at her, waved at the chair across from him. "What's your pleasure, Jedi? I'm buying."

"Thanks, but no." She sat. "I have to get back to the OT soon. What's the latest?"

He told her, and Barriss nodded. When it had happened, she hadn't felt a disturbance in the Force, and that bothered her immensely. There were days when, during battles on the planet's surface, she had read the swirling ethereal currents with uncanny detail. Master Yoda was said to be able to sense major disturbances parsecs away—even, sometimes, of things yet to happen, though Barriss wasn't sure if she believed that part. But of the explosion on the orbiting frigate, she had not gotten even a glimmer. She was but a Padawan, true, but still she counted her insensitivity as a personal failing. She felt certain that Obi-Wan Kenobi or Anakin Skywalker would have sensed it immediately. She had lived with the Force as long as she could remember—certainly longer than Anakin. How could she *not* have felt the event?

"You okay?" Den asked.

She nodded. No reason to burden him—there was nothing he could do to help. The little Sullustan shook his head, as if he knew better, but said nothing.

Then, perhaps because she was not expecting it, the Force abruptly rose swirling in her, and imparted to Barriss a sudden knowledge that stunned her: *The explosion on MedStar had not been an accident.*

The reporter must have seen her reaction in her face. "What?"

Barriss breathed deeply, trying to regain her center. The absolute *certainty* of the insight had left her shaken, unable for a moment to speak.

She had to do something with this knowledge. She had to tell somebody. Not Den, not a reporter, but somebody. Someone who was in a position to do something about it.

It was the same conviction she had felt when the transport had blown up months ago, before the relocation. They had never found out who had been responsible for that. She had reported her feelings to Colonel Vaetes, who had been polite but dismissive, obviously preferring to rely on more solid evidence than what he considered mysticism. Perhaps he would be bit more open-minded this time. This act of sabotage was a thousand times worse than the last one. *Something* had to be done.

15

Jos, exhausted but still too worried about Tolk to rest, wandered through the medical ward. The surgical patients in recovery were all as stable as they were going to get, and the operating tables were empty, for the time being. The thought of going back to his kiosk, of being by himself in the cold silence, was anathema. He needed something to do.

Ahead, one of The Silent stood impassively near one wall, a faint cloud of breath-fog issuing from within the cowl at slow and regular intervals. It was cooler here than in the OT, but at least they had enough blankets and heat-paks to keep the patients warm. The Silent seemed unaffected by the cold.

Barriss stood next to the bed of a trooper who had some new kind of infection. One of the local microbes had apparently undergone a mutagenic shift and become deadly, a cause of considerable concern. What could afflict one trooper could afflict them all.

"Hey," Jos said.

Barriss looked away from the sick trooper, who was either asleep or in a coma. "Hello," she said.

"How is he?"

"No change. None of our antibiotics, antivirals, or antimycotics seems to be working."

"Spectacillin?" Spectacillin was the current reigning champ, a broad-spectrum RNA polymerase inhibitor capable of stomping on the most virulent of the Drongaran bugs.

She shook her head. "He's got a fever we're barely keeping down with analgesic suppressors and coma induction, a white blood cell count off the charts, and his kidneys are starting to shut down. He's got fluid in his lungs, an erratic heartbeat secondary to cardiac tamponade, and his liver is working overtime and getting tired. Only good thing is, he doesn't seem to be shedding pathogens, so he's not contagious."

Jos moved in, looking at the patient, whose chart identified him as CT-802. "Fast as everything mutates here, it might cure itself."

"It better hurry, if it doesn't want to kill its host. I've done what I can, but it isn't enough. I've been keeping him stable by working on him through the Force, but I can't keep that up forever." Barriss's voice was calm and even, in contrast to her strained and haggard expression. "I don't think he'll see another sunrise, Jos."

Jos stood there for a moment, remembering a conversation he'd had with Zan Yant in this same room. He hadn't known Barriss that long, but here in the swamps, among the dead and dying, fast kinships were established among the medics. The war was the problem, and they all did their best to be part of the solution, any way they could, as little as that might be.

He took a deep breath. "There might be something else we can try."

She looked away from the patient to him, her gaze questioning.

When Zan had died, it had fallen to Jos to clean out his friend's belongings. He had packed up most of the

stuff—the quetarra, clothes, book readers, and the like—
and had it shipped to Zan's family, back on Talus. But
hidden away under Zan's cot had been something he
hadn't included in the personal effects package: Zan's
supply of processed bota.

It was illegal to possess the stuff here. All the harvested
and stabilized bota went to other worlds and systems,
where it was worth its weight in precious gems. Like out-
world plantations where the locals produced fruit and
crops too expensive for them to eat, or firestone pits
where every day miners found stones worth more than a
year of their pay, or anyplace else where those who did
the scut work reaped none of the rewards, bota was
deemed too valuable to waste on troopers.

But Zan hadn't accepted that. He'd managed to get
hold of a small amount of the miracle growth and field-
tested it as much as was feasible, given the necessarily
clandestine nature of his protocols. Even under less-than-
ideal conditions, bota had cured every resistant infection
a Fett-clone had developed on this world. The irony of
being on a planet where the plant grew like a weed and
not able to use it to save lives had not been lost on either
Zan or Jos. Zan had risked his career and liberty to secretly treat patients with it. Jos hadn't been willing to go
that far, but he had turned a blind eye to his friend's illegal actions.

He became aware that he had been standing there too
long without responding. *Time to make a decision, Jos.
Can you do anything less than what your friend did?*

"Wait here," he said. "I'll be right back."

He left the ward and headed for his kiosk. The snow
was knee-deep and still falling, but some of the mainte-
nance droids had been set to clearing walkways, so it
wasn't that big a problem—yet. Of far more immediate

concern was the lack of warm clothing for everyone. Jos was an ectomorph, tall and thin; his body radiated heat very effectively, which was useful in a tropical climate. But right now the temperature under the dome was about ten degrees less than either of the planetary poles, and for the first time in his life he found himself regretting his lack of body fat. He was wearing practically his entire wardrobe: two pairs of army-issue pants and socks, a heavy shirt, a durnis-hide vest, and a blanket as a makeshift poncho. He had two surgeon's caps keeping his head warm, a sweatband worn low to cover his ears, three pairs of thinskin gloves, and he was *still* cold.

If that harmonic malfunction wasn't fixed soon . . .

On his way to his quarters Jos noticed several members of Revoc's retinue heading for the cantina. He waved, and they waved back. Most of them were taking the unexpected exile fairly well. Trebor and the other headliners had been bivouacked in a quickly constructed barracks, and there they had mostly stayed. No one had been allowed to evacuate yet, either to another Rimsoo or to MedStar, because the more the malfunctioning dome was attenuated to allow transports through, the more discombobulated the harmonics seemed to become. The majority of the incoming lifters were being rerouted to Rimsoos Five and Fourteen, the closest nearby units, but they could only handle so many extra cases, so some still had to be allowed through here.

Zan's supply of processed bota was now under Jos's cot. He'd kept it, not quite sure what to do with it. Now he knew that, on some level, he'd been waiting for an opportunity like this.

What the Republic didn't know wouldn't hurt them, and it could save a trooper's life—a life that Jos now knew was worth as much as anyone's. At some point, you had to start taking a stand. Jos wasn't certain of much in his life, but he knew one thing for sure: letting a man die when you could save him was wrong. And vac take anybody who said otherwise.

"Jos?"

He looked up and saw Vaetes approaching.

His blood went icy faster than a cryovascular transfusion. He tried to steel himself for the news that Tolk had been in the wrong place at the wrong time on MedStar, that they had confirmed the ID, that he would never see her smile again—

"Tolk's okay. I just got word."

Jos' relief was so great that he almost sobbed. He felt like the legendary world-carrying giant Salta must have felt when he had transferred his burden to a pedestal of platinum cast for him by his brother Yorell.

"Thank you" was all he could manage.

Alive! Tolk was alive!

"She won't be coming back down anytime soon, I'm afraid. The explosion took out four decks in the ventral hull area, including, as I'm sure you know, the docking bays. She's helping tend to the injured."

"Doesn't matter," Jos said. "As long as she's safe."

"Merit's okay, too."

"I knew he was off base," Jos said. "Didn't know he'd gone upstairs." He noticed then that the colonel still wore a grim expression. "What?"

"I recently spoke with Jedi Offee, and, based on some tests we ran pursuant to her suggestions, we've confirmed that this was not an accident. It was sabotage. Probably the same person or persons who blew up the transport."

Jos stared at him, unable to process, for a moment, what Vaetes had just said. Sabotage? Again? They'd never found out who had destroyed the bota transport, and now the same thing had happened, this time on a much larger scale.

The news was shocking. There were supposed to be some rules, some accords, even in war. Hospital ships had been considered inviolate ever since the Great Hyperspace War. Even though the orbiting ships were easy targets, the concept of damaging or destroying one was anathema to civilized beings.

Or had been, until now . . .

16

Den seemed to be spending pretty much all his time in the cantina lately. He wasn't 100 percent okay with that, although it had its advantages. For one thing, it was the warmest place in the Rimsoo, by far. For another, it was the easiest place to meet people, and people were usually the starting points for the kind of stories that he did best.

And third, of course, there were the drinks.

It took a lot to get a Sullustan drunk—truly, seriously, falling-down-and-missing-the-floor drunk. Jos had tried to explain the physiology of it to him once, using a lot of jawbreaking words like *glycolysis, mitochondria,* and *polymorphic chemisorption*—the gist of it all being that his body's cells were very selective about which molecules they used and how. Which meant that an amount of liquor that would have most carbon-based species sitting with arms or tentacles around each other's shoulders, singing old Corellian drinking songs, merely gave him a pleasant buzz.

He was buzzed now, and saw no reason not to get a little bit more so. He'd cleared his bar tab when the payment for his last story—the puff piece for *Beings* holozine on Uli Divini, Boy Surgeon—had come in. Now he signaled Teedle, who rolled over to his table. "Another Johrian whiskey, Teedle—on the rocks."

"You got it, hon." She wheeled away, and Den shouted after her, "And I mean *ice*!" He'd learned the hard way that the serving droid's idiomatic programming in Basic was not as extensive as it could have been.

Teedle shot back over her shoulder, "I suppose you want it in a glass, too?"

Den laughed. The comeback had been unexpected— whoever'd initiated her neural programming had at least had a sense of humor.

He glanced at the remnants of green liquid in his glass and swirled it about, thinking about recent conversations he'd had with both Jos and I-Five. The droid had said once that all of his kind had a sense of humor. Den wondered how much of Teedle's personality had been programmed in, and how much was intrinsic. There was supposedly a very simple test, developed centuries ago, which postulated that if one could carry on a conversation with another, unseen entity and not be able to tell if that entity was organic or cybernetic, then said entity had to be considered self-aware.

He'd never really heard of any droid being put to that test—at least, not in a widely publicized way. Which wasn't surprising—after all, if you're the CEO of a huge manufacturing corporation like Cybot Galactica or Industrial Automaton, you don't want your product suddenly thinking it has the same rights as a sentient organic.

He was sure I-Five could pass the test easily. Perhaps Teedle could, too.

Teedle brought his drink. "On the rocks, hon. Solid H_2O."

Den took a sip of the whiskey. It was cold and yet fiery, warming his insides. He shook the glass, listened to the ice globes tinkle together. There certainly wasn't any shortage of the frozen stuff these days. It had been over a week now since the force-dome had first malfunctioned, and still no indication as to when it was going to be fixed. They had at least stabilized the temperature, albeit at a not-terribly-comfortable minus six degrees. It had stopped snowing, but only after three kiosks had buckled under the weight. It wasn't as bad as being stuck in an outpost on Hoth—that he knew from experience—but it definitely wasn't pleasant.

From what he'd heard, there were at least two vital parts that had to be brought in from outside the system. Until they were delivered, it was going to be a long, cold winter.

He noticed a couple of the entertainers at a table not too far from him. He'd love to work up something on them—they were getting antsy about being stuck here, and who could blame them? Their schedules were already hopelessly shot. Doing a story about their plight, however, would require revealing the dome's malfunction, and the powers-that-be had decided that, for now, that fact was classified. He'd gotten a bit persnickety about it, but Vaetes had been adamant. Den couldn't see how the Separatists could take advantage of the knowledge, since everyone was claiming it was a malfunction. Still, the lid remained firmly in place, and was likely to stay there for a while.

Little to do, then, except have another drink.

The sabotage of MedStar certainly wasn't expediting matters. As far as Den had been able to determine—which wasn't much, even with his sources—the explosion had definitely been intentionally set. That in itself was horrifying enough—blowing up a hospital ship was an act of barbarism, not war—but the fact that it might be linked to the earlier transport explosion seemed to indicate that, somehow, a spy walked among them.

Needless to say, he wasn't being allowed to file that bit of news, either. Not via official channels.

He shook his head. It seemed absurd—a spy, in an out-of-the-way Rimsoo on a star-forsaken world like this? To think that, when he'd drawn this assignment, he'd come steeling himself for boredom and enforced idleness. The time he'd spent at Rimsoo Seven had been anything but boring.

As he finished his drink, he saw I-Five enter the cantina. He made an inviting gesture, but the droid headed instead for the bar, where Teedle was.

The two droids spoke for a moment. Den was close enough to overhear the conversation. Usually he had no compunctions at all about eavesdropping, but since this conversation was in Binary instead of Basic, there wasn't a lot to be gleaned from the rapidfire clicks, beeps, and whistles exchanged.

After a moment, Teedle went on her way and I-Five joined Den at the table.

"Didn't know you spoke Binary," Den said.

"This comes as a surprise? Surely you know that protocol droids—even a discontinued line like mine—are programmed extensively with languages."

"Right. So I guess you were just making nice with the lady."

"Hardly. If you must know, I was asking for her model number and field substrate parameters."

Den was just drunk enough to find this hilarious. "Great line," he said between giggles. "Maybe I'll try it on that cute little dancer with the troupe. *C'mon back to my cube, doll—we'll discuss field substrate parameters.*" He laughed again.

"Organics are endlessly amusing," I-Five said. "If only to themselves."

Den managed to stop laughing, though his dewflaps fluttered with barely contained mirth. "Don't be stuffy. We never did get you drunk, did we? Had a few ideas, but nothing seemed to work."

"And I'm honestly not sure whether to be grateful or aggrieved about that. Klo Merit's suggestion would probably work, but only after I've retrieved all lost memory data. Until then, my nonlocal control dampeners would prevent any baseline alteration."

"Well, I'm still working on it. Have no fear." Den drained the last of his drink.

"How comforting. Is this where you pass out face-first in the bowl of shroomchips again? Because, much as I enjoy organic physical comedy, I do have many more non-challenging tasks to perform."

"I'm not *that* drunk," Den said. He set his empty glass on the table without overturning it, though it took a little effort.

"The important thing is that you believe that." The droid headed for the door, stepping aside to allow two beings to enter. Den squinted against the momentary dazzle of the snow's reflection. He recognized them after a moment as the Umbaran and the Falleen. Recent arrivals for some administrative task or other, if he recalled correctly. No doubt they answered to the new supply sergeant. He felt a moment's envy for them—at least they were performing some kind of function here. Until the blackout was lifted, he had little to do other than sit in the cantina and drink.

Come to think of it, that wasn't such a bad job after all . . .

17

It was done.

The spy stood before a viewport, looking down at the green-and-blue planet below. The initial cost had been thirty-three biological lives, seventeen droids, and several billion credits' worth of damage. And it would ultimately be far more. Because Column had been ordered to destroy the lower decks, reception of patients from the planet had been severely curtailed—sick and wounded would begin stacking up in Rimsoos, and some of those who would have lived had they been transferred to Med-Star would not make it. Bota shipments would be drastically slowed, as well—but not so much as to arouse Black Sun's ire. The gangsters were aware of Column's Separatist connections. It was a narrow line being walked here, no doubt about that. The spy had to make sure that the services performed for Black Sun outweighed inconveniences in the matter of the bota shipments, or Kaird of the Nediji might soon be knocking on Column's door as he had on Admiral Bleyd's.

It was indisputably a setback for the Republic. Enough by itself to win the war? No, of course not. But it was another block on the bantha's back, as the saying went. Who could say that this might not be the one that made the creature's burden too great? Or the one just shy of doing so?

Still, Column felt no satisfaction, no closure. To blow up a medical ship, or even part of one, was vile, heinous, reprehensible. There were people on Drongar who thought well of Column and, if they knew what the spy had done, would turn away in disgust. Or—more likely—cheer were Column to be executed in a sleet of blasterfire. Those who didn't clamor to be the ones who pulled the triggers . . .

Best not to dwell on it, the spy knew. Painful experiences left scars, and even years later they could throb and blaze, if one paid them too much mind. Best to put them in a closet and close and lock the door. They would always be there, but if one didn't look at them, there in the dark, they didn't hurt as much. Sometimes it was the only way to move on.

They still thought it was an accident, as far as the spy had been able to determine, so they weren't looking for a saboteur. Eventually, operations between the ship and the planet would return to normal. And Column would be allowed to leave and return to the Rimsoo.

To contemplate the next inevitable blow against the Republic.

To call the results of the intramuscular injection of bota extract into the dying trooper a miracle was perhaps stretching the meaning of the term as Barriss understood it; still, there was no denying that the man had been calling on death's door a few hours earlier, yet he was now awake and alert, his fever was gone, and his rapidly failing organ systems were on the mend, if the telemetric monitors were functioning correctly. His white cell count with its bacterial shift was markedly decreased, though still slightly elevated. He was, for all intents and purposes, nearly well.

Amazing.

Barriss had six more of the bota muscle-poppers given to her by Jos, and she knew several patients who could certainly benefit from them. Those who were more human in their species-tap seemed to derive the most antibacterial and antiviral benefits, but those for whom the drug functioned primarily as an analgesic, and who were in extensive pain that was unabated by ordinary narcotics, would appreciate the injections as well.

There were a lot more patients in the Rimsoo than usual—the explosion aboard MedStar had slowed their transfers, and while most of them were stable, some still needed more care than the Rimsoo could provide. The bota would help that. Problem was, it wouldn't last long.

Even as she made her rounds through the medical ward, Barriss was already wondering how she might get more of the miracle plant. The larger crops were, of course, guarded, but Jos had told her that there were smaller clumps still growing wild. These patches Zan had found, and used for his preparations. If she could find a wild patch and harvest even half a kilo or so, she could make a suspension that might treat fifty or a hundred patients. She didn't know the precise dosage and proportions of active ingredients to carrier solution, but she could analyze one of the remaining poppers and figure that out. Chemistry and pharmaceutical preparation hadn't been her two favorite subjects during medical training, but she had managed to learn enough in both to pass with honors. She would find a way to make it work.

Too bad Zan didn't leave notes, she thought. *That would have saved some time and trouble.*

Of course, leaving such notes around could get one in deep trouble if somebody found them. What Zan and Jos

had done, and what she had in mind to do, was technically illegal. It was not, however, immoral, and her Jedi
and medical training were in complete accord on such
matters. There were laws, and then there were laws.
Some of them had been passed for the wrong reasons,
and many were flawed—nearly every rule had some exception. When the choice came down to a legal act or a
moral act, the Jedi making the choice would ideally do
both. But circumstances were seldom ideal, and in such
cases one should always choose the moral way, and be
willing to suffer the consequences, if any.

In this case, it wasn't complicated. Saving lives was the
right thing to do. If the means to do that were at hand,
and one allowed people to die because of a law that had
been passed to favor the rich and powerful—well, that
was wrong.

She heard a low moan, and turned to see one of the several nonclone patients, a Rodian lieutenant called
Zheepho, thrashing in his bed, struggling against the
pressor field holding him in place. Zheepho had chronic
smashbone fever, which had apparently been dormant
for years, but had recently recurred. The intensity of the
muscular contractions caused by the pathogen—a form
of microorganism not quite a bacterium, nor exactly a
virus, but somewhere in between—was such that the infected's ligaments would tear and bones sometimes snap
during the more violent episodes of tetany. The illness
carried a 50 percent mortality rate, even when treated.
There was no cure, and most of the muscle relaxants they
had on hand were not effective on Rodians. A brain-stem
surgical disconnect would stop both afferent and efferent
nerve conduction, but—besides the small matter of leaving the patient totally paralyzed as far as voluntary

movement was concerned—it wouldn't stop the convulsions, because the infection was in the muscle tissue itself, not just the CNS.

Maybe the bota would help. Zheepho was in much pain, and could soon die if something wasn't done. In over half of the cases, the infection spread to the organs, and something vital—heart, liver, or lungs, most likely— would shut down. Barriss had checked, but the literature—at least what she could access here—held no mention of the effects of bota on Rodians.

But it wasn't as if he had much to lose. There were no fatal side effects of bota on any known species. And the continued episodes of tetany could very well damage Zheepho beyond the Rimsoo's ability to properly treat, even if he survived the illness itself.

She approached the thrashing Rodian. She'd have to drop the pressor field to inject him. A deltoid or thigh jab would do the job. The popper would blast the aerosolized drug right into the muscle tissue—if she could do it before he spasmed again. She might have to use the Force to hold him still.

She reached the bed. "Zheepho," she said. "I'm Barriss Offee, a Jedi healer."

"Ex-excuse m-m-me if I d-don't g-g-get up, H-H-Healer," he managed to say between gritted lip plates.

"I have a treatment here that might help you," she said. She held up the popper. "But there is some risk, which I can't calculate properly."

The Rodian clenched all over, tightening like a giant fist. The spasm lasted twenty seconds. Blue-green perspiration broke out on his tensed body. When the spasm subsided, he croaked, "Right n-now, Healer, I would g-gladly take p-p-*poison* if y-you offered it—*ahhh*—!"

Another contraction gripped him, shorter this time.

"I'll have to drop the field. Try to hold as still as you can."

"No p-p-problem," he managed.

She felt less confident than she sounded. She couldn't do this by swaying his mind, since the spasming muscles weren't under his control. She'd have to hold him in place physically, with a controlled and sustained Force push, and that would be tricky to do without injuring him, especially given the fragile condition he was already in.

She found the connection with the Force that she needed, and thrust forward with her mind, pinning him down. He lay still, and she readied the popper. She'd drop the restraining field, reach in fast, hit him, and be out in a second or two. Ready . . . *go!*

She thumbed off the pressor field and reached in with both hands, using one to steady his leg. She pressed the popper to his thigh and reached for the trigger—

A major spasm wracked the Rodian. The unexpected severity of it shook Barriss's grasp of the Force.

Hurry—!

But as she triggered the fire button on the popper, Zheepho's leg jerked, as if a thousand volts of electricity had galvanized it. The popper bounced off his thigh. She was still gripping his leg as a second spasm hit him, throwing her momentarily off balance. Barriss lurched forward, and the injector came down—*on the back of her other hand*.

The popper sprayed the suspension extract through her skin. Some of it went into a vein—she could feel the cold rush. Quickly, she pulled back, relit the pressor field, and grabbed another bota popper from her pocket. As Zheepho's muscles relaxed, she killed the field again, jammed the popper at his leg, and fired it.

This time her luck was better.

A moment later, the field was back in place, and Barriss stood there, staring down at the Rodian. He twitched again, but less than before, and after another two minutes, the spasms stopped.

Can it work that fast? she wondered.

"Whoo," he said. "Thanks, Healer. I don't know what you did, but I'll take a barrel of it."

She smiled. "I'll come back and check on you in a little while."

The Rodian had been in the Green Bed, the last one in this ward. Barriss walked through the sterilizing field and turned into a supply chamber. She sought the Force, intending to turn it inward, to monitor herself. While it was true that bota had not shown any adverse affects on humans, she had just taken a rather whopping dose. She didn't feel any different, but still—

Sudden sourceless light washed over her.

She blinked. And saw Master Luminara Unduli, standing three meters away against the far wall, watching her and smiling.

"*Master?* How did you—?"

Master Unduli went translucent, then transparent, and then blinked off like a light going out.

With her next breath, Barriss felt sudden energy flow into her—pure, raw, vast *power*. In that moment, she felt transcendent, almost omnipotent. She was simultaneously in her body and out of it, able to sense beyond three, even four dimensions. It felt as if she could grasp the fabric of space and time, and *turn* it, *twist* it, any way that suited her. For one blinding instant she could feel the Force as she had never done before—in its entirety. There was a kind of . . . cosmic consciousness, in which she felt connected to all things, everywhere, able to do anything, anything at all—

For that timeless moment, she *was* the Force.

Suns were born, planets spawned, civilizations rose, fell, the planets grew barren, the suns cold. Time flowed like a blaster bolt, like a ship at hyperspeed, but she was able to track it all. Every detail on every world in all the galaxies to the end of the universe.

It was indescribable. This must be what it felt like to be a god, did such things exist.

How long it lasted, she couldn't say. A few moments or a few eons, there was no way to time it . . .

Then it was over. Barriss staggered back against the wall and slid down it until she was sitting on the cold floor, stunned by the experience.

She could barely breathe. The surge passed, but remnants of it continued to swirl in her, potent patterns that eddied and danced throughout her being. She felt exhausted, but . . . *wiser,* somehow . . .

What *was* this? What had just *happened* to her?

18

Jos couldn't recall feeling more excited anytime since he'd been on this planet. The transport carrying Tolk was on the way down. He stood by the pad, peering upward—not that he could see anything for the blasted clouds that still covered the arch of the dome. The snow was chest-deep in places, even with the droids shoveling it away full time. Enough heaters had been rigged so that most of the indoor spaces were bearable, some even toasty, but it was more than a little inconvenient. Even at ground level, there was a condensation that fogged one's view—they were essentially living in an opaque bubble. There hadn't been any enemy attacks near the Rimsoo lately, no stray missiles or particle beams striking anywhere close, fortunately. Were it up to Jos, he would shut the force-dome off, let the snow melt—it certainly wouldn't take long—and do repairs with the system offline. But, of course, had it been up to Jos, they wouldn't *be* on this karking planet; there wouldn't be a need for protective domes because there wouldn't be a blasted *war*.

The invisible dome window dilated, allowing the transport in, along with a fast exchange of hot and cold air that swirled fog and clouds into a momentary cyclonic vortex. The small windwhirl spun down and died as the dome closed and the ship settled from the clouds to the cleared landing pad. The snow that dropped around the launch area was lightly variegated—a pale rainbow with red the dominant shade, tinted by spore colonies that had been blown in and instantly frozen.

It seemed to take forever for the vessel to land and the port to open, and five people got off before Tolk did, of course. She was wearing surgical scrubs, and her luggage was following in a baggage droid's hamper. Jos saw chilblains start to frost her bare arms.

He felt a rush of joy that was nearly vertiginous as he saw her, and he hurried to embrace her. She relaxed into his arms for a moment, then seemed to stiffen.

"Hey. You okay?"

"I am, yes." She looked around, and shivered. "You weren't joking about the weather, were you?"

"Isn't so bad right here—over near the rep-dep there's some kind of cold spot where the snow's piled higher than a wampa on stilts." Jos took her arm and steered her back toward the camp. "Let's get you inside. You'll warm right up." He held her close with one arm, and hurried toward his kiosk.

"Let's go to my place first," she said. "I have a jacket there."

Jos shrugged. "Sure."

Inside her kiosk, the heater Jos had installed and turned on earlier had taken most of the cold from the air. Tolk sat down on her cot. "Snow," she said. "On Drongar. Amazing."

"You get over that pretty quick," he said. "Then it just gets to be a big pain in the posterior. Especially given our triage situation. If they don't get the uplift back on schedule pretty soon, we're gonna be stacking patients in warehouses—we're running out of room in the wards."

She nodded. She looked tired, Jos realized. Tired and drawn.

"Pretty bad up there?"

She sighed. "Not for me. I was on the Command Level. All we got was a big vibration before we were sealed in. I didn't know any of the people who were killed, and the injured and survivors were triaged by the emergency response teams belowdecks."

Jos shook his head. "Unbelievable. Blowing up a medical ship."

"It's a terrible thing," she said. Her voice was flat and somewhat distant.

Silence stretched. "Want some stimcaf?"

"That'd be nice."

He busied himself preparing the drink. "How was Great-Uncle Erel?"

Tolk looked away from him, at her bag. "Fine."

Even allowing for the recent past horrors, something in her demeanor struck Jos as odd. "Tolk? Are you okay?"

She waved one hand. "Yeah, I'm fine. Just tired, is all. It's been a . . . trying time."

"Got that." He hesitated. "We could go down to the cantina, get something to eat, maybe a drink?"

She looked at him. "You know, Jos, I'm really not up for it."

"Okay, sure. We can stay in, no problem. Uh, I can go pick something up at the chow—"

"Jos," she said, and her voice had a slightly brittle tone to it, which he'd heard far too many times from far too many next-of-kin. "I—I think I just need to get some rest."

"Oh. Oh, okay, sure." He hesitated, unsure of what to say. She didn't seem particularly happy to see him. Yes, she was tired, and of course it had been traumatic—but Tolk was a surgical nurse. She had seen more people die in a month than many nurses saw pass away in a decade, and under far more unpleasant conditions. She was as tough as durasteel. How could an explosion that she hadn't even been directly involved in affect her so?

He glanced at his chrono. "My shift starts in a few minutes," he said, and was slightly shocked to realize he was grateful for an excuse to leave. "I'll . . . comm you when I'm done, if that's okay?"

"That—that would be fine," she said.

He hugged her, and again she seemed to stiffen under his hands. He kissed her, and she returned it, but it was like kissing his sister—there was not even a hint of fire in it.

As he walked through the falling snow toward the OT, Jos felt a sudden sense of nameless dread envelop him. Tolk had come off the transport changed. He didn't know how or why, but she wasn't the same woman who had gone up there.

Something was wrong. Something was very wrong . . .

Den sensed that something was different when he took his usual place at the sabacc table. It took him a moment to identify what it was. Then he started to order a drink, and realized that Teedle wasn't on duty.

That was odd. Droids didn't work in shifts like organics—Teedle was always there, whenever the cantina was open. Except that she wasn't, today.

Neither were Jos and Tolk, but that was to be expected, given that the latter had just made the drop from MedStar. The players, besides himself, were Klo, Barriss, I-Five, and a new face—one he was rather pleased to see:

Eyar Marath, the Sullustan singer from the troupe. Den took his seat, which was right across the table. She looked up from her drink at him and smiled.

Den smiled back. He'd been wondering how to casually run into her, and now here was a platinum opportunity. It had been so long since he'd seen another of his own species that he'd probably find the hag-witch of To'onalk attractive. No problem here, though—Eyar was drop-dead gorgeous. She was young, true—he was probably old enough to be her father—but, judging from the look she was giving him, she wasn't thinking of him in that way. She had lustrous eyes, dark as obsidian and large even for a Sullustan. Her ears were delicately shaped, with large whorls and lobes; her jowls glistened with saliva. They flushed a deeper shade of pink as she smiled at him.

Oh, yeah. What a sugarcane this one was!

"*Wa loota, maga nu,*" she said. "*Mi nama Eyar Ahtram.*"

Den blinked. She was speaking in the inferior inflective, just as a fem would to a mate.

"*Wa denga, see't boos'e. Mi nama Den Dhur.*"

She smiled again, and suddenly Den wasn't the least bit cold. Not the least bit. Nobody's father at *this* table.

"Where's Teedle?" he asked the table at large. He felt a sudden urge for a drink.

No one answered.

He glanced at Merit, saw the big Equani looking slightly discomfited. He said, "She is no longer with us."

"What? Reassigned? She just got here." He wanted a Blaster or two to loosen him up; it wasn't like he needed it, but still . . .

There came another uncomfortable silence. Then I-Five broke it: "The TDL-five-oh-one unit has been disassembled."

"Come again?"

"It was necessary to obtain the central drive component. The TDL-five-oh-one unit was one of the latest models from Cybot Galactica, and its YX-Ninety Drive's technical specs were compatible with the phase harmonics generator secondary drive of the force-dome. It was—"

Den held up his hands to stop the droid. "Hold up a minute—you're telling me she's been *cannibalized*?"

I-Five's expression and voice seemed flatter than usual, if that were possible. "Engineering Section learned that it would be a minimum of five standard weeks before a replacement drive for the damaged generator could be delivered, so they sought some suitable replacement, and requisitioned the TDL-five-oh-one's—"

"Teedle," Den said. "Her name's *Teedle*."

I-Five paused a moment, then continued: "They requisitioned the unit's YX-Ninety. Its field parameters are within the range needed to realign the phase harmonics generator."

Den stared at the droid, his jaw sagging. "I don't believe this. They broke her down for *parts*? How could they? She was more than just—" He stopped as the full implications of I-Five's statement hit him. "Field parameters. I remember. You asked her about that—"

Barriss said, "Den, I-Five isn't—"

Den ignored her and stared at the droid. "*You* fingered her?"

I-Five said, "I was ordered to determine the potential usefulness of the unit's drive."

"I can't believe it. One of your own kind."

"As much as I hate to rain on your righteous indignation," Barriss said, "there are one or two things about this that you don't know." There was something odd in her voice, Den noticed, but he didn't have time to worry about that. His best server was gone and her "friend" I-Five had been responsible.

"I know all I need to know—"

"Teedle volunteered, Den." That from Merit.

He stared at the minder. "Huh?"

Merit said, "She knew what the consequences would be. It was Teedle who noticed the range compatibility. I-Five merely confirmed it. It wasn't his idea."

Den shook his head. Gutted her. As sentient as anybody at the table, and funny besides, but—*rip!* just like that.

"I believe you owe I-Five an apology," Barriss said. Again, there was something in her voice, something he couldn't quite pin down. She seemed, well, older. Much older. But that was silly.

"Unnecessary," I-Five said. "I am, after all, merely a droid. Why should I take offense?"

Den sighed. "I'm sorry, I-Five. I was a parsec out of line. I, uh . . . oh, to deep with it. Let's play cards."

Klo began to deal—they had dispensed with the Card-Shark's services several games back, and now it usually sulked in a corner while they played.

So there it was, Den thought. Another reminder of the difference between droids and biologicals. Someone they interacted with as a person could be . . . shut down, just like that, because she had a widget that was more useful elsewhere. Of course, people died in wars all the time— companions with whom you shared drinks and laughs could be taken away in the blink of an eye, zip-zap, just like that, but this was different. It made a Sullustan stop and think.

Den picked up his hand, glancing at Eyar Marath as he did so. She smiled back. Good. At least his temper tantrum hadn't driven her off. She was beautiful. How long had it been since he'd even sat at a table with one of his own species, much less clapped flaps? Too long.

A thought occurred to him. "Well. Sorry. After all, once the drive they ordered arrives, they should be able to repair Teedle and she'll be as good as new, right?"

There was another moment of frozen silence. Then I-Five said, almost gently, "They didn't requisition the new drive, Den. The military will compensate the corporation that owns Teedle, but they see no need to pay for the repairs twice."

Den stared. "Kark," he said.

"An apt expression," I-Five replied.

Merit dealt the cards.

19

Jos had finally managed to obtain a jacket and a pair of thermal gloves, which meant that the dome would almost certainly be repaired soon. It seemed like it never failed that, if he went out of his way to prepare for something, the need soon vanished. But at least for the moment, he was better off.

He was on his way to the chow hall when his comlink beeped.

"Doctor Vandar, we have a problem in the OT."

"I'm off duty—" Jos began.

"Yes, sir, Colonel Vaetes knows that, but he asks if you'll please stop by."

"Okay. I'm coming."

At the operating theater, business was slow, with only a few patients. Half a dozen doctors and nurses were gathered around one of the tables, Vaetes among them. He turned, saw Jos, and stepped away from the patient, who was hidden from view by the group.

"Colonel? What's the problem?"

"You ever work on a Nikto?"

Jos's eyebrows went up. "You have a horn-face? I didn't know there were any on this world."

"Afraid so. One of the crew working the bota fields. Ran over a piece of unexploded ordnance and blew the harvester to pieces. Patient's full of shrapnel, and nobody here has ever opened a Nikto before. You've cut on a slew of species—any experience on this one?"

Jos blew out a sigh. "Not since my first-year surgical rotation. I'm not really qualified to—"

"Nobody else here has ever laid a blade on one, Jos. Not even Lieutenant Divini. Whatever you know is better than what we don't know."

He was right. "I'll scrub," Jos said.

"Thanks. Tolk is already here."

Jos nodded.

He hurried through his scrub, was gowned and gloved by the sterile circulating nurse, and stepped up to the field. He saw Tolk across the table, lining up instruments. He'd been hoping to get more of a sense of her mood, but they had a crowd watching, and that wasn't how he wanted to talk to her.

As if some bored war deity had read his thoughts, the drone of a medlifter dopplered up.

"Incoming, people!" Vaetes shouted. "Jos, you got this?"

"Probably not, but you looking over my shoulder isn't going to help much. Go. If I have a problem, I'll yell."

The watchers cleared out, leaving Jos, Tolk, and the circulating sterile droids. Jos looked across the field. The sparkle and shimmer of the overheads against the electrostatic boundary gave Tolk's masked face an almost otherworldly quality. *Even gowned and masked,* he thought, *she's beautiful.*

"Hey," he said.

"Hey," Tolk said. Her eyes, above her mask, didn't seem to be smiling. She wasn't looking at him.

Jos glanced at the patient. Nikto were reptilian in appearance, with a couple of dozen small horns haloed around the face and crown, and a larger pair on the chin. There were four or five different subspecies; this one had greenish gray skin, which meant it was a mountain and forest dweller. His clothes had been cut off, and there were several stanched wounds on his torso.

The procedure would be the same as with any patient, in that Jos would have to track the wound channels and mine the shrapnel, then repair injured organs. And he'd have to work with what was there, because he was pretty sure there weren't any cloned Nikto organs in the bank.

Getting to the shrapnel wouldn't be easy. The Nikto's scales had shifted to overlap the entry points. This was an autonomic reaction, evolved over millennia, to keep the wounds as sterile and protected as possible until they healed. Usually that worked quite well—but usually there weren't several big chunks of durasteel sealed in a Nikto's viscera.

"We need to relax the muscles enough to be able to lift his abdominal scale plates," he said to Paleel, the circulating nurse who wasn't scrubbed sterile. "Find out what does that to a Nikto."

"Already got it," the nurse said. "Myoplexaril, variant four. Three milligrams per kilo of body weight, IV."

"Okay. What does he weigh?"

"Sixty kilograms."

Jos did the math. "Give him one eighty of Myoplexaril, vee-four, IV push."

Somebody had started an intravenous big-bore, TKO, which was good. Running IVs was a primitive process at best, and, on top of that, Jos had never enjoyed starting them on reptiloids—finding a vein under scaled skin was always a challenge. But all the osmotic drips were in use at the moment, so he had to make do with what was available. Threndy, the other nurse, filled an injector with muscle relaxant, double-checked the medicine vial and dosage, and pressed the injector against the IV's Rx portal.

It would take a moment for the pharmaceutical to do the trick. Jos said, "Threndy, why don't you finish the instrument sort? Paleel, go and get a second reptiloid kit, just in case. Tolk, over here and help me categorize wounds."

The nurses moved.

With Tolk now standing next to him, if they kept their voices down, they could have a private conversation. "You okay?" he asked.

She kept her gaze on the patient. "I'm fine."

"You don't seem fine. Since you got back from Med-Star, you've seemed, well . . . distant."

She looked at him, then back at the patient. "Looks like this one got hit in the spleen—if they have spleens." She pointed at a puncture wound with a stat-patch.

"Tolk."

She sighed. "What do you want me to say, Jos? It wasn't a visit to a pleasure dome. I saw people spewed into space like ripe poptree seeds. The lucky ones died right away."

"People die here every day," he said. "You seem to be able to deal with that."

"Not the same," she said.

"It wasn't like you did it, Tolk."

She gave him a sharp glance, and was about to say something when the patient's abdominal plate relaxed and retracted—and a gush of purplish hemolymph from one of the now exposed wounds lanced out and hit him squarely in the chest.

The next few minutes were occupied with stopping the flow of vital fluid. The nurses and droids handled that, while Jos stepped away from the table. He'd have to change clothes and rescrub. Which meant a serious conversation with Tolk wasn't going to happen now.

Blast.

But he wasn't going to drop it. Something was wrong, something over and above the trauma of what had happened. There was something that Tolk wasn't telling him. And he wouldn't rest until he knew what it was.

Barriss Offee was having a hard time concentrating on her work.

In front of her, in a bed in the recovery ward, a trooper lay—or rather, most of him did. His legs had been chewed by shrapnel up to midthigh. The solution was to outfit the soldier with cybertronic prosthetics—robotic legs that, once covered with a layer of synthflesh, would be nearly indistinguishable from the real thing. Barriss's job was to use the Force to prepare the trooper for the circuit grafts and implants by easing systemic shock reaction. It was a fairly easy task—a simple matter of soothing the autonomic nervous system and stimulating biological response modifiers. She'd done it dozens of times before with no glitches. There was no reason to assume it would be any different this time.

Nevertheless, she could not do it.

Since experiencing that searing, that "cosmic" connection, Barriss had been afraid to reach out to the Force again. Though there was no logical reason to fear it, still she found herself paralyzed every time she attempted a link.

She was aware that this was not a good situation, especially given her position here on this war-ravaged world. Though the last few days had been light on casualties, Rimsoo Seven could be inundated again at any time, and when that happened her abilities would be needed to save lives. She couldn't afford to remain helpless.

Her mind knew all this. Her heart, however, still shied away from the bond that had been a part of her life for so long.

That couldn't *be* any more wrong.

She told the FX-7 droid on duty to put the clone back in short-term cryosupport. She'd be doing him no favors trying to modulate his BRMs now, given the uncertain state she was in. She needed to get out, to clear her head. Perhaps a game of sabacc was indicated . . .

Alone in her kiosk, Barriss sat and stared at the wall. She had sought out company, but being in the presence of her friends hadn't helped to resolve matters. The power of her experience—and she was sure it had been real, not a hallucination—still thrummed in her, though it was now but a faint echo of what it had been; the drip of a single raindrop after the roar of a storm.

Even so, playing cards in the cantina and exchanging small talk with the doctors and nurses hadn't helped her do anything other than put off dealing with it. She couldn't talk to any of her colleagues—what was she going to say? *Hey, Jos, I just became one with the entire galaxy . . . and how's that case of Ortolan rhinorrhea you've been dealing with?*

None of them could help her, and there was nobody else she knew of who had experienced it—certainly not anyone at hand.

If anyone else ever *had* experienced it . . .

Barriss knew she wasn't the smartest Jedi who had ever lived, but she wasn't anywhere close to the stupidest, either. She knew what had happened. She had taken a therapeutic, if accidental, dose of the bota extract. There was no doubt in her mind that the unintentional injection and her sudden, overpowering connection to the Force had been cause and effect. She didn't know the why or the how, but she was certain that the panaceatic chemical concoction had produced yet another miracle, this time by intensifying her connection to the Force by an order of magnitude she couldn't even begin to tally.

When, as a youngling, she had first learned to use the Force, it seemed to her as if she had been living in a dark cave, and had finally been given a lamp to light her way. She could, of a moment, see, whereas before she had been feeling her way in the murk. It had been a most intense and profound revelation.

Compared to that, the experience she'd had after the accident in the ward had been like trading in that lamp for her own personal sun—a difference comparable to being able to see a vast plain, all the way to the horizon, in every minute detail, as opposed to the corner of a single small room. It was as if she were a hawk-bat, capable of spotting a rock shrew the size of her thumb from a thousand meters away, as opposed to being a blind granite slug, grubbing myopically at the few millimeters directly before her.

What did it mean?

Her first reaction had been to comm her Master. Luminara Unduli would know, or she would have access to somebody with knowledge. In any event, there was certainly no reason to try to puzzle it out on her own, certainly not when she had the vast resources of the Temple's archives at her disposal.

And so she had tried—but her communications unit was not working. Everything seemed fine, all the circuits tested clean, but there was no signal. Something was jamming the frequency; she could not even get an offworld carrier hyperwave, and she had no idea why. Possibly it was due to some military operation—it was entirely feasible that the Republic or the Separatists had recently implemented some device that could blanket a planet and stop transmissions such as hers. Or could it be a natural phenomenon? There were magnetic and flux storms in realspace that sometimes cast subspatial reverberations and interrupted comm signals. Drongar Prime was a hot sun; its coronal discharges were certainly strong enough . . .

Barriss made a frustrated gesture. No point in theorizing—she had to talk to *somebody* who knew more about the Force than she did, to pass this along and decide what—if anything—needed to be done about it. She'd tried the unit again, as soon as she'd gotten back to her kiosk, but of course it still wasn't working.

There was another way, however, an elegantly simple way: take another blast of the bota. She was almost certain that she could figure out just about anything, once she returned to that ineffable state in which she had been before, if this time she was expecting it and prepared for it. The experience held within it all manner of knowledge; she could still feel the truth of that. Once she understood the parameters of the event, Barriss could present the Jedi Council with something of incalculable value. She couldn't even imagine the miracles that a true Jedi Master could perform while suffused with such power. Why, even the small handful of the Order remaining could turn the course of the war, could easily defeat Dooku's forces and restore galactic peace, did they but have access to the kind of power Barriss had experienced. She knew this to be true; she had felt as if she could accomplish all that by herself, so she knew that, with such mystical strength in the hands of Luminara or Obi-Wan or Yoda, *anything* would be possible.

But—could she prepare herself sufficiently to ride that massive and all-powerful wave again? It seemed entirely possible that the next time it might roll over her, and she wouldn't be able to struggle free. Maybe it would claim her for itself, and never let her go, transform her somehow into something totally outside the experience of her or anyone else . . .

Barriss sighed. This was beyond her skill, her talents, her ability. She needed help, but there wasn't anyone here capable of providing it. It seemed that, until she could talk to Master Unduli, she would be better off doing nothing.

But that wasn't as easy as it sounded, by any means. The memory of the power, frightening as it was, nevertheless cried out to her. Its call was so tempting. Even though she was afraid, she longed to try it again.

It would be easy. There were several skinpoppers filled with the distillate literally within arm's reach. It would be but a second's work to take one, push it against her flesh, trigger it . . .

So easy . . .

Barriss wrapped her arms around herself and shivered, feeling a cold that had nothing to do with the snow outside.

20

"Jos, my friend. How are you feeling?"

Jos looked at the minder. "Well, if truth be known, I've had better days. Better months. Decades."

"Oh?"

Jos squirmed uncomfortably—a difficult task in the formchair that fought to match his every move and make the position comfortable. "You, uh, know about me and Tolk."

The Equani steepled his fingers. "Fortunately, I have not gone blind or deaf recently."

"Yeah, well . . . I thought we were flying like a land-speeder with custom harmonics. Only lately she's . . . cooled."

"How so?"

Jos sighed. Everything about Klo and his office was designed to be calming—his manner, the decor, the patient's formchair—but Jos had yet to be able to relax when he came here. It wasn't that he felt distrustful of Klo, or of the whole minder process, the way many of his family did. Even though he came from a long line of medics, many of his immediate ancestors looked askance upon the concept of healing through mental therapy. Though his father would never come right out and admit it, Jos knew that the senior Vandar was much more comfortable curing depression, anxiety, schizophrenia and the like with adjustments of dopamine, serotonin, and somatostatin levels, rather than by empathetic feedback. Jos told himself he didn't share this bias, but even so, he was always tense in Merit's office.

He wasn't sure why he had come this time. He hadn't had an appointment, he'd just taken advantage of Merit's free time. He needed to bounce this problem off somebody, and his kiosk mate was not as old as some of Jos's boots.

"Tolk and I were doing fine . . . then she went up to take a CME class on MedStar. She was there when the decks blew—and since she's gotten back, she's been frostier than the snow outside your window."

Merit nodded. "Why do you think that is?"

"If I knew, I wouldn't be here, now would I?"

"Did you two argue about anything?"

"No."

Merit nodded, and leaned back in his own formchair, which adjusted to match his new balance and contours. "Well, the accident was distressing to a lot of people."

"The way I heard it," Jos said, "it wasn't an accident."

Merit shrugged. "I've heard those rumors as well. Of course, the powers-that-be might want people to think that way—after all, if it was sabotage, that lets Security off the hook. The Republic is not immune to watching-your-backside disease."

Jos knew that. He shrugged. "Barriss says it was deliberate. I believe her."

"Well, it doesn't really matter for the purposes of our discussion. Whether the blowout was an accident or on purpose, it seems that the trauma of it may have hit Tolk harder than she's letting on."

"I've thought of that. But I don't see how. We have more people die in this Rimsoo in any given month—in a week, sometimes—than died in the MedStar blast. Tolk is often working on them when they go, looking them right in the eyes. Why wouldn't that bother her more than a bunch of people she didn't know, and didn't have to deal with?"

"I can't say." Klo paused, as if considering something.

"What?"

"Nothing."

"I'm not a face reader, a Jedi, or a minder, Klo, but I didn't just fall off the melbulb freighter, either. What?"

"How well do you know Tolk? I mean, yes, you've worked with her during your tour here, and you have established a relationship that, I assume, is physical?"

"You can assume that."

"But—what do you know of her background? Her people, her politics, her social development?"

"What are you getting at?"

"Perhaps she has reasons to be upset that you can't see. Perhaps there's something in her background she hasn't revealed to you."

"I don't think I like the way this conversation is going."

The minder raised a pacifying hand. "I meant no insult to Tolk," he said. "I'm merely suggesting that, as you point out, there would seem no ostensible reason for her to be more upset about an explosion on the MedStar than she'd be in the day-to-day goings-on here in the Rimsoo. Therefore, there could be another reason."

Jos blinked at him. "Are you suggesting that she had something to *do* with it?"

"Of course not, Jos. Only that there is apparently something going on with Tolk about which you seem to be in the dark. If you had any idea what that might be, maybe you could resolve this. At the very least, you'd have more tools to work with."

Jos brooded. "So far, I haven't been able to get her to talk to me about anything of substance."

"And therefore you lack enough information to make even an educated guess. You might see if you can find out more. It could be nothing serious—some past trauma connected to her family or friends that triggered old memories, for example. But until you gather more data, all you have is speculation," Klo said. "There's no future in that."

Jos nodded. Klo was right. He needed to talk to Tolk about this, find out what was really bothering her. They could deal with it together, whatever it was.

Unless, of course, Tolk had had something to do with the bombing . . .

Jos shook his head. No way. He wasn't sure of much these days, but he was sure that Tolk could never have anything to do with such a horrendous crime, no matter what. What healer could? Their job was to save lives, not take them.

"Thanks, Klo. I won't take any more of your time."

"They're still playing cards in the cantina. I-Five was winning. Cleaned me to my daily limit," Klo said with a smile, "which is why I'm back here."

Jos stood. "Maybe I'll go have a drink and play a few hands."

"Why not?"

Jos smiled and left.

He didn't make it as far as the cantina.

When he was halfway there, crossing the open area referred to as the Quad, he and several others braving the cold stopped in their tracks, momentarily paralyzed by an ear-smiting crack of something very much like thunder. *What the—?*

A moment later, the temperature began to rise. It was easy to tell the difference because it was happening so quickly.

Jos knew very little about how weather worked, but he knew that when warm air collided with cold air, things happened. And things were definitely happening now. A thick mist formed almost immediately, making it impossible to see more than a few meters ahead. He was buffeted by microbursts of wind from different directions, some hot, some cold, that whipped up flurries of melting, spore-tinged snow. Hard spatters of rain hit the ground in staccato bursts. Through the mist he could see eerie flickers of light—electrical discharges that he'd heard referred to in the past as Jedi's Fire. It glimmered on the tips of his fingers. He stood still. The voltage required to break through the air was high, obviously, but his capacity to store a charge was relatively small. He was in no danger. He hoped . . .

The mist began to clear after a few moments. Jos felt the air becoming charged with moisture as the temperature continued to rise. He began to sweat, and started doffing layers of clothing: coat, vest, his outer pair of pants. Mud squished under his shoes.

"Looks like Teedle's sacrifice wasn't in vain," Den Dhur's voice said. Jos looked about, and saw the diminutive Sullustan slowly materialize as the fog thinned.

"Winter seems to be going away at a good clip."

Jos nodded. For better or worse, the malfunctioning force-dome had apparently been repaired. And already he was missing the cold.

Another humanoid form took shape a few paces

ahead. It was I-Five. The droid was looking up. Jos followed his gaze. For the first time in weeks the relentless glare of Drongar Prime was visible.

"Guess things are back to normal," he said to I-Five.

"Indeed."

Jos looked about the base. Icicles were dripping and disintegrating, the mud was getting deeper, and the ripe and fecund smells of the Jasserak Highlands were back with a rancid vengeance. All that was needed was the sound of incoming medlifters to provide the finishing touch.

Even as the thought crossed his mind, the heavy air began to pulse with the distant throb of repulsors.

"They're playing our song," he said to the droid as he turned back toward the OT. He felt unaccountably content. For better or worse, things seemed to be back to normal. No more surprises for a while, perhaps. Was that too much to ask?

Probably . . .

I-Five hadn't moved. "Come on," Jos called to him. "We've got jobs to do, remember?"

The droid turned and looked at Jos. The subtle light shadings of his photoreceptors gave his metallic face a look of wonder. "I remember," he said.

Jos stopped. "You remember what?"

"I remember *everything*."

21

On Kaird's payroll was the human in charge of the xenobotanists monitoring the bota. Kaird, always thinking ahead, his identity always hidden within his Kubaz disguise, had been paying the man handsomely for information regarding the state of the crop.

Kaird met the man in a refresher, the door blocked against unwanted company. The air scrubbers were, like so much of the Rimsoo's equipment, only intermittently functional, and so the place smelled very bad.

The news, however, smelled worse.

"It's not unprecedented," the xenobotanist said. "Have you ever heard of the ironwithe plants of Bogden?"

"No."

"Quite fascinating. Nearly as hard as durasteel, and very popular as an export for rooftop gardens on Coruscant and other Core worlds. Its shoots are the major part of the giant renda bear's diet, and—"

"Fascinating. Is there a point?"

"Sorry. Well, every few decades there's a planetwide die-off of ironwithe. No one's sure why. It's like there's some sort of plant telepathy that triggers a near-extinction event. The really amazing thing is that it even affects the ironwithe growth parsecs away, on other worlds. The theory is that there's some kind of quantum entanglement reaction in the DNA that—"

"Just tell me *exactly* what it means regarding the bota," Kaird said, resisting the urge to strangle the man.

"The plant life here is constantly mutating, and that includes bota. There is a new mutation, and from all appearances, it's planetwide. We don't know why; it could have been triggered by anything. The change seems to be altering the bota's adaptogenic properties."

"Which means . . . ?"

"If it continues in this direction—and there seems to be no reason why it won't—within another generation, bota will be, for all intents and purposes, inert. Useless."

Silently, inside his mask, Kaird cursed. How was he supposed to explain *this* to his vigo? It was not his fault, he could hardly control what had happened, but vigos had been known to blast messengers bearing bad news before.

"Who else knows of this?"

"Well, except for you and me, nobody yet. I haven't made my report to the military. I thought you would want to know first."

"Good. Can you delay this report?"

"Not for long. Botanical stations around the continent run periodic tests. These reports are funneled through my office, and I might be able to sit on them for a week or two, but no more. A few weak batches are not unusual, but something like this will get out." The human shrugged. "People talk."

For a moment, Kaird considered killing the botanist. It seemed the easiest way to keep this under wraps as long as possible. But—no. Killing him would only guarantee that he would be replaced, and the replacement might not be as venal. Better to have the man in charge working for him. Knowledge was, as always, power. Much could be accomplished in a short time with millions, maybe even billions, of credits at stake.

"All right," Kaird said. "There will be a large bonus for you. Keep this information quiet as long as you can."

The human fidgeted nervously. "They'll fire me if they find out."

"I'll get you a better job, making three times as much."

The botanist stared at him.

"Trust me. I have many useful contacts." Kaird pulled a credit cube from his pouch and tossed it to the man. The botanist triggered it. The amount appeared as a red number in the air in front of him. It was equal to his salary for two years.

"Whoa!"

"That, and that much more if you keep the lid on this for two weeks."

The man nodded. Greed shone from his face. "All right."

The man left, and Kaird lost no time in vacating the close, ill-smelling building as well.

As he tromped through the mud back to his quarters—too bad the lovely weather of the past couple of weeks had vanished with the dome's repair—Kaird thought about the situation. Bota had always been fragile, of course, and it wasn't surprising that the past few weeks of severe local climate change had resulted in a loss of the nearby crop. They'd planned on compensating for this by increasing production from the other fields. Much of the harvest on the Tanlassa continent was shipped through Rimsoo Seven, and with Thula and Squa Tront doctoring the manifests, Black Sun's take would not have been affected much. This could still be accomplished to a degree, and it might help keep the problem quiet for a few extra days.

But that was merely a stopgap solution. The only way to salvage this situation was to get as much of the bota encased in carbonite as quickly as possible, and on its way to Black Sun. If the plant shifted from a miracle drug to a useless weed, then however much of it was still potent would become that much more valuable.

When he'd been a youngling, he'd learned from a favorite aunt a trader's story: if you have the only case of a rare, vintage rimble-wine worth a thousand credits a bottle, and you want to maximize your profit, drink all but one of them, and put the last bottle in a secure vault. There were many rich people who would pay a fortune for something that was unique, but who wouldn't bother if there were a dozen, or even fewer, just like it in the whole galaxy. The single bottle would be worth more than the case.

Bota, because of its properties, was already one of the most valuable of drugs. If the possibility of obtaining fresh supplies was gone, what was left would appreciate in value faster than a ship going lightspeed. A rich and seriously ill person would pay a lot to stave off death. How many credits you had didn't mean anything when they stuck your corpse in the recycler.

Kaird considered his options: he could steal a large amount of the bota and try to smuggle it offworld on a military or commercial vessel . . .

No. Too risky. Too many elements he could not control.

He could contact Black Sun—assuming he could get his communicator working. He had been unable to make a connection the last few days, and while that might change, it was also a risk. Once the mutation became known, the military would triple the guards on it, and that would make things worse.

Taking it by force would be impossible, of course. Black Sun was a formidable criminal empire, but its ways were those of the poisoned chalice and the hidden dagger, not the blaster and the lightsaber. All of Black Sun's firepower couldn't match even that of the Republic's clone army on Drongar alone.

Kaird reached his kiosk, sealed the entrance, and gratefully stripped off the stifling disguise. He was still reviewing options. He had his agents in place, so the theft itself was doable. But for the escape and transport, he needed a ship—one that was fast enough to outrun pursuit if they discovered the theft before he had enough of a lead.

He'd have to steal one, along with the security codes that would allow it to escape.

His vigo would be unhappy about the situation, Kaird knew. But he also knew that fifty kilograms of still-potent and ever-more-valuable bota would go a long way toward calming him.

He exhaled in relief. Yes. Now that he had a general plan, the specifics would be easier. He could make it happen. People who stood in the path of Kaird of the Nediji never stayed there for long.

He would contact the Falleen and the Umbaran and set up the theft. Then he would find a suitable ship and set that operation in motion as well.

It felt good to be doing something more active after just standing around as one of The Silent for so long. Kaird was always better in motion than when he was still.

When Den awoke, his head was—not to any great surprise—throbbing like a Benwabulan gong. He'd completely forgotten to take a dose of hangover-stop before he fell asleep. Seemed he was forgetting a lot of things lately. Next thing you knew, he'd be losing his sense of direction—

"Good morn," came a bright female voice.

Den rubbed sleep from his eyes and saw Eyar Marath, standing in his 'fresher, drying off with a towel.

Good morn, indeed . . .

"Your sonic shower is broken," she said, smiling at him. "I had to use the water spray. Might take a little while for the heater to warm it up again, if you want to use it."

Den smiled. So it hadn't been a dream, after all.

Eyar came back into the main room of the kiosk and sat on the edge of the bed. "I really enjoyed being with you, Den-la," she said, adding the familiar-suffix to his name.

"Yes, indeed," he managed, sitting up to watch her. "Me, too."

"You have wives?" she asked.

"Never had time to get any," he said, waving one hand as if to encompass the war, his job, everything. "What about you? Husbands?"

"No. I'm still probably a year away from Ready."

They both smiled as she pulled on her boots. "Revoc says we'll be here until the military unlocks the security quarantine. Perhaps we can see each other again?"

"I'd like that."

That they had just met officially yesterday and moved immediately into a relationship was, of course, perfectly normal for Sullustans. The old joke was that Sullustans seldom got lost, and they could *always* find the nearest bedroom . . .

Eyar stood, did a quick dewflap wipe, and smiled broadly at Den. "How do I look?"

"Best-looking fem for fifty parsecs," he said.

"Probably the only one," she said, "but I'll take it."

She started to leave. It was about as perfect as it could get, as far as Den was concerned. Nice to know he still had the moves.

Eyar paused at the door, looked back, and smiled. "You remind me of my grandfather—he was such a sweet masc."

Then she was gone, and Den was left with his mouth gaping and his dewflaps sagging. *Her grandfather! Could have gone all month without hearing that . . .*

22

Barriss tried to practice her lightsaber drills, but she just couldn't seem to narrow her focus. Her timing was off, her balance, her breathing—everything. Even the simplest sequences felt as if she were encased in a tight-fitting metal shell, barely able to move.

She had found a dry patch of ground, so at least she wasn't standing ankle-deep in mud, but that didn't help much. She relit the blade and started a basic centerline parrying sequence. The ozone smell and power hum of the lightsaber were familiar, but not comforting.

Someone was approaching.

Though no one could walk without making noise in the mud and dead vegetation, the buzzing of the energy blade made it difficult to hear snapping twigs, squishing mud, and other quiet warnings. Fortunately, she didn't need such aids. Barriss shut off the lightsaber, hooked it to her belt, and turned to face Uli.

He grinned at her. "Boo."

She grinned back. "We have to stop meeting this way. Out collecting flare-wings for your mother again?"

"Trying to . . . the cold seems to have wiped out all those inside the dome. No luck today. Y'know, even though it was a pain in the posterior, I kinda miss the snow."

Barriss nodded. She felt the same way. Though it wasn't even midmorning yet, the tropical sun had already laid its hot hands on the camp. Even the osmotic weave of her robe wasn't enough to keep her cool.

"So, what's with your practicing? You seem . . ."

"Stiff? Tight? Unattuned?"

He nodded. "I was gonna go with *off your game,* but those'll do. It's not your foot, is it?"

"No. That's healed."

He nodded. "Good. Anything I can do to help?"

"Offering me a massage, Uli?"

He blushed. She found that charming. Then, abruptly, she decided to talk to him about her problem—in general terms, at least. He was a doctor, and good-hearted. Besides, she had about come to the conclusion that any help now would be better than none. And the boy might have something constructive to say. Out of the mouths of children, and all that . . .

She said, "How much do you know about the Force?"

He looked somewhat surprised. "Almost nothing," he said. "The few Jedi I've run into haven't talked about it. I mean, I know the medical theories about midi-chlorians being the organelles that somehow generate the connection and all, and I've heard the usual wild stories about it, but as to how it actually works and what it really is—" He shrugged.

She nodded. "Actually, the Force may create midichlorians, sort of as its conduits into our continuum, rather than the other way around. They're isomorphic on every world that has life. The Force, it appears, truly pervades the galaxy, if not the entire universe.

"But, when all is said and done, the Jedi don't really know how it actually works and what it really is, either. We know how to connect to it, how to channel it, but in a lot of ways we're like primitives standing on the bank of a rushing river. We can put our hands in it, even wade in and try to swim, but we don't know where it comes from—only that it exists, and that it is bound to life and consciousness more deeply than the quantum level."

He nodded slowly, waiting for her to continue.

She was lecturing, she knew, as she might to a class of nine-year-olds, but he did seem interested, and it was a roundabout way to approach her problem, even if she didn't make it that far.

"Part of becoming a Jedi Knight is learning how to become better connected to the Force. Jedi Masters are the best at it—coupled with their wisdom and experience, they are able to do things that Padawans, let alone those with no knowledge of the Force, find miraculous. It augments our strength, oxygenates our tissues, decreases reaction lag. Once, in Coruscant Park, I saw Master Yoda lift a rock as big as a family-sized electric cart, with what looked like nothing but a simple hand gesture. The results can be great and wonderful."

"But it isn't all good, is it?" he said. "We've talked about that before."

Young, but sharp, Uli was. "It's not all good. Count Dooku was a Jedi who turned to the dark side of the Force. Since the beginning of time there have been others who were tempted by and who gave into the desire for power. Four thousand years ago, Exar Kun, a Sith Lord, somehow destroyed an entire stellar system with his misuse of the Force. One has to constantly be aware of the temptation, and guard against it."

"But you're not the sort of person who would do that," Uli said. "I mean—I would think someone who knew it was wrong and went for it anyway—"

"Ah," Barriss said, "but that's the insidious part.

Those who embrace the dark side don't see themselves as evil. They believe that they are doing the right thing for the right reasons. The dark side warps their thinking, and they come to believe that the end justifies the means, no matter how awful those means might be."

Uli examined a thumbnail. "You're not, uh, by any chance, thinking of going over to this dark side, are you?"

A year ago, a month ago—even a week ago—she would have laughed at this suggestion. Now she just shook her head. "I hope not. But it isn't a path with a sign that says THIS WAY LIE MONSTERS. It's more like a steep, slippery slope, where a misstep might turn into an unstoppable fall."

There was another pause; then Uli said, "The Jedi have a moral code, right? You're taught the difference between right and wrong?"

"Yes, of course."

"It's been my experience—such as it is—that on some level, one usually knows the difference between right and wrong. Sometimes you pretend to yourself that you don't, so you can choose to eat that cream-fat puff-pie you ought to skip, but deep down, you know you shouldn't. I think you have to trust that part of yourself, when it comes to the big stuff."

"Yes, of course. But with the big stuff, you have to be sure," Barriss said. "Gorging on a rich dessert isn't exactly high up there on the list of galactic-scale evildoing."

"Depends on the dessert," he said, smiling. There was a soft *cheep,* and he glanced at his chrono. "Oops, look at the time. My shift starts in a few minutes. See you later, Barriss."

"Yes," she said. Uli waved and headed back toward the base.

After he was gone, she thought about their conversation. She hadn't spoken of her personal trial, nor had she really intended to, but the dialogue with Uli had sharpened her thoughts a little. Barriss considered going back to her kiosk to explore these thoughts further, but decided that, however sluggish and stupid she felt, she needed to do her lightsaber forms. Sometimes she just had to push through, no matter how much she felt like quitting.

The larger question was still there. Was taking more of the bota a good idea, or a bad one? Would that path lead to a glorious swim in the rushing river that was the Force, or would it lead to the dank pool of quicksand that was the dark side? Uli couldn't tell her that.

In truth, she didn't think anybody could tell her; as far as she knew, no Jedi had ever been faced with this particular choice before. Any help, from her Master or any other, would be theoretical. *Do—or not do,* as Master Yoda would say.

She had a feeling, small but nagging, that this choice was supposed to be up to her. Even choosing to wait and decide later might send her in the wrong direction.

She lit her lightsaber again. *Leave it for now. Do the dance you know you can do. The dilemma will still be there when you are done.*

Unfortunately . . .

Kaird was feeling much better now that he had a plan of action in place. In a different and new disguise, that of a corpulent human male, he met with his agents.

They sat together in the crowded chow hall during the midday meal. It was noisy and smelly—a lot of different species eating extremely varied dishes. Nobody was paying any attention to Kaird, Thula, and Squa Tront.

Sometimes the best place to hide was in the middle of a mob.

His thoughtshield solidly in place against mental prying, Kaird explained his desire, quietly and to the point.

As he expected, Thula and Squa Tront had some reservations.

"This will kill the operation here," Thula said. She nibbled on a greenish blue vegetable cutlet, made a face at the taste. "Gah. What a waste of good spigage. The cook should be boiled in his own pot."

"Which is exactly what would have happened to him, had his cuisine displeased the tetrarch of Anarak Four," Squa Tront said. "But he's not subject to quite such drastic repercussions here as on his homeworld."

"Lucky for him," Thula said, shoving her plate aside.

Kaird broke in on the banter. "That the operation will end has crossed my mind," he said in response to Squa. "We've decided that cutting an artery and filling our bucket is better than bleeding a few drops at a time. War is uncertain. Somebody on one side or the other might get stupid and accidentally wipe this planet out, and then nobody makes any profit."

This was technically true, if it had nothing to do with his reasons. The *we* in this case was more properly *I*, since Black Sun knew nothing of his plan.

"True," the Umbaran replied. "But you would get more the droplet way, in the long run, if things stay the same."

"Are you going to eat that?" Thula asked Kaird.

Kaird looked at the splatters of viscous brown, green, and white lumps on his plate. He had no idea what it was—some kind of human cuisine, served to him due to his disguise. In Kaird's opinion it smelled like a stopped-up recycler in an overcrowded spacer bar. "It's yours," he said, pushing the swill to the Falleen. He turned back to

Squa. "In the long run, we are all dust funneling into a singularity," he said. "It's my job to give Black Sun what it wants, and your jobs to give me what *I* want. Is this a problem?"

Thula and Squa Tront looked quickly at each other, then back at him. They shook their heads. "Nope," they said in chorus.

The human mask smiled. "Good. You'll make enough of a bonus that it will be worth the heat if they come after you."

They glanced at each other again. "Well, the thing is," Squa said, "we'll need to be spacing the lanes before anybody realizes the stuff is gone. After all, we're among the first people they'll come looking for. I trust you have a way offplanet?"

"Sorry. You'll have to make your own arrangements," Kaird said.

The fake flesh he wore itched. He was boiling in this thing! He'd worn it because it had a filtration system that kept those pesky Falleen pheromones from affecting him. That, at least, was working, but the fine skein of heat-exchanging tubules and cavities in the material wasn't. There was always *something* in these elaborate disguises that caused problems. The Silent robe was about as good as it got.

Thula swallowed and said, "In that case, timing will be critical. We either have to ship out on civilian transportation at least a couple of days before the offal hits the oscillator, or sneak onto a military transport and be well toward a nexus station when things get leggy here."

"You two aren't hatchlings just out of the egg," Kaird said. "You can work something out."

"Credits talk," Squa said. "I can see somebody being bribed in our future."

"True. And you will have enough credits to drown out a stadium full of politicians."

The Umbaran nodded. "When, then, and how much?"

"I'll need fifty or sixty kilos, in carbonite, and within a week. Something shaped like a big personal effects case, with a handle on it."

Thula looked at him. "We're talking another twenty kilos minimum for the carbonite shell. Can you haul seventy or eighty kilos around without rupturing something?"

"I'm stronger than I appear," Kaird said. "And you can put wheels or a small repulsor on it."

Thula looked at her companion. He nodded. "All right," she said. "We'll need two days' head start from the time you think the alarm will go off."

"Done. You have five days in which to set it up. That leaves you two days to track vac before I take off." He pulled a credit cube from his pocket and slid it across the table toward the Umbaran. Squa smiled at it. Thula reached over and took the cube. Squa said, "Thula handles all the money. I'm a terrible accountant."

"My, my," the Falleen said, looking at the projection of the cube's contents inside the palms of her cupped hands. "Black Sun is being more than generous."

The human shoulders shrugged. "Share the wealth," Kaird said. "It makes for good business. Everybody goes away happy."

All three of them smiled at each other. *Rictuses all around,* Kaird thought. *Humanoids are always baring their teeth and pretending it means friendship.*

Kaird made his way out of the dining area and to a cleaning closet with an inside lock. He went in as a fat human, and came out robed as one of The Silent, the artificial flesh having been dissolved in the ultrasonic compactor, as it had been designed to do once it was triggered. He had plenty more where that came from.

He wasn't worried about the Falleen and the Umbaran. Small-time winders, thieves, and con artists were nothing if not pragmatic. *The Nediji from Black Sun wants it and is willing to pay handsomely for it? No problem, boss. How many, how big, and how soon?*

The next part, however, was going to be a little more tricky. For this, Kaird needed to select a ship fast enough, and with enough range, that he could escape in it with his stolen cargo. It didn't need any kind of big capacity—at the most, he would get away with fifty, maybe sixty kilos of bota. Even encased in a carbonite block, it wouldn't be so large that he could not belt it into a copilot's chair if he had to. He could, of course, attach a repulsor to a block weighing a metric ton or two and move it as easily as pushing a balloon, but something that big would be much more apt to be noticed, and stealth was a major part of his plan. Even the fastest ship likely to be found on this backrocket planet couldn't outrun a heavy charged-particle cannon's beam, and he wanted to be well out of ground battery range and beyond orbital picket ships before anybody even started thinking about shooting.

Greed had been the downfall of more than a few thieves, and Kaird had no intention of joining them. Fifty kilos of bota worth thousands of credits a gram, secured in Black Sun's Coruscant vaults, was worth a lot more than a ton of the same blasted to atoms by some razor-eyed dead-shot Republic gunner—not to mention the ship and pilot that would burn with it. Kaird had not become one of Black Sun's best operatives, an assassin who had taken out scores of the organization's enemies without ever once being arrested or even suspected, by being greedy or stupid. You made a plan. Then you made a backup plan. Then you made a backup plan for the backup plan. He already had a ship in mind, and if he could manage it, it would be the perfect vessel. He would begin scouting it as soon as possible. He'd have to make the lift to MedStar, but the alert status had been dialed down somewhat by now, and as a member of a religious order he wouldn't have any problem getting in the air lock.

And after that, it would be smooth sailing. He could almost smell the sharp, clean air of the eyrie once more . . .

23

Jos wanted to grill I-Five about the details of his restored memory at length, but unfortunately it was turning out to be another long day patching up the troops. There was nothing especially difficult or enormously complicated about most of the procedures; the majority of them involved removing shrapnel, as battlefield surgeons had done on war fronts for the past few millennia. The Separatists knew one grim fact of war very well—kill a soldier, and all you've cost your foe is the price of a recycle. Incapacitate the soldier, and you put a drain on your enemy's supplies and personnel across the board.

Jos grafted burned skin, resected pulverized tissue, removed perforated organs and replaced them with fresh transplants. Time crawled by.

Tolk was working with another surgeon this day. Whenever he could, Jos tried to catch her gaze, but to no avail; she simply looked at him from over her mask, her eyes betraying nothing—then turned her attention back to her work.

By the time his shift was up, nine troopers had passed beneath his gloved hands, and he was about to fall asleep on his feet—something he hadn't done since his residency.

He went to the 'fresher and laved his face and hands, sieved tepid water through his hair. It helped push back the exhaustion a little. Was a time when he had been just like Uli—well, a little older—and pulling a shift like the one he just had would have slid off him like water off an Aqualish's back. But now, every time he looked in the mirror, it seemed he could find new lines in his face, more gray hairs in his stubble. He was beginning to look—

Creators help him, he was beginning to look like his uncle.

He hadn't had a chance to talk to Tolk—she'd gone off shift before him, and he hadn't seen her since.

When he left the 'fresher, he saw I-Five just emerging from the OT disinfection passage. The combination of UV light and ultrasound was complete enough to zap any pathogen that might have somehow made it through the sterile patient field, but the droid always complained that the sonics left him with the robotic equivalent of tinnitus for a few minutes afterward.

"So your memory's fully restored?" Jos said as the droid joined him.

"What?"

"Turn up your auditory sensors. You said you remembered everything," Jos said. "So tell me—are you really a lap-droid for some wealthy princess, or a groomer for a Shistavanen, or what?"

"I'm exactly what I was before, thank you very much for asking. I said there were gaps in my memory that needed to be filled. Now they have been. My internal cognitive function repairs are complete."

"I wish mine were. Anything in particular you recall? C'mon, I-Five. Share."

The droid cocked his head in a puzzled pose. "Why are you so anxious to know?"

"Well, because—" Jos thought about it. Just why *was* he so curious?

"Because," he said slowly, "because from what you *do* remember, you've had an adventurous time of it, first on Coruscant and then careening around the space lanes. As for me . . . the only worlds I've been to, other than here, are Coruscant and Alderaan. I look in the mirror, and I hardly recognize the aging hunk of protoplasm I see. I suppose that, when you said you remembered everything, that . . ." He shrugged.

"That you would seize the opportunity to do a little vicarious sightseeing?"

"Something like that. Also," Jos paused, looking again for words. "I suppose I should be telling all this to Klo—"

"He does rate far higher than I do on the intuition scale."

"Most doctors—especially the ones here and others like them—will tell you they don't fear death, because they've seen so much of it. That may be true, for them. But as far as I'm concerned, it's for just that reason that I *do* fear death. Or at least the boat that makes the crossing."

"Padawan Offee might also be more able to help you than—"

"It's usually painful and protracted, death. Seems odd, with all the painkillers and stim treatments available nowadays, but there's still about a billion quadrillion or so beings just getting by for every one with his own private skyhook. In that respect, the galaxy probably won't ever change."

"There are other options."

"True. If you're rich, there are options—a personality dump, being frozen in carbonite—all kinds of options. But I'm not within a parsec of being that rich, and probably never will be. So I—"

"Jos," I-Five said. Jos stopped, surprised. The droid's

voice hadn't really changed—it still had that slight, inde-finable touch that identified its origin as a vocabulator in-stead of a larynx—but it was different, somehow. *He hardly ever calls anyone by name,* he realized suddenly.

I-Five said, "From what I've studied of popular culture, I think this is the moment where I'm supposed to remind you of all the wonderful advantages you, as an organic, have over me, a mechanical. Unfortunately, I really can't think of any. Yes, you are capable of creativity, of flights of imagination that I am not—because my core program-ming doesn't encompass such ephemerals. But I don't miss them. I don't yearn to be able to understand beauty and art. The same goes for love—and existential life crises such as you seem to be currently experiencing."

"I don't believe that. You have, at the very least, a sense of humor—"

"I was *programmed* with one. Just about all droids that interact with organics on this level are."

"You wanted to get drunk!"

"True. I didn't say I wasn't programmed with emo-tions. Loyalty is one. Curiosity is another. And my lack of creativity dampers and my expanded synaptic grid al-low me to extrapolate feelings. Experiencing things that organics favor—such as mind-altering concoctions—would theoretically help me understand them. And, since I'm stuck in this galaxy with all of you, I need all the data I can get.

"But I'm not the little droid in the children's tale that wants to be an organic, Jos. I'm a machine. A very com-plex machine, capable of mimicking the thinking pro-cesses of a sentient to an astonishing degree, if I do say so. But a machine, nonetheless. And I have no real desire to be anything else."

Jos stared at I-Five. He couldn't have been more astonished if the droid had just turned into a three-headed Kaminoan. Then, somewhat to his surprise, he started to feel angry. He'd just recently had his worldview twisted, was only now starting to get comfortable with the idea that maybe droids shouldn't be treated like electrospanners with arms, and he was determined not to let I-Five mess with his head again.

He said slowly, "Do you remember, during one of the sabacc games, when we were discussing how a being knows if it's self-aware?"

"I remember."

"And you said something along the lines of, *To be self-aware enough to ask the question is to have answered it.* I think you're aware enough to answer that question, I-Five. In fact, I think you already have. But now you're pulling back—you're denying your *self,*" Jos said. "I wonder if it might have anything to do with your memory returning?"

I-Five was quiet for what seemed a long time. When he spoke again, Jos could hear a definite tone of wonder in his voice. "I think—comparing subjective neural activity with internal files on the subject—" the droid said, "I think I'm having an anxiety attack."

24

Sometimes the names did get a little confusing. Most of the time, it was the one the others in the Rimsoo used; after that it was Column, the op-nom bestowed by one of Count Dooku's Separatist spymasters. Lens, the code name by which Black Sun knew its agent, was the one least often utilized. None of them, of course, was the name bestowed upon the spy at birth, and that was but one of a long list that had changed time and again, as circumstances dictated.

However, *Lens* was the sobriquet being used now, that being the one the spy's guest was familiar with. The being sitting facing Lens was ostensibly human, but, in fact, concealed under the adipose rolls of a fat-suit disguise was Kaird, the Nediji assassin and enforcer. The two of them were in an empty office that belonged to a lab supervisor who had contracted a nasty, local form of pneumonia during the recent cold spell. The lab worker, an Askajian, was in the medical ward and wouldn't be using her room anytime soon.

The ersatz human had just laid out what sounded like the bare essence of a plan to steal a major amount of bota—and a ship in which to transport it. This didn't make any sense, and Lens was not at all hesitant to say so.

"We have our reasons."

"And you are telling me this . . . why?"

"You are our agent; it seemed only fair to warn you. The theft will cause investigation—best you are not caught unprepared."

Lens smiled. "My official persona here is quite blaster-proof. What's the real reason?"

The human disguise was quite good—the smile it produced looked genuine. "Eventually, as all wars must, this one will end. Business will continue. You have been a valuable asset to us and could be one again after this conflict is resolved. We hate to waste talent."

That made more sense, but it wasn't all of it, Lens figured. "Still not quite right, is it?"

The disguise's vox unit gave a realistic offering of a human laugh. "It is so refreshing to not have to deal with the dull and ignorant," Kaird said. He leaned forward. "Very well: in your official capacity here, you have access to certain data."

"True—but security codes for vacuum-worthy ships, especially those with hyperdrive units, are not among such data," Lens said.

"I didn't think they were. But you can get medical records."

"Anybody in the Rimsoo with standard clearance can view those files. I fail to see how that will help you steal a ship."

"Ever see a child's tumble-slabs? You can set them up in long and convoluted rows and whorls, the one at the end being a hundred or a thousand away from the one at the beginning. If you line them up right, however, tipping the first one over will eventually result in the last one falling."

Lens nodded again. "Yes. I see what you mean."

"I am going to do some very basic research," Kaird

said, "and after I have learned some things, I will ask you for specific files that I believe will be useful. Nothing that should be secured above your ability to scan."

"Not a problem," Lens said. "I will obtain what you need."

"Excellent." There was a pause. "Now I'm going to do you a favor, Lens. I realize you have other loyalties besides those to Black Sun, but those interests—and ours—here are about to cease to matter."

Lens frowned. "How so?"

"The reason we are all here is singular. That reason is already dwindling in importance, and, in a short time, will stop completely."

"I'm afraid you've lost me. You're talking about the bota?"

"Yes. The plant, it seems, is undergoing a new mutation, one that will radically alter its prized adaptogenic properties. By its next generation, bota will be no more valuable than any other weed growing on this hot rock—it will be chemically changed so far as to be useless as a drug. Since Drongar itself is of no use, strategic or otherwise, both the Republic and the Separatist forces will have no reason to remain here." The hands spread themselves, palms-up, in a gesture of freedom. "We can all go home."

"How do you know this?"

"That doesn't matter. I know it for a fact. I tell you this because, after I'm gone, you might be able to use the data to help your friends under Count Dooku's command. It might be worth a final, all-out battle to secure what's left of the bota fields—since once those are gone, there won't be any more to be had. Not around here, at least."

Lens, startled by this revelation, said nothing. There would be no reason for Kaird to lie about this. The theft of a goodly amount of bota would, at least indirectly, harm the Republic, and so Lens wished him success as far as that went. But if what he said was true, it would definitely be in the Separatists' interest to grab up as much of the crop as they could, even at the risk of destroying the rest of it. Better half a loaf than none.

Somehow, this information had to be verified.

"This is valuable knowledge," Lens said. "And yet you offer it freely."

The jowled head nodded ponderously. "As I said, the war will eventually be settled. Win or lose, it's all the same to us. If we do you a favor, someday you might be in a position to do one for us. Black Sun has a long memory, for enemies and for friends. We have plenty of both, but it never hurts to have more friends."

Lens nodded and smiled. The Nediji's statement made sense, although it came with a fairly high dosage of irony, since Black Sun had in the past played such deals from so many angles that it took a nine-dimensional slice of space–time just to contain them all.

The human suit stood, its rolls of foamcast fat quivering. "I'll contact you in a day or two," Kaird said.

"May frost never dim your vision."

Kaird left, and Lens considered what the Black Sun enforcer had said. If this revelation about the bota checked out, it would be a major bit of intelligence to pass along. The course of the war here would almost certainly be altered quickly.

Very quickly.

Jos plodded toward his kiosk. He no longer shared it with Tolk, nor with Uli. She'd moved back into her own three days ago, saying she needed space to think. Uli was still in the single unit that he'd moved to soon after Tolk moved in. These days, Jos spent most of his time either in the cantina or in the OT. He only went back to his quarters when he needed sleep—and he desperately needed it now.

The drone of medlifters began. They quickly built into such a cacophony that he couldn't even guess how many there were. He shook his head. That was going to be bad for whoever was on—

His comlink cheeped.

He answered, knowing it was bad news. "What?"

Uli said, "There's been an explosion and big fire at the AIA hydrogen plant, Jos. A hundred people seriously hurt. We've got nine lifters worth headed our way, thirty-some wounded, most of them bad burns and—"

"I just finished my shift. I can barely lift my hands, much less use them to operate."

"I know. But one of the droid surgeons just blew a gyrostabilizer, and it'll take hours to repair it. We're short-handed in the OT. Colonel Vaetes said to call."

Jos sighed. "Kark," he said. But there was no heat in the word, only a great weariness. Would this *never* end?

In the OT, the first patients from the fire started arriving as Jos gloved up. He saw Tolk, and this time she nodded at him. A small gesture, but it made him feel a little better. At least they had that much.

He moved to a table as a pair of droids slid a patient onto it from the gurney. A clone, and scorched pretty badly. "What do we have here?"

"Third-degree burns over twenty-six percent of his body," one of the droids, a surgical diagnostic unit, intoned. "Second-degree over an additional twenty-one percent. First-degree over seventeen percent. In addition, he has a lacerated small intestine from what seems to be a splinter from a shattered hydrogen tank, left lower quadrant, transversely; puncture wounds in his left lung, which is collapsed; and a fragment embedded in his left eye."

"Separatist droids attacked the plant?"

"No, sir," the SDU droid said. "It was an industrial accident."

Wonderful.

"Isn't bad enough the Seppies're killing people—now we're blowing ourselves up. Crack open a burn kit," Jos told Threndy. "Somebody hit him with enkephalin, a hundred milligrams. And get the ultrasonic scrubber— he's going to need at least half his skin replaced . . ."

Jos somehow managed to keep it together for another five patients, saving them all.

Then he killed the next one.

He was halfway through the first stage of a pneumonectomy, on a nonclone human patient, working on the left lung with a laser scalpel, when he nicked the man's aorta. Blood spewed from the clamped vessel in a geyser that shot nearly all the way to the ceiling.

"Get a pressor on that!"

Tolk and Threndy had been pulled away to help Uli and Vaetes, who were doing a heart transplant, but the surgical assistant droid quickly focused the pressor field on the cut artery with mechanical precision, a perfect placement. Unfortunately, the field strength was not quite sufficient, and the wound continued to ooze.

"Kick it up," Jos ordered. "What's the field strength?"

"Six-point-four," the droid said.

"Go to seven."

"But doctor, that will exceed tissue parameters—"

"Override. Seven, I said."

Even as the droid complied, Jos realized his mistake. The man lying before him was not a Fett-clone, one whose circulatory system's wall strengths had been augmented to help keep wounds from bleeding as much. This was an ordinary human, which meant—

The aorta exploded, shredding as if a small bomb had gone off inside it.

"I need some help here!"

All of the surgical heart–lung bypass roilers were in use, and an extra pair of hands wouldn't be enough. The field couldn't stop the blood, and even as he tried to tie off the blown artery, he knew it was too late. Massive shock took the man, and he flatlined before they could implement cerebrostasis. Jos tried to revive him, once he had a flexy-stat on the torn vessel and oxygenated expander flowing to replace the lost blood. Ten minutes he tried, but nothing seemed to work. He couldn't restart the heart.

He had four more patients lined up. He knew what he had to do.

Jos pronounced the man and had a droid haul him away. There was no other choice. If he kept working on this one, the patients waiting would almost certainly die.

Or maybe you'll kill them, too, the malicious little voice within whispered, as the next patient was placed before him.

He had never felt more tired in his life. *Blast* this war.

25

Den sat listening to the Ugnaught med-mechano special-ist, Rorand Zuzz, feeling as if he had just been handed the key to Coruscant on a platinum platter. Zuzz had supplied him with useful information in the past, but nothing like this.

"You're *sure*?"

"Y'kin take it t'the IGB 'n' swap it f'creds, Dhur. Oh, yar."

"How did you come by this information?"

Zuzz grinned. "Femnaught in Rimsoo Twelve, over'n Xenoby, she lustin' f'me. She runs alla d'test on d'local crop."

"Have another drink," Den said. This was big. Huge. Monstrous. So important, in fact, that . . .

"Why haven't I heard about this?"

The stubby little alien shrugged. "Dunno. Rachott, d'fem, say she runnin' d'tests, passin' 'em 'long, 'n' no feke, the stuff's gettin' weaker 'n' weaker. Somebody sit-tin' on d'results. Who knows why?"

The server arrived with a fresh drink, and Zuzz grabbed it as if it were the last drop of liquid on the day side of a nonrotating planet.

Den continued to think about this. If the bota was in-deed losing its potency, that was major news. The stuff was worth its weight in first-grade firestones, if not more, and if it died out, the price of any that still had full strength and full spectrum would rise right out of the galaxy. Once word got around, everybody and his ugly little sibling would be out there in the fields trying to grab up as much as they could. A being could retire on what he could hide in his *pockets* . . .

Yeah, this was a story, all right. A ticket-to-anywhere, the kind of piece that came along once in a Falleen's lifetime. Spin it right—and he knew he could—it might even be a Poracsa Prize winner, and that would set him up for life.

Den had to confirm it, and fast. He had to break it before somebody else leaked it. This would put him on the map. They'd name journalism colleges for him . . .

He paid for another three drinks for his Ugnaught source, got up, and left the cantina. He had to find at least two more confirmations. Maybe even just one. Once it had been confirmed, he would get the story out, somehow. Even if his comm unit was on the crackle at the moment, there had to be a way. He'd tattoo it on a soldier mustering out, if he had to. *Something*.

As he started to cross the hot and fetid compound, he saw Eyar heading toward the chow hall. He moved to intercept her.

No doubt about it—she was one gorgeous fem.

She smiled, and they exchanged ritual greetings.

"You look excited about something," she said.

"How could I be anything else but excited in your presence, Sweetflaps?"

She laughed. "I love a Sullustan who makes me laugh. But I ken something else in your attitude."

"A story," he admitted. "A big one, if it checks out."

"Good for you!" Her voice was warm, generous, sincere.

Den looked at her, and for a moment, he felt a pang of regret for the wives and families he had never had time to build. It had always been the work, first, last, and in the middle. The lane not taken included watching the younglings venture out of the caves for the first time, hearing the sounds of childish laughter, feeling the warmth of a spouse or spouses in a bed under a cooling sheet. Things he had planned to do, someday, when he had time. Only, it had never worked out that way.

"Your brow furrows in thought," she said.

He sighed. "A few regrets in my old age."

She grinned. "Not *that* old."

"I thought I reminded you of your grandfather."

"You do—but our family started young. He's still fit and active, my grandfather. Six wives, fourteen children, twenty-six grandchildren, and he took a new spouse just two seasons past. She's already with child."

"Impressive."

"Do you ever think about returning to the home-world?"

He nodded. "I have. More and more, lately. Chasing after wars does get old. I've considered quitting the field, getting a local news beat back on Sullust, and trying to find a few ancient fems desperate enough to consider me as a husband."

"They wouldn't have to be desperate," she said, looking down at the tops of her feet. "Or ancient."

Den stopped walking and looked at her. "Uh . . . perhaps my ear dampeners are malfunctioning. What are you saying, Eyar-la?"

Eyar glided to a halt as well, and turned to face him directly.

"After this war ends, and my tour breaks up, I plan on returning home and finding a cohabitation cave."

"What? And leave show business?"

She laughed again—it sounded like a cascade of tone-crystals—then continued. "The prospects I know are young, but serious mascs. Don't get me wrong; they'd be good fathers, and I hope to collect one or two more like them, but they're maybe lacking a bit in the sense-of-humor department. There would always be room for a Sullustan of your cut, Den-la."

Den was astonished. He grinned at Eyar. "That's the best offer I've had in a boukk's age."

"Then consider it formal," she said. "Younglings need fit and strong fathers, but they also need older and wiser ones. You would honor my cave if you chose to live in it."

Den blinked against the sudden welling in his eyes. Impossible that they could be tears—not for a crusty old cynic like him. Marriage? A family? A cave full of in-laws and younglings? He had thought all that was too far in his past, out of reach. Not for him. A hard-bitten reporter, decades away from the homeworld, he had always figured he'd die on a battlefield, or drunk in some pest-hole hive of scum and villainy.

But now, to be offered an alternative, especially by one so young and sweet . . .

"Please consider it," she said, mistaking his hesitation for a possible negative response.

"You know what? If I live past the end of this war, I believe I will try to find my way home." Den paused, took a deep breath, then said, "It would honor me to join my cave with yours."

She smiled, a broad, delightful expression. "Really? It would?"

Her enthusiasm washed over him, full of energy and cheer. "I can't wait to tell my family! Den Dhur, the famous reporter, joining us!"

"Not so famous."

"You hide your sconce under a shield, Den-la. I've been reading your stories for years. Everybody on Sullust knows who you are."

"Not nice to mock your elders," he said with false severity.

"Nonsense. It's true. In my home-warren there are younglings who want to grow up to be you."

"No mopak? Uh, I mean—"

She laughed. "No mopak," she said. She reached out and caught his hand. "Perhaps you'd like to come back to my cubicle and seal the vow? Unless, of course, you're too busy with your story . . . ?"

Den smiled. "The story can wait. It's not *that* important." And even as he said it, he realized it was true. In the end, there really were things more important than tomorrow's newsdisc, or even easy money.

Who would've thought it?

As Den left Eyar's kiosk, it was already getting dark. He saw I-Five standing outside the OT, talking to Jos. The surgeon said something to the droid, then turned and went back inside.

"I-Five, old buddy!"

The droid turned and saw him. Den swaggered up to him and punched him playfully in one arm. "Good t'see you. What's up?"

"Besides you?"

Den giggled as the two of them walked through the muggy evening air. Eyar had opened a bottle of fine Bothan grain wine to celebrate their possible nuptial agreement, and it had put up little resistance. He was feeling just fine, all around. While at Eyar's, he'd confirmed via his comm the bota story's probable veracity from three separate sources whom he trusted. He was now in a mood to celebrate.

"Hey, I'm just feeling a little friendly. Don't knock it till you've tried it," he told the droid. "Speaking of which, we still got to get you into the club."

"And what club might that be?"

Den wagged a finger at him. "Don't tell me you're backing out. You must experience the joys of intoxication. It'll be good for your silicon soul."

"Ah, yes. As a matter of fact, I believe I've come up with an absurdly simple way to do it. I'm embarrassed I didn't think of it before."

"Do tell, then."

"I am, as I was just reminding Doctor Vandar, a machine, essentially. My synaptic grid processor is heuristic—I extrapolate new data from known data. But I also have an algorithmic subprocessor that serves my autonomic needs."

"Okay . . ."

"You didn't understand a word of that, did you?"

"I believe I got *also,* and *my.*"

"It's like your parasympathetic nervous system, which controls your breathing, heartbeat, and so forth—functions your body needs that aren't under conscious control. While I don't need to breathe, I do need constant monitoring of things like balance, lubrication, powerbus functioning . . ."

"Right, got it," Den said. "But what's this got to do with tying one on?"

"Simple. My subprocessor is programmable. I can encode it to simulate a state of inebriation."

Den stopped and stared at him. "You can *program* yourself to get drunk? I thought you couldn't mess around with your systems."

"The hardware is protected. I have some leeway with the software, now that my full memories have returned."

"How long would it take you?"

There was a slight but unmistakable hint of snobbery in I-Five's voice as he answered. "I have a SyntheTech AA-One nanoprocessor, operating at seven petahertz, with a five-exabyte capacity. I wrote the program just after I mentioned it to you. It took me six-point-one picoseconds to encode the basic algorithm and calculate its functional parameters."

"Wow. That's . . . fast."

They stopped to let a small flock of R4 astromechs roll by, beeping and whistling at each other. "So, when are you going to implement the program? Or get mopak-faced, as we organics say."

"No time like the present. As you organics say."

Den considered. "Okay. I guess you could do it anywhere. But there's custom to be observed, trust me on this. Besides, I'd like to join you. I've got a nice little buzz on, and I don't mind keeping it going. And it's getting close to sabacc time. Everyone'll be there."

"Wonderful. Nothing like an audience."

Den made an *after-you* gesture toward the cantina, then fell in behind I-Five.

There was an old saying on Nedij—you are never more than seven wings away from the Great Raptor. Stretched to fit the entire galaxy, that number went up considerably, of course, but the principle was the same: talk to somebody who knew somebody who knew somebody else, and so on, until, in what was always an amazingly short list, you found that you were able to link up with just about anybody.

Kaird, now comfortably and gratefully back in the

robes of The Silent, stood in the gathering shade of a building thunderstorm, watching the food service tech leave the main chow hall kitchens and head for her communal kiosk. The proverb's truth was even simpler here, on a world peopled entirely by occupying forces, with no indigenes of its own. With this female, he was but two sets of hands away from the pilot of the ship he intended to steal.

The female, a Twi'lek named Ord Vorra, had a relationship with Biggs Bogan, a human pilot, who was one of a trio of such in the rotation to fly the admiral's personal ship. This Twi'lek–human relationship was noteworthy for an unusual—at least here on this world—reason: Vorra and Bogan were both Strag players, and both of them were ranked Adepts. The ancient game of strategy and tactics, played on a simple hologrammic board with a dozen pieces on each side, was an intellectual pursuit that required an excellent memory, and years of practice, to achieve mastery. Kaird himself was passing familiar with the game, but had never been able to give it the time necessary to reach the level of Adept. That there were two such on a planet like Drongar was most unusual, and so, naturally, they would have found each other.

A ship's pilot and a kitchen worker, both of them Strag Adepts. Just went to show you that the galaxy was a strange place—a fact of which Kaird had long been aware.

He moved across the compound, staying well back from the Twi'lek as he shadowed her. If she noticed him, likely she would not think much of one of The Silent out taking an evening stroll, but best not to take chances.

A warm breeze, heralding the coming rain, barely stirred the humidity, adding a small bit of freshness to the fetid air. He had already checked out the communal living quarters in which the Twi'lek lived—much too crowded for his uses, and always somebody around. But Vorra and Bogan had no doubt found places where they could be alone, since constant noise and motion were distractions that Strag players preferred to avoid. Not that they couldn't tune such things out—an Adept, it was said, could plan four moves ahead in the middle of a Piluvian salamander-storm—they just would rather not. So Kaird was confident that, sooner or later, the Twi'lek and the human would seek out a place where they could be together without other company, and that place would be a potential contact point for Kaird.

He had no interest in Vorra, save as a conduit to Bogan. Bogan, who, on the days when he was on standby for ferrying Admiral Kersos about, would have the new security codes for the admiral's ship. Kaird would learn when that was, and then it was just a matter of how and when to gather what he needed . . .

Ord Vorra stopped at the stores kiosk. Kaird drifted into the deep shadow of one of the industrial recyclers across the lane from the supply building and became effectively invisible.

The wind picked up, and the smell of the coming rain grew heavier. Kaird waited and sweated. The dome would not slow the rain coming, nor the evaporating puddles from leaving. When force-shields and -domes were first experimented with, ages ago, such things had not always been taken into consideration, and the result had often caused much discomfort—and worse—for the residents. A force-dome that filled with greenhouse gases that could not escape, allowing water vapor to condense on the inner aspect and causing thick fog or more rain—not to mention a sudden lack of breathable air—these were all bad things. And so the newly repaired dome had been set to pretty much the same environmental parameters as it had before the "winter glitch," as it was now referred to. Which meant they were back to weather that would steam the hide off a dewback.

The new admiral had apparently inherited the old admiral's personal vessel, or at least the use of it. Kaird approved of this. The vessel in question was a modified Surronian assault ship, a sleek craft powered by a quad cluster of A2- and A2.50-grade engines. It was fast in atmosphere, according to what Kaird had learned—comparable to a Naboo N-1 starfighter—but, more importantly, it was fast to lightspeed, also. Not to mention being armed with fire-linked ion and laser cannons, and, while less than thirty meters in length, sufficiently fueled and comfortable for a long flight, with more than enough range to get him off this mudball and back to Black Sun's headquarters on Coruscant.

Once he was there, and his business was done, it was his intention to somehow keep the ship and use it to get back to his real home.

Back to the snow-dusted mountains of Nedij . . .

The Twi'lek emerged from the store, carrying a small package. She was not unattractive, if one's desires ran to featherless bipeds, though she was much too heavy for Kaird's taste. Nediji females were hollow-boned and willowy, and that standard was hardwired into male Nediji's brains.

She moved off into the gathering dusk, and Kaird resisted the urge to follow immediately. No need to rush. He had his quarry, and now he would learn everything germane to his needs about them. He would obtain their medical records from Lens. From a clerk in Personnel, he would get their service information. A censor in Comm

Intercept would provide copies of communications, if any, the pair had sent or received from family or friends.

In a day, probably less, he would have amassed as much intel about these two as anybody here could possibly need to know. Then, when he had enough information, he would find a keystone, a link, a glitch—some small bit of data around which he would build a plan. Not a perfect plan, perhaps, but Kaird had learned many things in his years with Black Sun, and he counted this as one of the most important: it didn't have to be perfect. One always had to leave some looseness for variables.

He would also think of ways that would cover any contingencies, of course. Then he would put things into motion. All things going well, it would slide like a greased mynock over transparisteel. Even if there were problems, he could deal with them. It would still happen.

A few days from now, he would be in his new ship, with a cargo valued far beyond easy measure, on his way to turn it in, and then to take an early retirement. And to live happily thereafter, until the Final Flight . . .

There was a flash of lightning, an almost immediate clap of thunder to reveal how close the strike had been—very close—and the rain started falling, fat, heavy drops.

Time to get indoors, Kaird thought. He'd done enough for tonight. It was best, he knew, not to get too far ahead in his plans. It was always good to remember his eggmother's recipe for taboret stew: first, you must catch a taboret . . .

Column was not without regret, or even remorse, as the coded message was sent to the spy's Separatist superiors. There had been a moment of hesitation, a long and reflective pause—but in the end, one did what one had to do. The control function was initiated, the information transmitted. And it could not be recalled, once it was gone.

The transmission was accomplished without difficulty, even though communications all over the base had been subject recently to noise and loss of signal. This was because the area had been covered not long ago by a new, state-of-the-art broadband confounder stationed in the jungle about five kilometers away. The blockage wasn't consistent enough to arouse suspicion, but it did provide cover and protection when the spy had to send and receive. The official explanation, of course, was sunspots.

The code, as always, was cumbersome and overwrought, and most of the time a major waste of effort, but in this instance the intricacy of it was useful. One most certainly did not want the Republic to intercept and read this particular missive.

On the other end of the communication the deciphered message would undoubtedly cause much consternation—to put it mildly. That they would disbelieve it was to be expected. Column knew there would be follow-up exchanges, at least one or two, perhaps more, to verify the information. It was not a matter of trust, per se, but of certainty: if a large-scale attack was to be launched, if massive forces were to be gathered and expended, such things could not be done with any possibility of some code reader's simple error.

What? No, I didn't say that the bota is going bad, *I said Bothans are far too* sad . . .

Column smiled, but the smile quickly faded. The mission here was coming to an end. If not a blow that could topple the Republic, this last strike would at least be a barb in the beast's side worthy of a painful howl. It was tragic that many of the staff of this and of other Rimsoos would surely die as a result of this action. But it was done now, and there was no turning back. Best start getting prepared to exit this venue. There would be other places, other identities, wherein an agent of Column's skill and capability would be useful. Chipping away at the foundation of the Republic a bit at a time was slow but, over long enough a period, effective.

All this the spy knew to be true, of course. But the bottom line was that it was still going to be extremely difficult to look these people—one, in particular—in the eyes and pretend to know nothing about the impending doom.

It had to be done, however. To not meet their eyes, to act in any way departing from normal, any fashion that might cause the slightest bit of suspicion, could be disastrous. Column turned to the door. It was time to mingle with them, share their friendship, joy—and love—now, while there was still a little time left.

26

Of all moments, the instant of realization came to Barriss as she was washing up to join the sabacc table over at the cantina. She reached for a towel to dry the water from her face and hands—she preferred water-washing to ultrasonic, even when the latter was working in her kiosk. And, as she caught sight of her wet features in the mirror above the small sink, it abruptly came to her:

The answer is in the Force.

This shouldn't have been a revelation. It was something she had been told a thousand times, at least, a litany that every Jedi student grew up hearing: *When in doubt, trust the Force. You may not always interpret it correctly, but the Force never lies.*

She knew that. Had learned it early, had had it come to mean more and more to her as she had grown older, and had, at a very basic level, never doubted it. The Force doesn't let you down—it is eternal, infinite, and omnipresent. If you can figure out what to ask, where to look, how to get to it, the answer you need is always there.

How many times, after all, had Master Unduli said the words to her, gently and with the calmness of complete conviction?

Use the Force, Barriss.

Don't think, don't worry, don't get caught up in the small details, the nagging concerns, of it. Just use the Force, trust it, embrace it. Because that's where Jedi live. Not in the past, or the future, but in this eternal moment of joyous realization, this everlasting *now*. Don't let fear of failure keep you from taking the chance.

Barriss dried her face, hung up the towel, and looked into the mirror. Her face, calmer and more composed than it had appeared to her in a long time, looked back. Yes, of course. It was so simple, really: a perfect example of those enigmatic riddles that Master Yoda liked to pose as ways to help your mind let go of linear thoughts and concepts. The question was: how should she determine whether or not to use the bota again to increase her connection to the Force?

Ask the Force.

And what, so far in her life, had been the strongest, the most powerful, the best connection she had had to the Force?

The bota.

She could see Master Yoda, smiling and nodding gently, in her mind's eye. The bota was a key, a key that opened a door to new modes of perception. Beyond that door was a path that she could follow, to a place where she could find the answers she needed.

And there was no point in waiting. Barriss opened the lockbox next to her bed and removed one of the remaining poppers of bota extract. She took a deep breath, pressed it to her forearm, and triggered it.

As if her first experience had somehow *attuned* her, opening her receptors, as it were, the rush was almost immediate this time. That amazing sense of familiarity, coupled with awe and wonder at the newness of it, the astonishing, held-breath feeling, the breadth and depth of it, stretching to infinity . . .

She thought she was prepared for it, but she wasn't. It was just too . . . *big*. She couldn't see how anyone could accept it, take it all in, process it. It wouldn't fit into her limited comprehension; it was like trying to confine the blazing, multifaceted glory of a firestone into a flat 2-D image. Her senses, corseted into only three dimensions, couldn't even begin to make sense of it. But she didn't have to make sense of it, she realized. She had but to accept it, to be one with it. It was glorious, uplifting, and terrifying, all at the same time . . .

Her fear that this was an illusion vanished. There might be those who would say this was not a true connection to the Force because it had been induced by something outside herself, not arrived at through inner peace and meditation. She might even have said that at one time—but not now. This cosmic oneness could not be anything else *but* true—she could *feel* it to the core of her being.

It didn't matter how she got there. What mattered was being there.

It was if she were hungry, and, upon realizing this, was given a boundless table set with every kind of food imaginable. Choosing one dish over another was hard to do, and yet, on another level, she knew that she could.

Abruptly, the "table" swirled and shifted, melting into variegated colors like the mingling threads of spore colonies in Drongar's night sky. It become a giant, galaxywide tapestry, a woven fabric so intricate and complex as to bring tears to her eyes. A perfect piece of art, beautiful beyond description, beyond belief—

But wait. Yes, there *was* perfection here, but there was something else as well. She could sense flaws in the pattern, tiny, almost insignificant defects scattered throughout its immeasurable expanse. Barriss knew, instinctively, that these tiny mistakes were somehow *necessary*, that they were stitches in the skein of existence—imperfect ones, maybe, but nonetheless essential. Without them, the fabric would not hold together.

She reached for one of these small twisted threads with her mind, saw it expand and shift, so that it became . . . *readable*, somehow . . .

The concepts revealed to her were not words, or images; neither smells, tastes, sounds, nor touch. They were instead some kind of wondrous amalgam of all of these, plus senses no being of flesh had ever had . . .

In that moment, Barriss, herself a part of the grand pattern, *knew* the flaw in the tapestry:

The camp was in danger. There was a spy among them, the same one who had been responsible for the explosions of the shuttle, and on MedStar. Not dead, as they had thought, but still alive. This spy had initiated events that would, if left unattended, cause the destruction of all those who were there.

For the briefest of times, less than an eyeblink, she had more—she had the how and why and where and when of it—but then that was gone, swirled away in a burst of energy that she could not control. She couldn't remember the details.

She strained to regain them, aware of how supremely important it was. But now *something* somehow stood in her way . . .

Barriss abruptly found herself floundering, as if swept away by a raging, swollen river. She was tossed helplessly, like a twig—*in* it, but not *of* it.

It was the flaw, she realized. She had seen it, reached for it, but she had not had the power or the skill or whatever was needed to control it properly. And now, by trying, she had somehow disrupted the flow of the Force. She had lost her footing, her stance upon the firm ground that her serenity had given her. The roiling current had her now, was sweeping her along . . .

No. She had power. Great power. She would use it!

She tried to anchor herself, but there was nothing to grasp, nothing solid that she could perceive. She was caught in a flood, a gale, an avalanche that spun and disoriented her. Deep within, she knew that she was desperately seeking metaphors for that which could not be described, searching for some kind of mental analog that would enable her to separate herself from this chaos. She fought for calm, struggled to center herself, but she could not. Like a flood, it seemed to splash into her mouth, threatening to drown her; like a gale, it flung her in all directions, snatching the very breath from her lungs; like an avalanche, it threatened to crush her. It was like all those things, and none of them.

It was the Force.

She thought she heard someone speak then, a quiet and familiar voice, which she couldn't quite place.

Let go, it said. *Don't struggle against it. Take a breath and sink beneath it . . .*

No! I can control this, use it, wield it—!

Or—you could die.

Barriss felt the care and concern in that voice, and on some level below her conscious mind she knew it was right. Even as she inhaled a breath and relaxed into the mighty current, she recognized the speaker:

Master Unduli . . .

Barriss found herself sitting on her bed, blinking as if she had just come out of a deep sleep. She didn't need to check the room's chrono to know that time had passed. She had taken the bota injection at midday. She now sat in the dark.

She stood, walked to the window, cleared it, and looked out. The faint glimmer of the force-dome was not enough to hide the stars in the clear night sky above. The constellations were halfway through their nightly dance; it was around midnight. She had been . . . *gone* . . . for twelve hours, at least.

Gone to a place where she had never been. Where, she suspected, few, if any, had ever been.

She turned away from the window. She felt refreshed, as if she had slept soundly. She was not hungry, or thirsty; nor did she feel the need for the 'fresher. She smiled. The memory of the experience was still potent, pinwheeling in her mind in a glory of light and sound and smells and tastes and touch . . .

This was what her relationship with the Force could be. This was how it *should* be, all the time . . .

She frowned, feeling a tiny tug at her memory. The flaw. The coming disaster to the camp. In the cosmic totality of what she had just experienced, it was nothing, utterly insignificant when compared to the warp and woof of the whole; still, it was there, along with the uncountable other flaws. And she knew that, while they were somehow necessary in their total number, and they couldn't *all* be eliminated, in some cases individual ones could be—and should be—repaired.

The camp was in deadly danger. She had been shown this for a reason—this she *knew*. Just as she knew she had to do something about it.

27

The cantina was about as full as Den had ever seen it. After a moment, he realized why: the HNE troupe members were about to dust, as spacer lingo had it—they were on the morrow leaving Drongar to finish the remnants of their tour, and they were partying the night away.

As Den and I-Five entered, the reporter nearly staggered back, as though struck a physical blow. The sweet scent of spicestick and gum, the tang of various alcoholic beverages, and—most of all—the combined odors of a dozen or more species, all mixed into the heavy, wet air, produced a miasma as thick and strong as Gungan bouillabaisse. He glanced at I-Five. "You're sure you want to go through with this?"

"It seems the perfect atmosphere to me."

"To me it seems more like the kind of atmosphere you'd find twenty klicks or so down under the clouds on Bespin."

Den eyed the place askance. Many of the performers were dancing—or attempting to—egged on by the Modal Nodes doing a variety of favorites loud enough for the high notes to injure ears on MedStar. Den had been in a great many loud, crowded, and unruly bars over the course of his career, and he felt safe in ranking this one right down there among the worst.

I-Five seemed undisturbed. "Tradition, remember?" he said to Den. Then he squeezed between two dancing Ortolans and vanished.

Den sighed. *I'd better keep an eye on him, before someone or something decides to use him for a toothpick.*

How he was going to manage this was a good question: Sullustans were among the more height-challenged sentients in the civilized galaxy. Nonetheless, he pushed ahead, weaving and dodging legs, spurs, tentacles, and various other supporting limbs. He saw no sign of I-Five. Concerned about his own safety—at least as far as the issue of mashed toes went—Den finally climbed up on a table, next to a clone trooper who had passed out.

This action put him about at eye level with those who were of average height. Several species who were taller were mixed into the group as well, most notably a Wookiee member of the troupe he'd noticed at the first and only show. That one stood head and shoulders over just about everyone else. He seemed to be enjoying his ale very much, and was perfectly willing to share it with others, mostly by sloshing it on them from above.

A drunken Wookiee. That would no doubt make things more interesting at some point in the evening.

Den shifted his gaze, noticed Klo Merit near a wall, a drink in one furry hand and an introspective expression on his face. Equani weren't particularly tall, maybe half a dozen centimeters above most folks, but they were massive; Klo probably outweighed the Wookiee, with an Ugnaught or two tossed in. Den started to shout a greeting, then decided not to. From his expression, the minder looked like he could use a dose of his own medicine.

"Den?"

Surprised, he turned and saw Tolk le Trene by the table he was standing on. She, too, looked entirely too serious for such a party.

"Have you seen Jos?"

Den shook his head. "Just got here myself a minute ago."

"I need to find him," she said, more to herself than to him. The rest of her words were lost in the general vocal noise.

"What?" he shouted. But she just turned and disappeared into the crowd without another word.

There had been something in that look—Den wasn't sure just what it had been, but it put him in mind of the old Sakiyan saying about a flensor flying over one's bonepit. It made his dewflaps horripilate. Brrr!

Finally, he spotted I-Five.

The droid was standing not too far from Epoh Trebor, speaking to the human entertainer. He was gesticulating with far more emphasis than was customary with him. Den couldn't tell what I-Five was saying—even Sullustan hearing couldn't help when there was this much ambient noise in a room—but whatever it was, Trebor was laughing at it.

Seems pretty obvious that the elemental's out of the magnetic bottle, he thought. I-Five had obviously already implemented what the reporter had already come to think of as the "inebriation algorithm."

I-Five was, not to put too fast a spin on it, drunk.

It was also quite apparent that the droid hadn't shirked on the writing of his program. Den could see that his friend's photoreceptors were shining more brightly. That, coupled with the excess body language, and the laughs I-Five was getting out of a veteran entertainer, made it obvious that the droid was anything but a surly drunk.

Den grinned. Mission accomplished. He'd wanted to do his friend a favor by helping him find a way to cast off the shackles of propriety, to loosen up. Good. I-Five deserved no less. After all, if organic sentients chafed in those shackles, how much more must the artificially intelligent suffer?

And the really good news was that I-Five wouldn't even wake up with a hangover.

Den decided it was high time he joined the party.

He jumped off the table and began to weave his way to the bar. "Excuse me. Coming through here. Low being walking. Pardon, citizen. Hey, watch the ears, floob . . . !"

Jos sat on his cot, staring at the wall, feeling as miserable as he ever had in his life. His days were spent wading in blood, up to his armpits in the mangled bodies of clone troopers who were little more than particle cannon fodder. His one real friend, a brilliant musician and surgeon, had been killed by the war, snuffed out in a heartbeat. The only other bright spot in this sea of bleakness, the woman he loved, had pulled away from him—and she wouldn't even tell him why.

Jos stared, unseeing. He was a surgeon, he had seen people die before the Republic had called him into its service—he'd dealt with it. He'd just shrugged it off.

But he'd been wrong to think that helped. On days when death was with him from the moment he started work to the moment he finished, when he worked to the point of bleary-eyed dullness, over and over and over, it still took its toll.

Tolk had been the antidote. Tolk had stood beside him,

and regardless of how the relationship might ostracize him from his family and friends back home, she had been worth it.

But now . . .

Now his days were dark, and the nights darker. He could see no end to it. This war could go on for years, decades; it had happened before. He could grow old here, cutting and pasting ruined bodies until one hot morning he would fall over and die himself.

What was the point?

As a doctor, Jos knew about depression. Postsurgical patients were often low after life-altering events, and, while he would send the seriously affected ones to minders, he had been trained to deal with the symptoms if there wasn't proper backup available. But understanding depression didn't make him immune to it. There was knowing, and then there was *feeling*.

The idea of leaving it all behind was tempting, oh, yes. He was capable of it, if it came to that. He knew just where a slight nick with a vibroscalpel would bleed the most. Take a little anticoagulant, open a major blood vessel, then slowly fall asleep—and not wake up. Death would be painless that way, or with any of a dozen drugs he could take off the shelf that would do the trick just as well. A final salute, and then the Big Jump . . .

Suicide was rare among his people—few Corellians took that route, and none of Jos's family had ever done so, as far as he knew.

At the moment, it didn't feel like the worst thing that could happen to him. He could easily make it look like an accident, thus sparing his family the shame, and at least some of the grief.

Jos shook his head again. How had he come here? This

was a place he had never dreamed he could be, thinking in detail about how to end his own life.

He remembered what he had been trained to tell those patients who had fallen so low: *wait.* Don't do something that can't be reversed. Life is long; things change. A month, a year, five years from now, your situation could reverse—look at how many people came from nothing, grew rich, lost it all, and then rebuilt their fortunes. Look at those who were afflicted with a debilitating or even fatal illness, who stayed around long enough for a cure. Even those who lost a spouse, or a child or a parent, and later found happiness. The bottom line was: alive, you have a chance. There are no possibilities for the dead.

Jos sighed, a deep and ragged breath. Yes. Those were the things he told his patients, and they were all true.

An old memory rose up from his days at Coruscant Med. The instructor, a grizzled and gray human named Leig Duwan, who must have been well over a hundred standard years old, had spoken of his days on Alderaan. The old man smiled a lot, and he was grinning as he told the story.

There had been a bad time in Duwan's life—his father had died, his mother had been hospitalized, and his sister had gone missing on a frontier expedition. Duwan had failed an exam, and it looked as if he might be dropped from medical school. He had, he'd told the class, seriously considered suicide. Instead, he'd muddled through somehow, and eventually things did get better.

One day, he met a man on the street. The man stopped him and said, "I want to thank you, Doctor Duwan, for saving my life."

Duwan had heard this many times, of course, and he had deflected the praise with practiced ease: "It's my job, citizen. No thanks are—"

"No," the man interrupted. "I wasn't your patient. I was undergoing a period of deep depression and was suicidal. I had decided to end it—I'd already obtained the means—and was on my way to a private place where I would do it. But I gave myself one out: if, on my journey, any person I passed was to smile at me—just one—I would not go through with it.

"I was on the street, outside the hospital, and you were on your way in. You smiled and nodded at me. And here I am."

The point of his story, Duwan said, was not whether his medical expertise had saved someone. The point was that, because he had gone through his own darkness, and had kept going long enough to be able to smile at a stranger, he had saved that man's life. There were thousands more over the years whom he had, with some skill and much luck, also managed to keep alive. Being useful to others was not an unworthy thing, even if you had nothing else.

Jos looked at the chrono. He had rounds to make, postop patients to check. If he killed himself, somebody else would have to take over his rounds. That would be an imposition, causing somebody to have to cover for him.

It would be . . . impolite.

He could manage to face another hour. *That's all you have to do*, he told himself. *Just an hour, the next hour. Do your rounds, make your reports.*

He could get through another hour. And after that . . .

Well. Time enough to worry about that when he got there. For now, this hour was all that mattered.

28

Jos finished his rounds. He knew about the farewell party for the HNE troupe, and normally there would be little reluctance on his part to join them. But now . . .

What if Tolk was there?

Seeing her in the OT was bad enough; he wasn't sure he could handle seeing her in a social setting. What if she was there with someone else?

He shook his head. At least in the cantina he wouldn't be drinking alone. Sooner or later he would run into her again. It just wasn't that big a base.

To deep with it. Jos marched out of the OT, feeling much like a man walking to his own execution.

It was crowded in the cantina. Also hot, noisy, and smelly. Maybe Jos wouldn't encounter Tolk after all in this crowd.

That hope didn't last long. It was, in fact, Tolk who found him, before he could get his first drink. He turned around and there she was, right there, her gaze fixed on his face, searching it for—what?

He didn't know what to say. He knew he should say something, but she was so lovely, even just in her scrubs, with her hair up and exhaustion evident in her face, that she stole the breath from his lungs.

"Tolk . . . ," he managed. "I—"

"I've been thinking a lot, Jos. There's more to all this than just how we feel about each other. There's more to this war than just here, what we do—who we are to each other. I need some time to process it, on my own." She took a breath. "I'm requesting a transfer to Rimsoo Three."

His mouth was dry. Rimsoo Three was over a thousand klicks north, across the Sea of Sponges. "What are you saying? Can't we at least talk about it?"

"No, not yet."

Jos blew out a big breath. He didn't want to say it, but it had to be said: "Does this mean we're through?"

She hesitated. "It means we're apart for a while."

There was no way to dissuade her, he saw. But if she transferred out, he'd never see her again. Of that he was sure.

"I have to go," she said. And with that, she was gone.

Jos made his way to the bar. He was numb. *What had happened? What had gone wrong? What had he said or done?*

He still couldn't believe it. Done. Gone. Just like that.

His mind scrambled frantically for some purchase, something to hold on to. As chief surgeon, he could refuse to let her transfer out, could say she was too valuable here—but what good would that do? How could they work together? Play sabacc together? How could they—

Questions swirled around in his head like dust motes, like a swarm of fire gnats.

He needed a drink.

He reached the bar, but before he could order anything, he heard a deep growl. He turned to look.

Now there's something you don't see every day, he thought. *A droid and a Wookiee playing hologames.*

The game was called dejarik; although Jos didn't play, he was familiar with it. I-Five and the Wookiee sat at a small corner table amid all the commotion. The Wookiee was covered with coal-black shaggy fur, save for a star-shaped white patch high on the left quadrant of his chest. And at the moment, he seemed really upset, even for a Wookiee—and that was saying something.

"Never a boring minute, eh?"

Jos looked down and saw Den Dhur standing beside him. Den gestured toward the dejarik table and sighed. "You might remember my mentioning once or twice before that I was trying to help I-Five get drunk?"

"Yeah?"

"Well . . ."

Kaird was, after a fashion, enjoying himself, even though he was of necessity wearing the Kubaz suit. He didn't mind seeing people have a good time, and the fact that he knew—and would do—something that would ruin their high spirits did not diminish his enjoyment. When news of the change in the bota became widespread, chaos would most likely ensue. The misfortunes of war.

Too bad. While he wasn't sentimentally attached to anyone here—sentimentality being a luxury he could ill afford—he admired a great many of the doctors and soldiers and techs who populated this place. They were, for the most part, honorable folk. Honor, as most people seemed to think of it, was a code that limited one's options severely and, even worse, was a good way to return to the Great Egg at hyperspeed. Kaird was a practical being—he couldn't afford to have honor. But he surely did admire it in others. If nothing else, it made it far easier to predict their actions.

It was harder dealing with scalawags in some ways, easier in others. Take Thula and Squa Tront, for example. Kaird would be quite surprised—almost disappointed, in fact—if those two hadn't thought of ways to shortchange him and Black Sun on the upcoming transaction. Not that he really minded if they found a way to skim a little for themselves—that was the nature of business, and to be expected. But he wasn't overly concerned. Rogues they might be, but they also seemed smart enough to realize the lunacy of attempting any major deception on Black Sun.

He dipped the mask's snout into his drink—one reason he liked the Kubaz identity was because he could drink while in it. Pity he couldn't just let go and enjoy the party to the fullest, but he was also here for a practical reason. As it turned out, the human pilot Bogan had taken a double shift recently, and as a result he would not be on standby for the admiral's ship when Kaird needed him. This was easily remedied, however. There were another two pilots in the rotation, and one of them was here in this cantina, right now. This pilot, also a human—a lot of those around the galaxy, Kaird had noticed—was behaving in a responsible manner: since he was on standby, he was not drinking, smoking, or sniffing anything intoxicating. Sebairns, his name was, and while he seemed to be having a good time, smiling and laughing, he had restricted himself to some kind of steeped brew made from a local plant.

Because Kaird had access to all kinds of information, including medical records, he had learned that Sebairns had an allergic condition for which there was no cure or preventive treatment. If exposed to a certain common legume, the human would develop a fairly severe anaphylactic reaction, the symptoms of which might include urticaria and syncope secondary to ascites. Kaird had gotten this information translated via the HoloNet. It meant that the human could break out in a serious, itchy rash that could include large hives; he could faint and, if left untreated, might even choke to death as his windpipe closed. Not that it would get that bad in the middle of a Rimsoo full of doctors—he'd be whisked off to a ward in a hurry, and all his symptoms could be treated easily. But he wouldn't be able to work for a day or two, which was more than enough for Kaird's purposes.

Kaird had watched the servers with care, and his moment came. He stood and started away from his single-unit table, as if to answer a call of nature. The droid server bearing a tray for Sebairns's table started in that direction as well. Their paths would intersect, as Kaird had planned.

As Kaird neared the server, he said, "Pardon me, could you point out the 'fresher?"

Even though the refresher was clearly marked in half a dozen languages and graphic images, the droid had no doubt heard the question more than a few times from inebriated patrons. It swiveled its head slightly and pointed with its free appendage. "That way, sir. The door under the glowing sign."

While the droid was thus engaged, Kaird brought his hand around, as if to scratch his snout, and in so doing allowed a small pinch of legume powder to fall into the man's drink.

He then headed toward the 'fresher. He would return to his table in a moment to make sure his target drank from the doctored cup and reacted appropriately. Once that was done, his objective for tonight would be accomplished.

It was unlikely that anyone would suspect the man's drink had been tampered with—it wasn't poison, after all, and the attending medics would recognize the reaction for what it was. Even if they did suspect it had been deliberate, it wouldn't matter. There was no way to tie Kaird to the deed. Even if the serving droid was questioned, and happened to recall a Kubaz asking directions to the 'fresher, the Kubaz in question didn't exist. After tonight, Kaird would have no more need for this particular costume, and it would be rendered down to its molecular level by a recycling unit. Can't find what doesn't exist.

He had, in one of his fat human disguises, obtained from one of the entertainment group's members a copy of the most recent recording of *Galactic Sports Update*. Upon this *GSU* recording was a recent Strag Sector Match Championship. If you were not a skilled player, watching a game of Strag was less interesting than watching mold grow; if you were ranked, however, such matches were fascinating. Neither the Twi'lek Vorra, nor the human pilot Bogan, would have seen this particular match; it hadn't been holocast this far out yet. The corpulent human, whom Kaird had named Mont Shomu, would arrange soon to be heard talking about this match, which he happened to have a recording of, within Vorra's hearing. She would fall all over herself to obtain it from him. The fat man would be loath to part with it, however, being a fan of the game himself. Of course, he would be willing to share a viewing of the match with her. And, naturally, she could bring a friend . . .

Kaird smiled as he exited the 'fresher and returned to his table amid the noise and heat of the busy cantina. There was a real joy in watching a carefully made plan unfold.

* * *

"Let me get this straight," Jos said. "I-Five is *drunk*?"

"I've been watching him for hours," Den said, "and believe me, he's soused. If that's the proper term for a droid."

"From a *program*."

"Yeah."

"Which *he* wrote."

"Right."

Jos looked over at the game table, where the various transparent holocreatures that were the pieces of the game shifted and scratched restlessly on their squares. I-Five didn't look any different from here, save for a slightly increased luminosity in his photoreceptors and more exaggerated movement. Jos shook his head. "It just keeps getting weirder." He turned back to the bar and hoisted his drink.

"*Ha!*" I-Five said loudly. "My molator takes your houjix! I win!"

The Wookiee roared with rage. Jos looked back at the game just in time to see the Wookiee stand, grab I-Five's right arm, and wrench it from the droid's shoulder. Circuitry and servomotor couplings broke free in a shower of sparks and sprays of lubricating fluid.

My, my.

"Bad loser," Den said.

"Looks like," Jos agreed.

They both leapt forward, grabbed the droid, and pulled him away from the game board as the furious Wookiee harned and moaned in his own language and waved the mechanical arm over his head. Jos glimpsed several of the showfolk, including a burly Trandoshan, moving in quickly to calm down their colleague.

I-Five felt no pain, of course. He seemed more confused than anything else.

"I seem to be missing an arm," he said to Jos. "I'm sure I had it when I came in."

Jos pushed I-Five into an empty booth. "Your gamer friend borrowed it."

"I-Five," Den said, "I think maybe it's time to sober up now."

I-Five shrugged. Jos wouldn't have thought the gesture possible for a drunken droid with only one arm. "If you say so." His photoreceptors flickered for a moment, then resumed what Jos thought of as their normal glow.

The droid looked about him in mild surprise. "Interesting."

"Wish sobering up was that easy for me," Jos said.

A human female brought the arm over to them, handing it to Jos. "Here," she said. "You might want to program your droid to avoid games with Wookiees in the future. They're, uh, very competitive."

I-Five looked at the arm. "So I have determined."

Jos examined the arm's exposed end. "I'm no cybertech," he said, "but it looks like this can be reattached fairly easily." He looked at the droid. "You're lucky he didn't pull your head off."

"True," I-Five agreed. "That would have been considerably harder to fix."

"What were you thinking, challenging a Wookiee to a dejarik game?"

"I wasn't thinking. That was the point. I was drunk— or at least as close to it as I could program."

Jos shook his head in amazement. "Come on," he said. "Let's head over to the shop and see if anyone's still there who can fix you up. Reattaching mechanical limbs is a bit beyond my expertise."

The three left the cantina and walked through the hot night air, I-Five holding his dismembered arm. Den said,

"I'd feel terrible if I was responsible for you getting drunk and into a bar fight—if it turned out not to be worth it."

"I think it was," I-Five said. "I think it was very worthwhile." He looked at Jos. "Remember my mentioning that I seemed to be having an anxiety attack?"

Jos nodded.

"I believe it was born out of conflicting impulses based on new data garnered from regaining all of my memory files—including several regarding my erstwhile friend and partner, Lorn Pavan.

"I remembered that I have an obligation to fulfill—one that involves my returning to Coruscant as soon as possible. But to do so would be to abandon my responsibilities here. This was a problem that could not be solved by an application of logic. I needed intuition—the ability to sense what was right by mechanisms far older than logic and application of data.

"I needed, somehow, to jar my synaptic grid cortex into another mode—a totally nonlinear mode. Thus, the concept of altering my sensory input and perception of data."

"Did it work?" Den asked.

"I believe so. I have decided on a course of action."

"You leaving us, I-Five?" Jos asked.

"Not immediately." The droid did not amplify his comment.

Jos couldn't resist. "But," he said, "you're a machine, remember? Programmed to be an automaton, no more. So what does it matter how you reach a decision?"

I-Five looked at him. "You're enjoying this, aren't you?"

"Oh, yeah."

"All of what I have said before is technically true," the

droid said. "But I've come to realize it's possible for things to be more than the sum of their parts. And that a difference that makes no difference is, for all practical purposes, moot. I think I was, for lack of a better term, afraid. I believe that I was trying to convince myself, more than you, that I am not what you, Barriss, and a few others here see me as. I was, however, lacking necessary information to reach the right conclusion."

"And that would be . . . ?"

"That I am indeed sentient," I-Five said.

Jos grinned, and slapped the droid on his durasteel back. "Took you long enough to figure it out."

They found an Ishi Tib tech, half asleep under a tool bench. At first he was surly, but the bottle of Corellian wine that Den had grabbed as they'd left proved an effective bribe.

As the tech was reattaching I-Five's arm, spot-welding snapped junctions and splicing sensory cables and hydraulic circulatory piping, Jos said, "By the way, it's none of my business, but I'm curious—just what is the obligation you remembered?"

I-Five didn't answer right away, and the silence stretched long enough for Jos to begin to wish he hadn't asked. Then the droid said, "It was a request of Lorn's. He asked me to watch over his son."

29

Barriss could not sleep. Her experience with the Force continued to echo in her, stronger by far than after the first time, bringing up powerful flashes of the wondrous cosmic consciousness she had been a part of—along with the feeling of important things going undone. She wanted to return to that place—to stay there, if at all possible.

Maybe it was cumulative. Maybe it would come to pass that, eventually, she could swim in that magical sea on her own, at will, and without the bota to deliver and keep her there.

There hadn't been any new revelations. The danger to the camp was approaching, but it was not yet at hand. On some level, she knew she had enough time to decide upon a course of action. On another level, what that course of action would be seemed utterly beyond her capabilities.

Beyond her *unamplified* capabilities. But nothing seemed too big for her to handle while connected in the Force by the miracle of the bota. She *knew,* right to the depths of her bones, that what she could do with the Force in that state would be astounding, once she got used to it. Once she learned to not control it, but to flow with it, to *be* it.

She now understood how it was that the greatest Jedi Masters could sense things even parsecs away, information gained far faster than by subspace packet; she had now the knowledge—the certainty—that the universe was of an entire piece, each part connected to all the others, webbed together by vibrating strands of the Force that stretched through dimensions utterly beyond the ken of her senses—and she knew her place in it, and that all things, great and small, were precisely in position. As they had always been, and as they always would be, worlds without end.

There was a temptation to rush out and harvest bota by the bale, render it into fluid, and install a constant-feed pump on her arm to trickle it into her system continuously. She wondered if that was the desire of a seeker, or an addict.

She wondered if there was any difference.

In any event, she could take this new knowledge back to the Jedi Council, and with it the Jedi could become more powerful than anyone could possibly imagine. They could stop this war, as well as prevent others from starting. They could abolish slavery, transform barren worlds into lush paradises, chase evil to the ends of the galaxy and strike it down! *Nothing* would be beyond their capabilities—the power was that immense!

It all swam in Barriss, overwhelming in its intensity. Even now, she could barely contain the memory of it.

But first, before she went too far into the void, she had to deal with the camp situation. That would be easily accomplished. Then, she could address the larger issues . . .

Den hurried through the camp to the launch platform, hoping that he wasn't too late. *Milking fool,* he thought, *of all the days to oversleep—!*

He hardly ever bothered with alarm chronos—like most of his kind, Den had an inner timekeeper that went along with his keen sense of direction. Usually it adjusted to the day-and-night cycles of whatever world he was on fairly quickly, taking no more than a standard week at most, and he'd been on this planet a lot longer than that.

But on the one day he needed it the most, wouldn't you just know it would kick out on him, and he'd sleep just long enough to maybe miss the transport departure of the HNE folk, including Eyar?

After the proposal she had made and he had accepted, he couldn't let her leave without saying good-bye. It was hard to know just when he would see her again. And when he did, it would be as part of the extended family that would include, by all accounts, a truly staggering number of younglings.

He was to be a patriarch, a hoary old dispenser of wisdom. To sit somewhere deep in the warren and dole out nuggets of sage advice to the young and foolish.

The whole thing didn't seem quite as appealing now as it had when Eyar had described it to him.

The entertainers were being ferried up to MedStar, where their own transport was docked. Eyar had been scheduled for the first lift up.

Den came around the corner of the launch facility's main building in time to see the few members of the troupe moving up the ramp. Eyar was one of them.

He ran forward, pushing his way through the taller beings that surrounded him, mostly techs and other workers. "Hey!" he shouted. "Eyar! Wait!" Blast it, he couldn't see anything but legs—legs covered with clothing, fur, or scales; digitigrade legs, plantigrade legs; a veritable forest of supporting limbs. At last he reached the gate.

"*Eyar!*"

She was walking sadly up the ramp, the last to leave. At

his cry she whirled, and when she saw him, her eyes, her face, her whole body lit up.

"Den-la!"

He was so relieved she hadn't left yet that he didn't care that she'd attached the familiar-suffix to his name in public. They embraced.

"I was afraid you wouldn't come! What happened?"

To tell her he'd overslept would be a bad idea—this he knew almost instinctively. She'd be offended that he'd nearly missed her leave-taking for so trivial a reason. "Had a comm from HNE," he said. "Some talk about one of my articles from last year being made into a holo. Finally had to cut 'em off and run all the way to get here."

Amazing how easily the lie came out of him—amazing, and not a little bit dismaying. But it worked. She looked at him with starry-eyed love. "Come back to Sullust soon," she whispered. She nuzzled his dewflaps one more time, and then turned and ran up the ramp.

Den moved back behind the field radius. The transport, silent save for the *thrum* of the repulsorlifts, rose quickly and disappeared into the glare of Drongar Prime.

Den walked slowly back to his kiosk. It had been so easy to lie to her. One could argue that it was a small incident, trivial and unimportant. One could argue that he'd lied out of beneficence, to save her from hurt feelings. One could argue all kinds of things, but none of them had any more validity or authenticity than a Neimoidian's handshake.

He was a scoundrel.

Eyar was sweet and sincere and trusting. He admired those qualities in her. But how long would it be before those same attributes filled him with impatience, or annoyance . . .

Or contempt?

He was hardly worthy of Eyar's admiration.

Den stopped in the middle of the compound. This was bad. He was having cold feet all the way up to his armpits, and he had no idea what to do about it.

He looked about. From where he was standing, he had two options, each of which lay in practically opposite directions. To his left was the cantina, with its amazing and highly therapeutic varieties of distillates. To his right was Klo Merit's office, where he could talk to the minder, or at the very least make an appointment to do so later. He needed to work this out.

How?

It took Den nearly two minutes of standing in the broiling sun before he turned and trotted off, a direction finally chosen.

30

The throbbing of the medlifters, the shouts and cross talk of personnel running to the triage area, the screams and groans of the troopers—it was a litany of sounds and cries that Jos had responded to so many times that it seemed he could do it in his sleep by now.

Sleep. There was a laugh. The truncated periods of naps and dozing that the medics of Rimsoo Seven managed to snag on good days wasn't anything even close to good sleep hygiene. Of course, they had delta wave inducers, but cramming six to eight hours of uninterrupted cycling through the four stages and REM periods into a ten-minute nap just didn't replenish the brain the same way that real-time sleep did. The only solution was a proper night's rest, and that was a luxury seldom afforded.

Most of the time, the patients were clone troopers. For Jos, the hardest cases were not the completely alien species. They were the nonclone individual humans, because their anatomies were familiar to him, and yet subtly different from one another. When operating on such a human patient, he had to be very careful not to let his hands and brain fall back into familiar patterns that might work on a clone, but be just off enough to kill another human being. It had already happened once.

Truly alien individuals didn't come through the OT

very often. The few who did were usually on Drongar in some kind of observation or clerical capacity. And they often provided most of the moments of both humor and horror.

The last time they'd had an unexpected incident like that had been when Jos had been drenched in the Nikto's life fluids. This time, it had been Uli who experienced the shock of the new.

The young surgeon had been working on a female Oni. The Oni were a fairly bellicose species, by all accounts, that hailed from the Outer Rim world of Uru. What this one was doing on Drongar no one seemed to know for sure—probably a mercenary. In any event, she had caught a projectile from a slugthrower, and Uli was probing for it when there was a blue-white flash, a sound like someone whacking a nest of angry wingstingers, and the young surgeon bounced backward and hit the wall.

He wasn't hurt that much, as was evidenced by a stream of curses. The usual buzz of instrument requests and readout quotes came to a stop. Threndy, the nurse who had been assisting, helped Uli to his feet.

"You okay, Uli? Need any help?" Jos called.

"I'm good, thanks. But what in the seven skies of Sumarin was that? I never—"

He was interrupted by a tripedal medical droid that came in, moved to Uli's side, and spoke briefly to him. Jos couldn't hear the conversation, but after a moment Uli and Threndy both broke into laughter.

"What's up?" Jos asked.

"Apparently, Oni females are electrophoretic. I must've brushed against a lobe of her capacitor organ during my probe." Uli shrugged. "Kinda wish I'd known about it sooner . . ."

Jos chuckled. "Maybe we should keep her around in case our droids need a jump start."

His shift and Uli's were over at the same time, and, on impulse, Jos asked the younger man if he wanted to join them at sabacc. They'd been short several players the last couple of times. Tolk didn't show up anymore, and Barriss seemed lately to be too absorbed in "Jedi-ing," as Den put it, to sit in on every game. Even Klo had been too busy to put in more than an occasional appearance.

Uli grinned, a smile that spread over his entire face. "Sure!" he said enthusiastically. "I've been hoping one of you'd ask."

Jos grinned back. "Glad to have you." It would be nice to have something approaching a full set of players again. On one level, though, he did feel bad about it. Uli was so open and guileless, he was sure to be eaten alive by the others. Sabacc could be a tough game.

Jos, Den, Barriss, and I-Five walked out of the cantina.

"Wow," Jos said. "Who knew?"

"Not you, I'm assuming," Den replied. "Unless you're in cahoots with the little—"

"Hey, I had no idea he could play like that. I mean, look at him. He looks like a holorep for some nice wholesome farmworld somewhere." Jos shrugged. "Besides, we've been losing players. And I felt sorry for him."

"Yeah? Well, feel sorry for *me*. I lost three hundred creds in there." Den shook his head.

"Just a suggestion," I-Five said to Jos, "but the next time you're tempted to be altruistic in matters like these—don't."

"Aw, clamp your vocabulator," Den told him sourly.

"You're the only one who didn't lose his shirt. Not that you have one to lose."

"This is true. However, for the first time in some weeks I have not won anything, either."

Jos swatted futilely at a buzzing cloud of fire gnats. "Again I ask: what do you need money for? You're a droid."

"A fact that seldom escapes my notice, thank you. My need for money is quite simple—it costs large amounts of credits to travel. Especially as far as Coruscant."

"You're really going, then?" Barriss asked.

"Yes."

"But you're military property," Jos said. "Even if you could find a way to get transferred to Coruscant, you'll have limited freedom to search for Pavan's son."

"Also true. Which means," I-Five said calmly, "I might have to desert."

For a long moment the silence was unbroken save by the gnats. Then Jos said, "If you do, and you're caught, they'll wipe your memory down to the last quantum shell."

"*If* I'm caught. My time on Coruscant wasn't completely misspent—I know a variety of ways to slip through the cracks, especially in a megalopolis that large."

Den sucked on a hydropak for a moment, then said, "No doubt—but first you have to get off Drongar. And won't you arouse suspicion, traveling by yourself?"

"Droids, particularly protocol droids, make interstellar journeys all the time. We're not children. No one will look twice at me—especially if I carry the papers of an envoy en route to the Coruscant Temple on Jedi business."

He looked at Barriss. She looked back quite seriously.

"You are willing to risk everything—your very *self*—to do this?" she asked.

"It's something I promised Lorn many years ago, when his son Jax was first taken from him. He asked me to make sure that, should anything ever happen to him, I would do my best to keep watch over Jax, even though he was under the protection of the Jedi. Lorn did not trust Jedi."

"I must remind you, I-Five, that the Jedi are sworn to uphold the laws of the Republic." Barriss paused, then added, "There are times, however, when such laws come into conflict with the moral codes that we espouse. These conflicts often require difficult decisions to be made."

"And how do the Jedi make these decisions?"

"Well," she said with a slight smile, "some have been known to get drunk."

Jos laughed. He couldn't help it. And it felt good.

"It so happens," Barriss continued, "that I have something I wish to see delivered to the Temple on Coruscant as soon as possible. There are very few to whom I would entrust such a mission. If you would be willing . . . ?"

I-Five said, "I would be honored."

31

Column stared at the message on the desktop. It had taken several hours to decipher the cumbersome triple code, but this time it had been worth the effort. The Separatists had gotten the missive sent from this location earlier. They had checked it out, and found that the bota was indeed losing its potency. Much quicker than the spy had expected, they had come to a decision: there would be an all-out attack on the Republic forces on Drongar in the next few days. Every mech and mercenary the other side could field would participate in the battle, with but one purpose: to capture and collect the remaining bota for the Separatists. Many would die or be destroyed on both sides; much of the bota in the fields might be ruined—but the message, short as it was, was quite unambiguous and explicit. They were coming. This Rimsoo, along with all the others, would shortly be overrun. They would not be taking prisoners—at least, none they intended to keep alive.

Column stared at the note with labile emotions and mixed feelings. Yes, it had been expected, if not so soon. Yes, it would be a blow to the Republic, which was the reason that Column had come to be here in the first place. This didn't change the fact that the responsibility for the loss of life and matériel would be on Column's head.

The decrypted message, printed on a plastisheet templast, started to curl at the edges. In another minute the process, a combustible oxidation that began the moment the plastisheet was exposed to air, would evaporate the note into nothingness.

Just as the spy's third identity would soon come to an end.

No matter, either way. The note had served its purpose—Column had committed the contents to memory. The war here would also be effectively over, quite soon. The bota would be collected or destroyed or mutated into uselessness—they all came to the same result, insofar as the combatants were concerned.

Column would be gone by the time the attack came in force. There would be a reason to visit MedStar, and the transport supposed to take the spy there would be . . . diverted, so that it delivered its cargo to the Separatists' territory. Column would, of course, have the vouchsafe codes that would allow the ship to pass unscathed. Then, the jump to hyperspace, and those left behind here would be no more than sad memories.

There would be another assignment, on another world, soon enough. The war elsewhere would continue, and Column, under another false identity, would go forth to continue to aid in the destruction of the Republic. However long the task took, it would happen, the spy knew. It *would* happen.

Column sighed. There was still much to be done here, and little time in which to accomplish it. Records, files, information, some of which might prove of value to Column's masters, all must be gathered and condensed into data packets one could slip into one's pocket or travel case. The end—at least here and now—was quite near.

* * *

It was nearly midnight. The long-snouted Kubaz costume was gone, and the fat suit was a lot of trouble to flesh up and don, so Kaird had his meeting with Thula dressed as The Silent monk. It was not as if anybody would see them together, so he wasn't concerned about the impropriety of speaking.

He stood with his back against a thin-walled storage shed just past the main dining hall, apparently alone. Thula was inside the shed, invisible to anybody who might be passing in the hot tropical dark, but easily heard past a screened grille designed to let air circulate through the wall while keeping out the rain.

"You have what I need?"

"Yes."

"Then you and your friend have your two days' warning. I suggest you use the time wisely."

Thula's voice was a soft, feral purr. "And the balance of our payment?"

"Look atop the inside ledge of the door's frame."

There was a brief pause. Kaird's ears were keen enough to detect the sound of the Falleen's footfalls as she quickly moved to the door, paused a moment, then returned to the wall. He caught a faint glimmer of light through the mesh as she triggered the credit cube he'd left over the door and checked the holoproj for the sum it contained.

"Most generous," she said.

"Where is my case?" he asked.

"By now it's in your kiosk, next to your other luggage. It was a pleasure doing business with you, friend."

"You have a way to depart?"

"Yes. We've secured tentative passage on a small transport vessel, leaving tomorrow. There is a pilot open to bribes."

"A surface-to-ship transport won't take you far."

"Far enough to obtain something else that will. Money is a powerful lubricant."

"Perhaps we'll met again someday," Kaird said.

"Perhaps," she said.

Kaird moved away from the shed and back to his kiosk. The door had been locked, but such locks as were used here were hardly proof against professional thieves, as Squa Tront and Thula were—among their many other talents.

The carbonite slab stood next to his other bag, disguised so as to resemble a moderately priced travel case. It was almost a perfect match to his luggage. Frozen in carbonite, the bota would keep until somebody triggered the melter. After that, it would have to be processed quickly to avoid the rapid rot that would follow, but that was not his problem. Black Sun had the best chemists in the galaxy on tap; all he had to do was get it to them.

He hefted the case. It was heavy, nearly seventy kilos, he judged, but easily within his ability to pick up and carry.

Kaird felt better in that moment than he had since he had arrived on this pestilent planet. He had done the best he could, given the circumstances, and when all was said and done, he felt he would come out of it looking very good indeed. Just a couple more days of subterfuge, and then on to his homeworld and peace.

A well-deserved peace.

Jos woke up in the middle of the night, grainy from his most recent bout of drinking. He sat up on his cot and rubbed his eyes. He had dreamed of Tolk, and in the dream she had told him why she wanted to go away. Only now, he couldn't remember what she had said.

Jos stood, padded to the 'fresher, and splashed water on his face. He rinsed his mouth out. He had been drinking lately to such an extent that even the anti-veisalgia drugs that normally quashed hangovers were losing their effectiveness. He looked at himself in the mirror.

What a sad sight you are.

He sighed. No question about that.

What a pitiful excuse for a man, too. Are you just going to let her go? Without a fight?

He frowned at his reflection. Aloud, he said, "What am I supposed to do? She won't talk to me! And I don't know why!"

So? You're not stupid! Figure out why! You couldn't stop Zan dying—are you just going to let Tolk walk away without even knowing why?

Jos turned away from the mirror and went back to his cot. He stood there, staring at the bed. There was the question, wasn't it? The big one, the only one: why? What had caused Tolk, the woman who said she loved him, to just up and leave? She had cited the explosion on MedStar, the dozens of deaths—but that didn't make sense. Tolk had seen worse, far worse, and a lot closer at hand. No, this was different. It was almost as if she'd received a revelation from some primitive planetary deity . . .

The sudden realization hit him hard enough to make him sit down. It was as if he had been punched in the solar plexus, his wind stolen, so that he couldn't take another breath. He knew. He *knew*!

Great-Uncle Erel. He had talked to Tolk. He had told her what it was like to give up family and home forever. *He* had poisoned Tolk's thoughts!

It made perfect sense. She had figured the old man

would speak to her. Jos had, too, but somehow that knowledge had slipped from his mind—he had been so tired and overworked. In hindsight, it seemed unbelievable that he could have put that possibility out of his thoughts, but he had. Tolk had talked about the explosion, the deaths, the horror of it all, and Jos had fastened upon that and thought about her reasons no further.

Uncle Erel.

Rage rose in him like a hot tide. He stood, went back to the 'fresher, and flipped the sonic shower on. He stepped into the stall, feeling the grime and sleep and sour smell of alcohol that still seeped from his pores begin to sluice away, rolling down his body in dirty waves to the drain. He looked at his chrono—the next transport was scheduled to lift midmorning. Time enough to shower and dress, and then, by everything that was righteous, he would pull rank, call in favors . . . grow wings and fly if that's what it took to pay a visit to his loving uncle and have the truth from him—one way or another.

32

Kaird, or Mont Shomu, as he was known in his fat human disguise, smiled as the human pilot and the Twi'lek food service tech sipped from the bottle of local wine he had brought along. It wasn't bad wine, made from a round, reddish purple fruit about the size of a human's closed fist that grew on the funguslike trees of the Jasserak Highlands. Called avedame, the pulp was crispy when ripe, and had a tart, yet sweet taste; the wine reflected this.

That the wine was drugged with myocaine didn't affect the flavor at all, given that in the liquid oral form, the muscle relaxant was tasteless, odorless, and colorless. To allay any suspicion, Kaird also drank the wine. The difference was that a pinch of neutralizer had gone into his glass, along with the straw-colored wine, ensuring that he would feel no effect from the chemical.

"Let's get started, shall we?" the Twi'lek female said. The excitement was high in her voice. Kaird smiled, and the fat face smiled with him. How sweet and naive . . .

Bogan, the human pilot, was just as ramped. He swallowed half his glass of fruit wine and impatiently waved the holoprojector to life. Not as conscientious as the other pilot, to drink wine, even though it wasn't much.

The image of a large hall filled with tables, at each of

which two players sat, blossomed in the air above them.
The holoproj was sharp, and they would get to enjoy the
first twenty or thirty minutes of it. After that, once the
pharmaceutical took hold, they would be awake and
alert, but simply unable to move.

After fifteen minutes, the pair of them began to slump,
and, while they no doubt wondered and worried at this,
they simply did not have the energy to do anything about
it, save to frown. At twenty minutes, they couldn't even
flex their facial muscles enough for that. Were he to give
each of them a blaster, neither could summon the
strength to raise it and shoot him.

Kaird moved to the human. "Can you speak?"

"Y-y-y . . . yesssss," Bogan managed, his voice a
dragged-out slur. "Wh-wh-whaaat . . . ?"

"I'll keep it short and simple. I've drugged you. I want
the codes to the admiral's personal ship—access, security, operational, everything. The drug I gave you is not
fatal; however, if you don't give me the codes, or if you
give me false ones, I will kill you and your friend. Do you
understand?"

"Y-y-yesss . . ."

"Good." Kaird produced a recorder from his pocket.
He knew that the man's slurs wouldn't matter—the security codes were not vox-specific, so anybody could make
them work. "Give me the codes. Take your time, identify
each one clearly. If they work, you and your girlfriend
will have a pleasant evening watching the Strag match,
and by noon tomorrow, you'll be able to move well
enough to call for help.

"If any of the codes fails, however . . ." Kaird removed
a small thermal detonator from his pocket. Used to trigger a larger bomb, a unit this size, if it went off in this
room, would shred everything in it, paint the walls with

blood and vaporized flesh, and then knock down the walls. All in about a thousandth of a second.

He held it so the man could see it clearly. "Do you recognize this?"

"Y-y-y—"

"Good," Kaird said, cutting him off. "I have a transmitter for the detonator that has a range of two hundred kilometers." He produced a small device, held it up, then pocketed it again. "If, as I leave in the stolen ship—yes, I am stealing it—anything awry happens with the codes you give me, and I mean *any*thing at all—then I will trigger this." He stood, moved to the holoprojector, and set the thermal bomb on top of the device.

Bogan had begun sweating, which was good.

"Now, I know you're a pilot and thus a brave fellow, Bogan, and probably not afraid to die yourself," he said. "But your Twi'lek Strag mate here is an innocent noncombatant. You wouldn't want her to be turned into bloody paste now, would you?"

"N-no . . ."

"Well, then, we're in accord. The codes?"

After Bogan had spoken the words and numbers aloud—a long and slow process—"Mont Shomu" took several of the couch cushions and used them to prop the boneless couple up and against each other, so that they were looking at the holoproj. He wiped the sweat from Bogan's face. "Enjoy the match. I've set the projector to repeat, so you won't get bored—at least, not for the first dozen or so times." Kaird bowed slightly, then exited.

He could have killed them outright, of course, and there were many in his profession who would have done so without a second thought. Nor would it have bothered him particularly to do so; he had sent more than his share of people back to the Cosmic Egg in his time, so two more would hardly affect the total very much. But there were reasons not to kill them. First off, nobody had paid him to do so; second, it wasn't necessary. The two were out of commission, inside a locked kiosk, and by the time anybody missed them, Kaird would be long gone. They had no idea he was a Nediji, and the fat human they had met would be recycled synthflesh in a few minutes. He'd made sure there were no currents leading to his nest.

He grinned inside his disguise. Actually, the thermal detonator was a trainer—mechanically and electrically identical to a live grenade, but without an explosive charge, and thus harmless. The "transmitter" he had waved at Bogan was a personal featherette groomer. As far as Kaird knew, there weren't any handheld transmitters that size with a range anywhere near two hundred klicks. More importantly, if the codes didn't work and he was somehow captured, he certainly didn't want to be brought back to answer charges of intentional murder. They'd jam him into the brig for stealing a ship, of course, but that wasn't a death-sentence crime, even for stealing an admiral's rig during a war. Eventually, Black Sun would send somebody to find out what had happened to him, and they would get him released. A wartime tribunal that found him guilty of murder, on the other hand, would have him cooked and recycled long before Black Sun even began to wonder where he was.

In addition, there was the matter of that former Med-Star admiral he had taken out, the Sakiyan Tarnisse Bleyd, and it wouldn't do at all for them to be prying into his brain and discover that. But even in war, there were rules, and brain scans were not supposed to happen without proper authorizations. If it did come to that, it would be better to shut himself down than talk, Kaird knew, since he'd be dead either way, and doing it himself would be quick and painless—which was not at all how it would be if Black Sun was unhappy and involved.

The best plan was, of course, to not get caught.

Kaird headed for a 'fresher to lose the last of the heavy human suits. And good riddance. Mont Shomu, like Hunandin the Kubaz, had served him well, but he was quite happy not to have to wear the heavy disguise again. He wondered how humans who really did carry that much extra fatty tissue functioned. As far as Kaird was concerned, he'd rather be plucked and roasted over a slow fire.

Jos was as angry as he could ever remember being. He saw the man before him almost as if there were a red haze in front of his eyes. He said, through gritted teeth, "Were you not my great-uncle and my commanding officer, I'd knock you on your butt!"

"In your place, I expect I would feel the same way."

They were in the admiral's office on MedStar, and they were alone, but Jos somehow suspected that if he started smashing Erel's face in, somebody might come to see what the noise was about. Several somebodies, in fact, all of them military security, large, humorless, and armed.

Not that it mattered. The way he felt right now, no one and nothing could stop him if he wanted to slug his long-lost uncle.

"How *dare* you interfere between us this way? What gives you the right?

"I only wanted to spare you grief."

"Spare me *grief*? By driving off the woman I love? Sorry, Doctor, but I don't quite see the medical indication there. Tolk is the cure for so much of what bothers me, hurts me, scares me, that I cannot *begin* to explain it to you!" Jos paced up and down, seething, for a moment. "I still can't believe she listened to you!"

"That she did this is a measure of her love and regard for you, Jos."

"How do you figure that?"

"She doesn't want to see you ostracized from your family and friends."

"Because you painted for her such a grim and ugly picture of what it would be like. You made it sound like we'd be looked at as the scum of the entire galaxy."

"I admit that I did."

Jos had to consciously unclench his hands. He took a deep breath, let it out, took another. *Easy*, he told himself. Smashing the admiral's nose might be very satisfying, but it would also be a bad move, no matter how much the man deserved it. *He's a doctor*, Jos reminded himself. *He was doing what he thought best*. But it was still hard. He wanted to deck the old man. A lot.

Even so, his anger was not quite at nova intensity anymore. Jos took another deep breath and said, "Well, Uncle, if my family is not willing to accept the woman I love, then they're family in name only, and I'm better off without them."

Kersos shook his head, a gesture of infinite weariness. "I thought so, too. I've been down this path, Jos."

"But you are not me. I might have lived to regret it— though I doubt it—but even if I did, it would have been *my* choice. I should get to make it."

"It isn't that easy, son. You speak of cultural mores that have been around for thousands of years. There is much tradition to justify them."

"And sixty or eighty years from now, much of that culture and tradition, including the prohibitions against ensters and eksters, will be gone." Jos paused, struggling to gather his anger back in. He could explain this to his uncle. He was smart and articulate; if he could explain a complicated procedure to a nervous patient, he could surely couch this in understandable terms.

"Listen," he said. "You were far ahead of your time, and I'm still ahead of it. But my children and their children will not have to deal with such mindless mopek."

Uncle Erel shook his head. "I find this difficult to believe. Are you able to foresee the future?"

Jos shook his head, sighed. "I can see the *present*, Uncle." He paused again. "It's been a long while since you were on the homeworld. Have you ever heard the term *Hustru fönster*?"

His uncle shook his head. "It sounds like Hoodish."

"Close. It's Vulanish, a similar obscure dialect from the Great Southern Reaches. I believe the last native speakers of the language on our world passed away fifty years ago. Anyway, *Hustru fönster* means 'the wife in the window.' It's a term that's come into usage in the last few years, and not one spoken in polite gatherings."

His great-uncle looked puzzled.

Jos continued. "Suppose we have a young man of good family who finds himself drawn to an ekster girl. Okay, so, everyone winks and nods and glances away while he gives in to his wild urges and gets his drive tubes scoured. It's not condoned, but it's permitted, as long as he comes back to the fold.

"But more and more of late, the good sons, and the good daughters, as well, are going offworld and finding eksters with whom they wish to continue relationships. Yes, custom forbids it, but those with sufficient means have found a way around custom.

"The good son or daughter comes home and takes an

enster spouse. But this is a wife or husband who enters into the marriage for reasons of commerce or position only. The newlyweds hire a housekeeper or a gardener or cook who just happens to be an ekster—you can see where I'm going with this."

His uncle said nothing.

"Technically," Jos continued, "there's not even a prohibition against that kind of arrangement. And so everyone's happy. No scandal, no shame, and if the 'housekeeper' becomes pregnant through an unknown liaison, why, her child could be raised by her employers almost as if it's one of their own—such is their care and concern for a valued employee. Perhaps even adopted legally, since more and more of these enster marriages seem to be turning out barren.

"And, of course, if the child of a good wife resembles the gardener, or the issue of the maid looks like her employer, well, that can only be a coincidence."

His uncle shook his head. "This is being practiced on the homeworld?"

"Widely and more frequently all the time."

Erel looked as if he'd bitten into something sour. "Well. There's your answer, then."

"No, sir, it is not!" Jos replied. His tone grew hot again, but this time he didn't throttle back. "I will *not* subject my spouse to such a practice—living a lie that fools no one, just to maintain an archaic and anachronistic practice that no longer serves any purpose. I would take Tolk to myself as wife everlasting, and any who find that unacceptable can open their hatches and sniff vacuum, for all I care."

"Your family—"

"*Tolk* is my family! She ranks first and foremost. Everyone else from now on comes in second. I love her. I cannot see any life without her. And if I have to crawl across an obsidian razor field on my hands and knees to convince her of this, I *will*."

The older man smiled.

"Something amusing?" Jos felt his anger surge hotter. He was going to hit the man, great-uncle, commanding officer, or not—!

"I made that same speech to my brother, long before you were born." He stood. "Congratulations, nephew. I will support your choice in any way that I can."

Jos blinked, feeling like he'd been whiplashed by one of those hard banks against vacuum he'd seen fighter pilots pull. "What?"

"To go against thousands of years of custom is not a task for the weak. If Tolk meant anything less to you, you'd ultimately regret it. As you say, you might anyway—but at least you're starting from a position of strength."

Jos leaned across the desk and looked the older man in the eye. "At the moment, Uncle, thanks to your meddling, I'm starting from *nowhere*. Tolk is going to transfer to another Rimsoo. She isn't talking to me now. Somehow I don't see things getting better with a thousand klicks of water between us."

"Son, nobody in the Republic Expeditionary Medical Force goes anywhere on this planet without my leave. If the woman you love is worth giving up everything else you have to be with, then you have something that's worth doing. I'll correct my mistake. She'll be around."

"But—*how*? The damage has already been done. How can you—?"

"By letting Tolk watch the recording of this conversation," Admiral Kersos said. "She was willing to give you up because she loves you. If she sees and hears how much you love her, it *will* make a difference."

Jos sat down, feeling like he'd just climbed a skyhook. Could Uncle Erel rectify his mistake? Or was it already too late?

"Don't worry, Jos. What I break, I fix."

And for the first time in days, Jos felt a sense of hope stirring in him.

33

Den Dhur sat by himself in the cantina and brooded.

He had finished drafting his piece on the mutating bota, and, all modesty aside, he considered it one of his best efforts. He'd managed to tie some being-interest angles into it, by examining the potential ways in which various species would be affected by the loss of the miracle adaptogenic, using a number of case studies verified via the HoloNet. In addition, he'd worked in a hard-hitting bit on the irony of fighting a war for a plant that then mutates and makes said war pointless.

All in all, it was the kind of journalism that garnered notices. His byline on something like it could very well put him back on the radar again, land him an assignment someplace less . . . exciting than Drongar. Or, if he did indeed return to Sullust and take Eyar up on her offer, it would be a great story to go out on.

There was only one problem. Upon reflection, he didn't see how he could file it.

Once it became common knowledge that the bota was useless, Den foresaw two things happening. The second thing would be the cessation of hostilities and eventual evacuation of Drongar, since there would be nothing else on this simmering dungball to fight over. Which was just fine with him.

The first thing, however, would be a no-holds-barred final battle between the Separatists and the Republic over the last viable patches of the plant. Since bota grew pretty much only in this one area of Southern Tanlassa—about a thousand square klicks—the fighting would be concentrated all around them. The fifteen Rimsoos charged with the duties of caring for the wounded and, in the cases of Rimsoo Seven and a few others, of harvesting bota, as well, would be overrun by enemy troops. Battle droids, droidekas, mercenaries of all kinds, and just about anyone else with dreams of quick wealth would come howling over the barricades like a swarm of swamp shoats. It wouldn't be pretty.

He'd realized from the moment he'd heard the rumor that such was going to happen. Still, the story would break anyway, sooner or later—why shouldn't he be the one to reap the benefits?

But he knew the answer to that, much as he hated to admit it. Somehow, during his sojourn here, he'd become infected with a germ more deadly than any bug to be found in Drongar's pestilential ecosystem: a conscience.

Den could get the story out secretly, he knew that. But he would be at least partially responsible for a shipload of bantha poodoo falling on the people he'd come to consider his friends.

Den sighed gustily, dewflaps fluttering in vexation. Whether the leak came from him or someone else, the calamity was certain to come eventually. And when it did it would be the sort of thing best viewed from a few parsecs away. Which meant he should be finding a bunk on an outbound vessel. Soon. Which is why the thought of accompanying I-Five on his journey to Coruscant was quite appealing. It would be easy to connect from there to Sullust or just about anywhere else.

Den was still undecided on the whole retirement issue. In fact, compared to him, a two-headed Troig was a paragon of single-mindedness. Chuck it all and become the patriarch of Eyar's warren-clan? Or hurl himself back into the job he'd done all his adult life? There were still good stories to uncover, after all.

On the other hand, Eyar was a most lovely and desirable fem . . .

He would have to decide soon. I-Five was leaving on his mission for Barriss Offee. There would be no problem with Den going along—he was a noncom, a civilian, free to come and go as much as was practical. They could reach the Core worlds in forty-eight standard hours, maybe less.

There was no reason for him to stay, unless it was to risk almost certain death by remaining to report on the last chaotic hours. And, as he'd pointed out more than once to just about anyone who'd listen, he was no hero.

But something about going, about leaving people like Jos, and Barriss, and Tolk, Klo, Uli . . . it just didn't go down easily.

How had things gotten this bad? That he suddenly had all these people to care about?

As one of The Silent, getting up to MedStar was easy. Religious and meditative orders—particularly ones that had beneficial effects on the ill and wounded—were usually given preferential treatment. Once on board and checked in properly, Kaird took his travel case and proceeded directly to the main bay. Since The Silent didn't speak, he handed the guard a stat flimsi with his request, flashed his false identichip, and was allowed to proceed. Ostensibly, the departing Silent was going to stow his luggage on a military transport that was leaving for the

Core worlds in another day or so. There would be a guard there, too, but since the guard wasn't expecting company—at least, not company like Kaird in his disguise—the robed figure of The Silent passing by would mean nothing.

The admiral's ship was berthed away from the other shuttles and transports, which wasn't surprising. One had to approach it down a long and private corridor.

There wasn't a guard posted at the bay, because there was no perceived need for one: without the codes, you couldn't get into the ship, or operate it, or bypass Flight Control, or get past the picket ships, and the only people who had the codes were the official pilots, so—why worry?

Kaird moved slowly, with the preoccupation of someone meditating constantly on weighty matters. He knew that there was a dead zone ahead, right where the corridor turned—he'd found it while studying the MedStar's plans, for which he had paid dearly—and there were no cams covering the spot. It was a small area, only a few meters by a few meters, but that was all he needed.

When Kaird reached the spot, he looked around, didn't see anyone, and quickly shucked his robe. Underneath, he wore one of Bogan's uniforms and a simple human skin mask. The mask was generic—it looked like a human, and wouldn't fool anybody up close into thinking he was the real Bogan, but it should if viewed by a surveillance cam at a distance. The only thing that might be remarked on was the filtration mask he had to wear, which had been hollowed to accommodate his beaklike mouth. His other human disguise had been fleshy enough to disguise its three-centimeter jut; Bogan, however, was an exomorph, and so Kaird had had to be a bit more creative. Still, such masks were common sights aboard Med-

Star, especially in the wake of the explosion, since trace amounts of dust and possibly toxic particles lingered in the ship's atmosphere.

The last hundred meters was the most dangerous part of his trip. If anybody happened to pass him in the final steps, he would have to kill them fast and run for it. He didn't expect to meet anybody, however, and as he reached the ship's lock, he began a sigh of relief.

"Hey, is that you, Bogan?" somebody yelled from behind.

An icy shard of fear stabbed Kaird, killing the relief stillborn. He took a quick breath, and turned just enough to allow a glimpse of the mask. He waved at the speaker, who was thirty meters away. Then he quickly entered the access code on the keypad.

"Don't hit the walls on your way out!" the speaker called, ending in a laugh.

Kaird made a hand gesture of questionable taste, and the voice laughed again, louder.

The hatch unsealed and opened. Kaird moved hurriedly up the steps. Once inside the ship, he dropped the case of bota and hurried to the cockpit area. He punched in the security codes, powered up the mains, and began the launch sequence checks.

Flight Control came on the comm: "A-one, this is Flight Control; we show you powering up. That you, Lieutenant Bogan?"

Here was another tricky part, but one that Kaird had planned no less carefully than the rest. He could imitate Bogan's voice—humans were easy, with their limited vocal cord system—but doing a mask good enough to fool somebody looking at you on a ship's holocam was problematic at best. On Coruscant, with a face-mold and a good skin artist to do the hair and coloring—and a few hours of makeup time—it would be no problem, but here in the wilds Kaird didn't have that option, and they would want to see his face. Bogan's face, rather.

He quickly loaded a chip and tapped a control. The image of the human pilot, wearing the air mask, appeared on the comm's monitor, fuzzing in and out.

"Yeah, it's me," Kaird said in Bogan's voice. "I—kark! The cam's messing up." With that, he cut the transmitter off. It had only been on a couple of seconds, just long enough so Flight Control could glimpse a human face. That, along with Bogan's voice, should be enough to convince them that it was who they thought it was.

"You're just gonna have to imagine my handsome face, Flight."

The controller chuckled; a human female, Kaird realized. "I've seen nerf herders who were more handsome. In fact, I've seen *nerfs* who were." The voice grew more serious. "What are you doing, Bogan? We don't show any flight plans for the admiral today."

"I need practice time," Kaird replied as Bogan, "if I want to fly commercial liners after I get out of the navy. I'll only be gone a couple hours. A few loops, a couple of rolls, I get to log it, everybody's happy."

"And the admiral doesn't mind?"

"He said he wasn't going anywhere. I think he was headed for the soak tubs after I saw him, but you can call him and clear it, if you want."

"Get the admiral out of a soak tub? Yeah, right. Give me the airlock codes."

Kaird grinned his raptor's grin and rattled off the code.

"Check," Flight replied. "Cleared to vacuum chamber."

The doors between the pressurized chamber and the airlock opened. A slight breeze stirred bits of trash as Kaird rolled the ship into the gigantic lock. The massive doors shut behind him, a warning siren hooted, and a red light flashed. The comm's autovox said, "Warning, warning— hold depressurizing. All unprotected personnel must clear the chamber immediately. Warning, warning—"

The voxbox repeated its alert drone until the siren stopped and the red light went out. After another moment the outer doors opened, revealing the blackness of space, with its pinpricks of distant stars.

"A-one, give me your launch codes."

Kaird complied.

"A-one, you are cleared for launch. Try not to hit the walls on the way out."

Kaird grinned again, and reached for the controls. The ship began to ease out of the lock. He was leaving Drongar, by the Cosmic Egg, and bearing valuable gifts for his masters—gifts that would soon free him, and let him go home at long last. What could be better?

34

There wasn't much to pack—Den's years as a field correspondent had taught him how to live lightly. It wasn't down to the point where all he needed was his dewflap brush, but it was pretty close. His multiclimate clothes were all compressible fabrics, his voxwriter not much bigger than his thumb. Two pieces of luggage, both small, were all he needed. Load it up, move it out. He'd done it a thousand times. At least.

The announcer chimed.

"Come in."

The entry panel slid open, revealing I-Five.

"Just the droid I was looking for," Den said.

I-Five's left photoreceptor made the droid equivalent of a raised eyebrow. He looked around. "You seem to be packed and ready for departure—though it's somewhat difficult to tell, given the general . . . ambience."

Den grinned. "I'm not the best housekeeper on this planet," he admitted. "Probably not on most of the known planets. Or, I expect, the unknown ones."

"Oh, it's not *that* bad," the droid said. "Give me thirty minutes and a flamethrower attachment, and—"

"You know, there's still one more transport lifting soon, with the last of the entertainers. I'm sure a droid who does stand-up would be high on their list of needs."

"No doubt. And, as it happens, I will be on the next shuttle after that."

Den nodded. He'd expected as much. "You have your mission from Barriss, then?"

"Yes. Information—eyes-only, very hush-hush—and a vial that I must also deliver." I-Five extended a hand. "I came to say good-bye."

Den did not take the droid's hand. "No need. I'm coming with you."

Another subtle shift of luminosity, this one registering surprise. "Indeed? To what do I owe this honor?"

"To the fact that, very soon, this place will be overrun with Separatist droids, mercs, and anything else they've got that's smart enough to move and shoot at the same time." Den explained briefly about the bota mutation, and what the likely outcome would be once this became common knowledge.

"The mutation comes as no surprise," I-Five said. "This entire planet is one huge transgenic experiment. Given all the cross-pollination of the spores and the undifferentiated potential of the local DNA, I'm only surprised it remained stable for this long."

"Well, *stability* is a word that won't be bandied about too much in the next few days. Which is why I'm headed back to Coruscant." Den shrugged. "I thought maybe we could travel together."

"I have no objection. Though I doubt most of the other droids will speak to me if I'm accompanied by an organic."

"Y'know, you might want to prune back that prickly side of your programming just a little. Otherwise, someone's likely to do it for you—with a vibroknife. Very few people like a smart-mouthed droid."

"As you might imagine, you're by no means the first

person to tell me this. However, I find it adds a bit of piquancy to an otherwise bland existence. And I can take care of myself, thank you."

Den looked at his chrono. "Just about nine hours before the shuttle lifts. Any plans for the interim?"

"It would seem appropriate for me to spend it in the operating theater, aiding Jos and the others. That was, after all, my primary assignment."

"Myself, I have another destination in mind. But even though we'll be spending our last hours here in two separate locations, there is one thing that both places have in common," Den said with a grin.

"Alcohol." The droid paused. "Are you planning to tell anybody about your knowledge of the bota mutation?"

Den regarded I-Five. No doubt about it, he was as sharp as a lightsaber, this one. "Officially—no. And if I put fire gnats into any ears among the staff, that wouldn't do much good, since they aren't in a position to do anything about it except worry."

"I sense an unspoken addendum."

"Yeah, well, some of the card players and I have gotten friendly, and I'm thinking maybe I don't want them to be caught from behind."

"But if, as you say, they can't affect the situation, why say anything?"

Den shrugged. "Wouldn't you want to know?"

"Of course. The more data one has, the better equipped one is to function."

"There you go." Den started for the door. "I'm going to have a drink or six, then tell my friends the news. See you at the pad."

35

Barriss tried her communicator again. Whatever conditions had blocked her attempts to establish a connection with the Jedi Temple had been constant for days, and she didn't want to get her hopes up too high. She remembered something Jos had said one night while playing sabacc, quoting a homily he had gotten in a restaurant once: "Minimize expectations to avoid being disappointed."

There's a realistic philosophy, she thought.

Then, perhaps because she wasn't expecting it, her comm went through. The holoproj flowered at one-sixth scale, and Barriss found herself looking at the image of Master Luminara Unduli. She felt a surge of joy at the sight.

"Master!"

"Who else? You did call me, didn't you?"

Barriss grinned, anticipating the moment of sharing this great and terrible secret. Astonishing how mental and spiritual burdens could be made lighter by dividing them up, just as physical loads could be.

"Yes." Abruptly, Barriss felt as if her mind was too full and jumbled to speak. She hesitated. She had to sort it out, had to make sure she was presenting it properly. This secret had the potential to affect the entire galaxy, after all . . .

Before she could speak, Luminara said, "Barriss, what is the situation there? Are you all right?"

"Oh, sorry. I'm just trying to figure out where to begin. There's, uh, there's a lot going on here."

"Pick a starting point." Was that the slightest hint of asperity in her Master's voice, or merely a glitch in the transmission? The latter, she hoped. "You can go forward or back from there," Master Unduli continued.

Barriss took a deep breath. "Very well. I've discovered something remarkable about the bota . . ."

Quickly she laid out her experiences, telling her Master the story, trying to keep it coherent. Trying also to convey, not just what had happened, but also how she had felt, the sense of total *connection* to the Force, the wonder of it all.

Master Unduli listened without interrupting. Now and then she would nod encouragingly, but she remained silent, not prompting Barriss whenever the latter paused to collect her thoughts.

"—and that's pretty much all there is to tell," Barriss finished. "Well, except that a protocol droid called I-Five will likely show up there eventually with an encoded message covering what I've just said. I was worried that something might happen to keep me from passing this along, I've been unable to reach you via comlink, and I-Five needed a reason to get to Coruscant anyway, so we joined forces. He's a most unusual droid, and he has a connection to the Temple—he once belonged to the father of one of our Padawans. You may find him useful." She realized that she was babbling somewhat, and stopped.

Master Unduli stood quietly for another moment. Then she said, "You feel certain that what you experienced was not some kind of . . . illusion?"

"It was no illusion, Master," Barriss said. "It was a joining with the Force more powerful than I could ever imagine possible. It was *real*. Of that, I am as sure as I am of speaking to you now." *More so*, she wanted to add, but didn't.

Her Master nodded. "An extraordinary event." After a moment, she added, "Master Yoda and several others on the Council mentioned recently that they sensed—not a disturbance, exactly, more like a *surge*—in the Force. Perhaps this is the explanation."

Barriss waited a moment, but the other woman remained silently preoccupied. At last the Padawan said, "I feel great danger for these people, Master. As I told you, the 'accident' aboard the MedStar was no accident. Whoever is responsible will strike again, and I also feel—no, I *know*—that, using this new connection, I can prevent it. I have not the least doubt of that. The power is staggering. Even now, I feel the echoes of it reverberating within me."

"Why have you not already used it toward this end, then?" Master Unduli asked.

"Because I'm not qualified—I don't have the experience or the wisdom to make this kind of decision, or to take this kind of action." Barriss spread her hands. "Master, what should I do?"

The small hologram of her Master stood silent for a moment. Her expression, given the image's size and resolution, was hard to fathom. Then she said, "This is not an easy question to answer, Barriss. You are there, I am here, and I cannot know your situation as you know it. But, taking that into account, I think that you should—"

The hologram wavered, blinked, and scan lines ran up it in a pulsing wave. Master Unduli's voice warbled, cutting in and out: "—try—find—know the truth, because—" Then the image vanished and the voice stopped.

No! Barriss wanted to scream. *Come back!*

She tapped the controls on the unit, her movements just short of frantic, but it was no use. The connection was sundered. Gone.

Gone.

Barriss ran her fingers through her hair distractedly. The weight of responsibility she had thought she was about to have lifted, or at least partitioned, settled down on her again, even heavier than before.

What was she supposed to do? Had any Padawan ever been given such a thorny problem to solve?

There was but one bright spot, and that one wasn't as bright as all that—at least the Jedi now knew the situation with regard to the bota. Whatever happened here on Drongar, they would be able to consider and make a decision, backed by the wisest and most adept of the Jedi Council. That didn't make her personal choice any easier, of course, but it was something.

And, she reminded herself, *eventually I-Five will get there with the full story, and the vial full of extract. Surely I have fulfilled whatever my obligation is regarding the Council's knowledge of this. It isn't just on me anymore.*

But the weight she felt seemed no less. Indeed, before it had seemed like a yoke of wood; now, like one of stone.

She wondered how much longer she could stand beneath it.

36

Once he had cleared the last of the picket ships, Kaird felt a definite sense of relief. Yes, he was a professional, and facing death was ever a part of his life. He wasn't afraid of the return to the Egg. Sooner or later, all must make that journey, and he had put the trip off many times more than most. Still, being in deep space and about to make the jump to lightspeed meant that he had once again survived, and feeling a certain pride in so doing was permissible.

He was going back to Coruscant, bearing an extremely valuable gift for his chosen flock. There was a sense of accomplishment in that, as well. He had made the best of a bad situation, had managed to salvage something out of what had initially seemed to be complete disaster. Truly, it was as the old saying put it: there was no carrion so bad but that it offered some scavenger sustenance.

With the ship on automatic pilot, Kaird refreshed himself, ate a meal of synthesized bool grubs, and went through a short series of martial exercises. Feeling less stale with his muscles warm and his breath deepened, he went back to the entry lock in which he had left the faux case with its precious cargo. He would rather have it where he could see it, even though he was alone on the ship. The fewer things left to chance, the fewer things that could go wrong.

The case was where he had left it. It was heavy—not so much that he couldn't lift and haul it, but enough so that the set of wheels on it was useful. Kaird rolled it back toward the control cabin.

The ship boasted a series of pressure doors down the main corridor. In the event of a hull breach, these doors would quickly and automatically seal to maintain integrity in the separate compartments. Each had a slightly raised threshold to better effect an airtight seal. The ridges were only a couple of centimeters high, but he had to remember to step over them to avoid tripping when the A-Grav field was on. Kaird did this almost unconsciously after years of space travel. Luggage makers were well aware of these threshold obstacles, and thus standard luggage wheels were of a flexible compound that would roll over the pressure door lips with ease.

Not so the wheels of the fake case. Kaird didn't know where his former partners in crime had found these wheels, but they were definitely made of harder stuff, for when he hit the first threshold, the case stopped with a jolt, and one of the wheels broke.

Kaird shook his head. He'd have to carry it after all.

He lifted the case—and both the wheel and its axle fell off, taking with them a fist-sized chunk of carbonite that dropped onto the deck with a *clunk!*

Something metallic glinted from the edge of the broken case.

Kaird stared at it. A sudden jolt of hormones raced through his system, erecting his featherettes in atavistic fear, fluffing them to make him look larger to any predator that might be considering him prey. The fact that there was nothing even remotely resembling a predator within the several thousand cubic kilometers of empty

space surrounding him did nothing to allay his instinc-
tive fear.

There was not supposed to be any metal inside the
carbonite.

Bota was fragile. Even when packed into compressed
bricks, it would rot eventually, which was of course why
the contraband was transported in carbonite—the
carbon-freezing process suspended nearly all organic
molecular action. Bota did not become really stable until
further processing made it into an injectable or tablet
form. In the compressed-brick form normally used for
shipping, anything packed along with it might cause unwanted chemical reactions. Great pains were taken at
this stage to make sure the product was shipped as pure
as possible, and he had insisted similar care be taken by
the black marketeers.

So why was he staring at something made of metal
within the carbonite block?

His featherettes began to smooth as Kaird took several
deep, calming breaths, making sure his exhalations were
a second or two longer than the inhalations, so as to flush
carbon dioxide from his system. It worked; he felt his
pulse rate starting to slow as his anxiety level dropped.

He considered the possibilities. First possibility: something was inside the carbonite with the bota.

Second: something was inside the carbonite *instead* of
the bota . . .

The assault ship had an onboard medical unit, and it
included a diagnoster. Kaird carefully lifted the case in
both arms and made his way to the autodoc. In the course
of his profession, he had, on occasion, needed to use
such devices to attend to injuries, either his or those of his
comrades. He was no expert, but the machines had been

designed to be used by those with minimal medical training, and they came equipped with simple instructions.

This model had an axial image resonator built into it.

Kaird carefully put the case onto the diagnoster's table. He called up the instructions for the device on the computer, scanned them, and found the maximum settings. He touched the proper controls.

A clear, hoop-shaped transparisteel radiation shield lowered over the case. There came a power hum. It was but the work of a moment for the medical device to produce an image of what was within, and what the scanner showed was not bricks of compressed bota.

What it showed was a bomb.

Kaird studied the image that floated in the air over the computer with a practiced eye. He saw four thermal detonators linked in series with a timer—more than enough to vaporize the carbonite and everything between them and the ship's hull if they went off together. Maybe even powerful enough to blow the ship itself apart. It was the corner of one of the detonators that had showed where the carbonite had chipped away next to the wheel and axle. Since carbonite did little to suspend electronic or mechanical processes, there was every reason to expect that it would go off as planned.

Thula and Squa Tront had betrayed him. They had taken the bota for themselves and given him a death sentence instead. And he had paid them well to do it!

Luck was a funny thing. Had he chosen to carry the case instead of rolling it—and had it not been for that poorly made wheel, and the hatch lip that broke it, then the bomb would almost certainly have been sitting right next to him in the control cabin when it went off.

It had been a bold move. Had it worked, the pair

would have been very rich, and nobody anywhere would be the wiser.

It might still *work, if you just keep standing there staring at it like a sunstruck fledgling—!*

Kaird lifted the case and headed briskly for the nearest airlock. He did not know when the timer was set to detonate the device. He could feel himself beginning to sweat as he deposited the case in the lock, stepped back to the other side of the hatch, turned off the A-Grav in the airlock and slapped the cycle button.

The winds were at Kaird's back this time. The rush of air from the depressurized lock carried the bomb away from the ship, into vacuum. He returned to the cabin, and in a few seconds he had accelerated enough to leave the case safely behind. It might not go off for hours, days even—

The soundless flare was picked up by his rear array less than two minutes after jettisoning the bomb. The readout showed a yield of half a kiloton. The bomb would have turned him and the ship into a cloud of incandescent plasma.

Kaird leaned back in the seat. He had made a mistake, a large one, and it could easily have cost him his life. He had succumbed to hubris. He had assumed that Thula and Squa Tront were smart enough to realize that crossing him would be foolish; that he would hunt them down and make them pay in blood, no matter how long it took, no matter how far they fled. Black Sun had eyes and ears everywhere, and sooner or later, he *would* find them.

What he hadn't counted on was the pair having the nerve to attempt to assassinate an assassin. They were low-rent, small-time criminals, with no history of violence. He hadn't guessed that they'd had it in them, and that had very nearly been a fatal mistake. It was always better to overestimate a potential enemy's strength than to underestimate it. If one was prepared for the worst, the least was easy to manage.

What really stuck in his craw was that he had very nearly proven them right in their estimation of him. He had been lucky, and as everyone knew, there were times when luck was better than skill. He accepted this.

The loss of the bota was not in itself a fatal error, since his vigo would never know it had been on the table. Kaird could twirl it so that the story would not reflect too badly upon him: yes, he had discovered that the plant had mutated, but, unfortunately, by the time he'd found that out, the military had clamped down hard, and there was no way to collect any. The vigos would be disappointed, but it was part of the business, and in the end Kaird was too valuable a tool to punish for a misfortune not of his causing. There was always another way to make money.

Nobody would ever know that he had erred, save Kaird himself and two others.

What it meant, he realized grimly, was that he was still in thrall to Black Sun. Being given leave to retire by a grateful and enriched master was also no longer on the table, and one did not just walk away from Kaird's kind of work without permission.

There was nothing to be done about that part.

Kaird clenched a fist, looked at it as if it already held the two scoundrels' fates. He hoped Thula and Squa Tront enjoyed their riches fully, for whatever time was left to them. That time would not be nearly as long as they thought, and their end would be most unpleasant.

Most unpleasant.

Kaird fed the coordinates into the nav computer, then

activated the hyperdrive. The ship lurched as its gravity field flickered, the starfield in the forward viewport blue-shifted into long spectral streaks, the engines screamed, and he was gone.

37

Colonel D'Arc Vaetes, as head of Rimsoo Seven, was the highest-ranking military officer close to hand. Barriss went to see him during a lull in the surgeries. It had been suprisingly quiet the last day or two. Was it, she wondered, the calm before a storm?

She could have, even as a Padawan, asked for and probably gotten an audience with the new admiral on Med-Star, but there was a long-standing protocol when dealing with the armed services, and Barriss had seen how it worked often enough to know it was smarter to try the chain of command first. The Republic military was many things, but *flexible* was not the first word that came to mind when one thought of dealing with the army or navy. There was the right way, the wrong way, and the military way . . .

"What can I do for you, Padawan Offee?"

"This base is in danger, Colonel," she said.

The colonel smiled. "Really? A Rimsoo in an active theater of war in danger? Imagine that."

"No, sir. I mean it is in more danger than usual—whatever level 'usual' might be."

Vaetes was a first-class surgeon, a career officer, and nobody's fool. His smile vanished, and he turned his full attention to her. "Please explain."

"I believe that the person responsible for the explosion of the bota shuttle some time back is the same person responsible for the attack on MedStar, and that this person is about to become instrumental in an action that will put everybody here at risk. And not just this Rimsoo."

"The shuttle investigation was closed some time ago," Vaetes said. "It was determined that Filba the Hutt was a spy, and the one responsible for the sabotage. That was the conclusion of Colonel Doil, the officer in charge of the investigation."

"I don't believe that's so. Or, at least, it's not the whole story."

"All right. Then who is responsible? And what is he or she about to do that puts us at risk?"

Barriss sighed. "I don't know exactly who yet. Nor exactly how it will happen."

Vaetes looked at her. "How do you know what you do know, then? Intuition?"

"I learned it through the Force. It's hard to explain to someone who has not felt it, but it is far more than intuition."

She could hardly tell him that her connection with the Force had been augmented by using a drug—and one that she wasn't supposed to have access to, at that. Any credibility she might have would evaporate fast if she went down that path. Vaetes was a military man, pragmatic in the extreme, and a surgeon. It had been her experience with most surgeons that, as far as they were concerned, if a problem couldn't be excised with a scalpel, it didn't exist.

Vaetes said, "Padawan Offee, I know that the Force is a big part of your organization's . . . operational method, but . . ." He shrugged. "What am I going to tell the admiral to justify any action? And given the, uh, lack of specific information, even if he agreed to trust you on this, what exactly are we supposed to *do*?"

Barriss felt a sense of frustration envelop her. What could she say? He was right. And if she couldn't convince Vaetes—a man who knew her and, she felt, liked her— what were her chances of convincing somebody who didn't know her at all? It did sound all too vague.

"Colonel, would it be possible for you to contact Coruscant? My comm unit can't seem to hold a sustainable connection."

He shook his head. "It's supposed to be a military secret, Padawan Offee, but at the moment, we can't call home, either. Some kind of subetheric disturbance, jamming long-range communications. Our comm-techs can't seem to get a grip on it."

Barriss nodded. She had hoped that if the military could talk to the Jedi Council, they might vouch for her, at least enough to justify an alert. But that apparently wasn't going to happen.

"Listen," he said, "I tell you what—I'll talk to the commander of the troop unit attached here, tell him we heard something from an enemy patient who died that something is up, and that he should ramp up his patrols. I'm afraid that's the best I can do unless you can give us something solid we can check out."

Something was better than nothing. "Thank you, sir."

As she left his office, she saw Jos Vandar walking away from the landing pad. It was cloudy, probably going to rain again soon, but Jos's aura was lighter, his energy higher, than she'd felt it in a long time. Certainly lighter than her own at the moment.

She moved to intersect his path.

"Jos. How are you?"

He grinned at her. "Better than I've been in a while, I think. I hope, anyway. I'll find out soon enough."

"I'm glad to hear that."

He looked at her. "What's bothering you?"

She was surprised at his question. "What makes you think something is bothering me?"

"You do—your body language, facial expression, general demeanor, all tell me you're distressed. What's up?"

It wouldn't hurt to tell him, and he already knew about her having access to the bota. Maybe another mind working on the problem would help. At this point, any help she could get, she would take.

She explained as they walked, telling him about her Force experience, the bota, and her certainty about the approaching danger. Almost without realizing it, by the time she finished, they were at his kiosk.

"That's the story," she said.

"Sweet Sookie's maiden aunt," he said. "That's pretty amazing."

"Yes. I feel like the mythological seer Daranas, from Alderaan—I can see the future, but no one will believe my warnings."

Jos said, "Well, you've told Vaetes, and he's passing it along to the guys on the ground. If there is going to be a threat, that's probably where it'll come from. At least they have a heads-up."

She nodded.

"And you really think the bota is augmenting and focusing your connection with the Force?"

"Absolutely," she said. "I know that it offers great power. I believe that with that connection, I can somehow stop the danger. I might even be able to stop the war on this world completely."

He didn't say anything, but she could feel his doubt through the Force. "You think it's some kind of hallucination, don't you?"

"I didn't say that."

"But you believe it."

He rubbed at his face. "Barriss, you're a doctor. You know that medicine does different things to different people. Giving a Devaronian two cc's of plethyl nitrate will cure a lobar pneumonia and open up his congested lungs with virtually no side effects. Give that same dose to a human and it'll drop his blood pressure into the syncope zone. Give it to a Bothan—"

"And he'll be dead before he hits the floor," she finished. "Your point?"

"Bota is *the* wonder drug of our age—every time we turn around, we wonder at some new effect it has on some species that's never tried it before. Maybe it *does* connect you to the Force in some mysterious and powerful way. Or maybe you imagined it. A scientist would have to run an experiment with objective protocols to be sure which it was. We've both worked with patients in the throes of psychedelic delusion. They believe what they see and hear and feel, too."

She nodded. "Yes. But the Force is not something that easily pinned to an experimenter's board and dissected. I *know* that what I experienced was real."

"But you're the only one who does."

"Master Unduli said that several Council members felt the ripples of it."

"I hate to play Sith's advocate, but if I'm correctly understanding what you're telling me, there's no way to prove that what they felt was an echo of your experience. It's all just too subjective. Still, let's assume, for argument's sake, that it *is* all true—what are the risks of you having that much power? What might you do by accident?"

Barriss nodded. Yes. He'd put his finger squarely on the crux of the problem. Who was she to wield a weapon that was, perhaps, tantamount to a lightsaber that could shear through a planet? What might she do by accident? There was no telling. Even the wisest Jedi Master would have to approach such power with great caution and a lifetime of experience. And she was but a Padawan, lacking any great skill or wisdom.

So, the choice: take up the flaming torch offered her by the Force, use it to keep the pack of dire cats from her door—and, in doing so, run the risk of burning down her house.

One way or another, she would have to make a decision soon. Because one thing she was certain of: time was running out.

38

Jos was in the middle of shrapnel removal from a trooper. In this case, a bowel resection was necessary. The building's refrigeration units were offline again, so the air was clammy and hot, and the necessity of being up to his elbows in the trooper's pungent intestines wasn't helping things any. It was, Jos thought, as he wrestled yet another chunk of durasteel from the recumbent abdomen before him, mimn'yet surgery at its best. Or worst.

And yet, even as Jos worked away at his grisly task, he was smiling. His heart seemed to have its own tiny anti-grav unit; it threatened to burst free of his chest and float away, up to the bands of rust and verdigris girdling the sky. He felt like he could handle any case, repair any injury, no matter how extensive. The reason for this sense of joy was quite simple:

He and Tolk were back together again.

Uncle Erel had been as good as his word. He had fixed that which had been broken—in this case, Jos's heart.

He could feel her presence beside him, attentive and ready to hand him whatever surgical tool was needed. They hadn't had a chance to speak all that much before the incoming medlifters had driven them into the OT. Just a whispered apology, a quick kiss, and then they had to scrub and gown up.

That was all. But it was more than enough.

He finished the resection. The trooper was stabilized and gurneyed off, making room for another, this one's chest raddled with dried blood.

"Y'know what?" Jos said to the room in general. "I think this galaxy would be a whole lot nicer and more pleasant place to live if we could all just *stop killing one another*. Who's with me on this?"

A few chuckles and a couple of faux cheers were the response.

"You're a visionary," I-Five told him.

"Float it past Palpatine, see what he thinks," Uli suggested.

Yes, it was gallows humor, but at least it was humor. There had been other smiles in the OT, if only for a moment.

Jos and Tolk grinned at each other through their masks. Jos felt six meters tall and invulnerable. He was back with the woman he loved. That was all he needed—he knew he could handle anything thrown at him now.

Something smashed into the force-dome and exploded.

Outside, the rain had stopped, and Barriss waded through puddles from the OT to her practice spot. She had allowed herself to feel fear, worry, and she knew that only a calm mind could allow her to regain her mental balance.

With the lightsaber in hand, she danced. She put everything else out of her thoughts, shut it all out, and focused entirely on her moves. *Trust the Force.*

After a few minutes, she was sweaty, but doing something she had not been able to do of late—she was not thinking, only *doing*.

Her spirit calmed. The Force was there. Not the boundless power she had felt before, but the familiar, comfortable beacon in the darkness, the presence that had been with her since she'd been a child. An old friend with hand outstretched, offering what Barriss sorely needed:

Peace.

And with that peace came a clarity. Not forged of durasteel, not announced by the clarion shouts of trumpets, as it had been when she'd been tossed in the tumultuous current of the Force, but rather a still, quiet confidence: she could do this. She could do what she needed to do.

Barriss switched the lightsaber off and hung it at her belt.

These people had become part of her responsibility. She had the tools to protect them, she knew, even without the bota. She was a Jedi. Maybe still only a Padawan, but she still had abilities most people did not.

There was a spy in the camp, of that she was sure. Who was it? If she could puzzle out him or her, or it, she could likely find out what the coming danger was.

She had been here on Drongar long enough, and her use of the Force was certainly developed sufficiently that she could eliminate some people as suspects. She was a healer, and that gave her a connection to others that even Jedi more senior than her, who were not healers, sometimes did not have. She had been in close proximity with many of the medical staff, and their essences—their thoughts and feelings—were apparent to one with her training.

There were too many people in this Rimsoo for her to personally speak to them all and use the Force to try to read them. But she could eliminate some here by common sense: the spy, whoever it was, wouldn't be a trooper, was unlikely to be a droid, and had to be somebody in a position wherein he or she could access valuable information. Somebody in authority.

And here in Rimsoo Seven, that meant it was very probably somebody she knew.

Barriss started toward her kiosk. She did not know who the spy was, but perhaps, by the process of elimination, she could determine who it wasn't.

First, it had to be somebody who had been in place here before she had arrived on this planet, because suspicious actions had already happened. Certainly the explosion of the bota transport had taken some time to arrange.

So that immediately removed Uli from the pool, since he had arrived only recently.

Jos? No. She had been with him long enough to know it wasn't in him to be a murderer.

Zan was dead, and his heart had been too pure in any event.

Colonel Vaetes? He was in a position to gather intelligence, better than anyone else here, perhaps, but—no. He had no thoughtshield, and she sensed no great malice in him.

Who did that leave? Den Dhur? The reporter posed as a cynic, but clearly was not; nor did Barriss feel he was evil enough to kill people.

So. Of the people that Barriss had contact with, who would be in a position to gather the most useful information? Who could coldly murder people with whom he— or she—worked?

Nobody she had touched via the Force was capable of that. These were doctors, nurses, medical techs—all of them people dedicated to saving lives. She had felt that imperative strongly within each of them, and the Force didn't lie.

Wait. It was true that the Force didn't lie—but it didn't always reveal everything, either. There were two people here whom she knew, but could not scan deeper than the surface: Tolk le Trene, the Lorrdian, who could read a face like a child's textbook, but who kept a tight cover over her own thoughts and emotions; and Klo Merit, the Equani minder, who also had, by dint of assiduous training, a thoughtshield that protected his thoughts and feelings, hiding them behind his smile.

Tolk was a lieutenant, a nurse, but it wasn't impossible for her to gain access to privileged intelligence, especially given her face-reading abilities. Merit, as a minder, was well positioned to do so.

But how could it be either of them? Tolk and Jos were in love; Barriss could see that in their every gesture and glance toward each other. Could somebody who could love another like that be capable of wholesale murder?

Yes indeed, if history was to be believed. You could love your sister and still kill your brother. It happened all the time.

Still, Barriss did not want to believe this of Tolk. If she were a spy, that would mean there would be at least one more death on her conscience—for the revelation of her perfidy would surely kill Jos. If not immediately, eventually. He would never recover from such a wound.

And Merit? The minder who healed psychic injuries, who soothed anguish and psychological pain day in and day out? How could *he* possibly be the one?

Both candidates seemed impossible. And yet, as Barriss considered it with all the calmness and dispassion at her beck, it seemed more and more likely to be one or the other.

She suddenly recalled another fact—both Tolk and Merit had been on the MedStar when the explosion had occurred. Tolk had come back changed. She had withdrawn from Jos. That now seemed to be on the mend, but—what did it mean? Had Tolk been genuinely traumatized by the disaster? Or was she wracked with guilt?

Merit had not spoken of his feelings about the sabotage, that she was aware of—certainly not at the sabacc games. As far as she'd been able to tell, the big Equani had maintained the same, somewhat bland and professional concern for his patients after his trip upstairs that he had before. But did this indicate the callousness of a professional killer, or simply the ability to disconnect and so avoid burnout, which was a constant threat to a minder?

At this point, she had no proof that would convict either of them.

There would be records—if anybody else in this Rimsoo had been on the orbiting ship when the sabotage had taken place, they'd have to be included on the suspect list. But if not . . . ?

Tolk? Or Merit?

The more Barriss thought about it, the more it seemed to her that the secret agent *had* to be one or the other. Nothing else made sense. Any killer with a mind open to her touch would have been like a black lamp among all these healing folk. She couldn't have missed it.

There was, she knew, an immediate way for her to find the truth. She stopped walking toward her kiosk, turned, and headed for the OT. A simple, direct way. Often these were the best—

A flash of light flared overhead, followed almost instantly by a loud *boom!* Barriss looked up and saw the heat-wash of an exploding artillery round splashing against the force-dome.

They were under attack!

She ran for the operating theater.

* * *

Den ran out of the cantina, drink still in hand, and cleared the building just as another mortar shell impacted on the force-dome above, filling the air with eye-smiting light and noise.

He grimaced. It looked like he wouldn't have to tell anybody about the bota going roots-up after all. It seemed pretty obvious that word had gotten out.

A small unit of troopers double-timed along the dome's inner perimeter, heading for the exit, along with a couple of small vehicles hauling spare ammunition and armor. Outside the dome, larger forces had also begun to gather.

Den stood and sipped his Bantha Blaster thoughtfully. "Looks like my flight's going to be delayed," he murmured.

In the OT, as the echoes of the latest explosion slowly died, Jos said, "I'm getting *really* tired of this mopak." He looked up at the roof and yelled, "Hey! We're a medical unit—we don't have anything worth blowing up in here!"

Another explosion came, but it didn't seem to affect the OT much. A few bedpans rattled, and the bacta tanks sloshed.

"I don't think they heard you," I-Five said.

He saw Tolk smile through her mask. It felt like sunlight. He didn't want anything to happen to her, but if *he* died now, he'd do so a happy man.

He glanced up, and saw Den Dhur's face outside the viewing window of the OT's door. The little reporter must be standing on a chair or something.

Den raised a glass full of something greenish and offered Jos a silent toast, then drank.

Jos nodded at him, then turned back to his work. He

was almost done with this patient. Best to get him patched up, then try to figure out what was going on.

Barriss reached the OT. She saw Den standing on a table in front of the viewport, and moved to him. It wouldn't hurt to double-check what she thought she already knew.

"Den, I need you to do something for me."

"Name it."

"Open your thoughts to me."

He frowned. "Why?"

"Please."

"All right. But if you see anything embarrassing, it's your own fault."

She extended the Force toward him . . .

This was a person who had risked his life to save Zan Yant's musical instrument, a selfless act of heroism he continued to deny. She felt his mind—sharp, agile, bright. There were dark areas in it as well, regrets and loss, but nothing as dark as murder.

"Thank you," she said.

Another explosion rumbled over them. Den looked up, then back at her. "Two-hundred-millimeter mortar. They can throw those at us until the local sun burns out—won't dent the shield. But when they crank up the charged particle spitters and the gigawatt lasers, then we'll be in trouble. And they'll crank 'em. They're just pounding us now to get our attention, soften us up." He paused, finished his drink, and threw the glass at the nearest wall. It was made of something tough—it bounced, but didn't break.

"Why do you say that?" she asked. "Do you know why this is happening?"

"I've got a pretty good idea. Not that it matters now.

The bota is going bad, losing its potency. The new plants are morphing into something that won't work as a drug anymore. I'm guessing the Separatists figured it out and are coming to try to collect whatever's left."

"How do you know this?"

"It's my job to know things, Barriss. I was gonna tell the gang before I-Five and I shipped out, but . . ." He shrugged and looked up. "Someday you'll tell me what that *open your mind* stuff was all about, right?"

"Someday," she promised. *If we survive.* Then she moved down the hall and into the OT scrub room, slipped into a surgical gown, but didn't bother to scrub or glove. She wouldn't be getting that close to a patient.

She headed for Jos and Tolk.

"Barriss. What's twirlin'?" Jos said. She could hear the change in his voice. Whatever his demons, they had been greatly diminished.

"I need to speak to Tolk for a moment."

Tolk raised a quizzical eyebrow.

Barriss took a deep breath. Here was a risk. If Tolk was the spy, asking her to drop her thoughtshield would give away the fact that Barriss suspected. She might have a weapon, and if she was the spy, she wouldn't have any problems with using it. Barriss could protect herself—she could reach her lightsaber under her surgical gown through the slit on the side in a heartbeat—but it might put the others here at risk. A stray blaster bolt could hit anybody.

Another mortar round impacted upon the shield. Den was correct, the dome would shrug it off—assuming it didn't malfunction again—but it was nerve-wracking, to say the least. And there was no way to tell when the attacks would escalate.

The confrontation was a risk, but Barriss felt it was a

small one. And she knew she had to take it—life was not always about safe harbors. Sometimes you had to sail on stormy seas and risk the chance of sinking. There was no time to wait for a more opportune moment. Who knew what other vile plans the spy might have already put into play?

"Barriss?"

"Tolk, I need you to drop your thoughtshield and open yourself to me. It's important."

Tolk did not hesitate. "Okay."

With that single word, Barriss knew she already had her answer. The mind-probe merely confirmed it. What poured from Tolk was suffused with love for Jos Vandar and her own self-respect and pride in herself as a healer. It had nothing to do with espionage or sabotage.

That meant there was only one person left who was a reasonable suspect.

"Thank you, Tolk."

Tolk said, "And we're doing this . . . why?"

Barriss looked at her and Jos. Decided they deserved to know—Jos, especially.

She took a deep breath, and told them.

Klo Merit—also known as Column and Lens—looked around his office for the final time. The artillery rounds bursting more or less harmlessly against the protective force-dome were no threat, but once again nobody had bothered to let him know precisely when they would begin their real attack, and it was irritating in the extreme. He was a valuable resource to the Separatists—why did they continue to risk him so?

Well. He would take that up with them later. For now, he had a bribed driver standing by. He would sneak out in a supply vehicle and get away from the Rimsoo. Once he was out of range, he would get rid of the driver, then trigger his coded transponder. Any battle droid that came across him would recognize him as a friendly, not an enemy, and he could make his way back through the lines with no trouble. Hardly the same as having a parade thrown in his honor when he arrived, but that was a spy's lot. In quietly, out quietly, and if you did what you were supposed to do, nobody ever knew who you really were.

"Time to go," he said out loud. He had done what needed to be done, and while he had some regrets, the situation was what it was. He headed for the door, opened it—

And stopped in surprise. Jos Vandar stood before him, a blaster in his hand, pointed right at him.

39

The mortar rounds fell more often, and Den's comment about particle beam and laser weaponry was proving to be valid—even in the bright sunshine, the destructive rays of coherent energy were visible in the distance, reflecting off the dust particles and spores in the air. So far, none of them had passed close to the dome, but their luck wouldn't hold forever. As Barriss hurried to find Vaetes and report her suspicion—her certainty—of Merit's guilt, she noticed that a thunderstorm was heading their way. That was good—heavy rain interfered with tactical beam weapons, absorbing or deflecting much of their force. Probably didn't do battle droids any good to be hit by lightning, either. But as the sky darkened, the weaponry flashes seemed to be coming more and more frequently, mixed with those of the natural lightning.

War, in all its deadly aspects, was coming on swift feet.

The sense of impending doom was nearly palpable. It was too late now for the capture of the Separatist spy to do them much good, Barriss knew. He could be made to answer for his crimes—assuming any of the Republic forces survived to do that—but with the attack obviously in full swing, Merit wasn't Barriss's biggest worry. The survival of the camp was. Unless a miracle came to pass, the combined mortar and energy weapon attacks would pound them all into paste.

You can stop it.

It was an almost tangible voice in her head. She was carrying a popper of bota in her pocket. Just take it out, inject it into her arm, and in a few seconds she would have the ability to turn the tide of conflict, no question about it. She knew this. She couldn't say how it would manifest, exactly; probably it wouldn't be as simple as just waving her hands and watching all the attacking battle droids shut down and fall over. A pity they weren't controlled by a single orbiting broadcast power source, like the army the Trade Federation had fielded during the Battle of Naboo, but someone had wised up since then. Nevertheless, somewhere in the vast and omnipotent energies of the Force there was a way to stop them, and she could, with the bota's help, reach it.

She *knew* this. There was no doubt.

How would it feel to have that much power, to be able to stop a war? To go from being a Padawan to becoming the most powerful Jedi in the galaxy in a matter of moments—one who could use the Force in ways no one had ever been able to even comprehend, much less use, before? To direct vast energies, primal powers, like an active volcano channeling molten rock and hurling it in erupting fountains of lava? Nothing could stand before it. There was nothing in the galaxy that could resist the Force, if it could but be channeled properly, shaped and primed and driven by her will.

She reached into her pocket and gripped the injector.

Think of all the lives you can save.

Yes. That was what she did, wasn't it? That was her primary mission. She was a healer. She saved lives. Only this time, it would be on an enormously larger scale.

The storm drew close. Lightning flashed, thunder boomed, to join the sound of mortars exploding against the protective force-dome. It was true that Master Unduli or Master Yoda or Master Windu would be so much better suited to this task, but they weren't here. Barriss was the only Jedi in a hundred cubic parsecs, as far as she knew.

The moment had come. She had to choose—now.

Take the bota and save them all, or—

Don't take the bota, and know that countless beings—including some whom she had come to know as friends—would certainly die.

Barriss pulled the injector from her pocket. By now the environment had become virtually apocalyptic—the exploding mortars, thunder, and lightning were almost constant, and in addition lasers and particle beams were starting to strike the dome itself. One hit almost directly above her, and the resulting cascade of high-energy pulses along the dome's outer aspect was nearly blinding. Supposedly the field kept out gamma rays, alpha particles, and other deadly radiation, but for how much longer? Already she could feel her skin tingling in the ionized air, could taste the residual ozone.

The choice was simple enough, wasn't it? Why even hesitate? The gain here far outweighed the risks; the end more than justified the means. She had been to the heart of the Force already—how could it be wrong to go back now and seize it, use it for such a noble purpose? It would feel good, so good, it was *right* . . .

She cleared her left sleeve, held the injector in her right hand. She positioned it over the inside of her wrist. Another buzzing lance of energy—she couldn't tell if it was a laser or a particle beam—hit, and more fireworks resulted. Barriss touched the popper to her skin. She put her thumb on the firing stud—

And, as she was about to trigger it, a memory rose within her, a memory of Oa Park on Coruscant, of a lesson she had learned there, one that she had already applied here on Drongar, when facing the deadly fighter Phow Ji.

The memory of a conversation between her and her teacher about the dark side:

There may come a time when you experience this, Barriss. I hope not, but if ever it happens, you must recognize and resist it.

It will feel evil?

Oh, no. It will feel better than anything you have ever experienced, better than you would have thought anything could feel. It will feel empowering, fulfilling, satisfying. Worst of all, it will feel right. And therein lies the real danger.

Barriss Offee stood under stormy and violent skies, only the slightest pressure of her finger away from rejoining the Force in a way that had been more wonderful than anything she had ever felt, or had ever imagined anything could feel.

And in that moment—a heartbeat, an eon—she understood what her teacher had been trying to tell her that day in the park. To give in to the dark side was the path to ruination, to corruption worse even than death. Dead, you could not harm anyone. But alive, and with the dark side driving you, you could become a monster.

She remembered as well something she had told Uli a couple of weeks ago:

Those who embrace the dark side don't see themselves as evil. They believe that they are doing the right thing for the right reasons. The dark side warps their thinking, and they come to believe that the end justifies the means, no matter how awful those means might be.

Had her previous experience truly been of the dark side? No, she decided. As she had also told Uli, the Force did not choose sides. But to wield that kind of power, *no matter how noble the intent,* would almost certainly lead to ruination—if not today, then tomorrow, or the day after. Each time, the temptation to use it would become more compelling, the reasons for doing so more justifiable. She could feel the truth of that to her core. That kind of power could not help but be addicting. It would consume anyone who was less than absolutely pure, less than all-wise, less than wholly selfless. Barriss was by no means a bad person, she knew that. But she was not perfect, and such contact with the Force on a regular basis needed perfection to survive uncorrupted.

Did it make sense to have the powers of a god, without the wisdom of a god?

"Barriss?"

She had been so deep in her thoughts that she hadn't noticed Uli trotting toward her. Startled, she looked at him.

"You okay?" he called, through another crash of thunder.

She smiled. Carefully, she lifted the popper from her arm and put it back into her pocket. "Yes," she said. "Yes, actually, I am."

Another beam strike, another chromatic spill of ionization. Uli glanced up nervously. "Everybody is supposed to get inside. Use a dosimeter to make sure you're not getting cooked by backscatter radiation—they expect the dome to go soon. And you'd better pack—just the absolute essentials, one small bag per person. If the droid infantry gets through the troops, we'll have to move—

fast. Right now, word is that it's an even fight, but who knows which way it might go?"

"I understand. Thanks, Uli."

He nodded and hurried away into the gathering gloom. She turned to go as well, but something stopped her. In that moment, Barriss felt something new rise within her, a certainty as strong and real as her journey to the center of the Force had been: she was a Padawan no longer.

And the knowledge of *why* welled in her, equally unmistakable:

You truly became a Jedi Knight on the day when you realized that you already *were* one.

Standing there, amid the chaos and cacophony of the storm and the Separatist attack, Barriss Offee threw back her head and laughed.

40

Merit said, "Jos? What is it?"

He stared at the human blocking his way. The blaster in Jos's hand was dead still, as if the man's arm had been carved from wood.

"You killed Zan," Jos said, tonelessly.

Fear blossomed in Merit's gut, a flower made of frozen nitrogen. He let none of it show. Somehow, Jos had become suspicious. It didn't mean his cover had been blown—were that the case, he would most likely be facing Colonel Vaetes and several military secs instead of the Rimsoo's chief surgeon. This wouldn't be the first time he'd had to talk his way out of a tight spot, and, unless his powers of empathy and persuasion had vanished completely, it wouldn't be the last.

His expression was mildly quizzical, his tone solicitous as he said, "No. Zan died when the Separatists attacked. The transport was hit by a stray round. You were there, Jos. So was I, remember?"

"I remember," Jos said. Another beam of focused energy struck the dome, and the resulting pyrotechnic display momentarily backlit him. It almost seemed as if he had come here from some other, higher plane, a demon bent on vengeance.

"I remember," he said again. "I remember also how

you showed me how to work through my grief, Klo. How your understanding, your ability to do your job so well helped me heal, helped me put it behind me. I owe you for that, Klo. Or I would—but, since you were involved in calling in the Separatist strike, I think that kinda zeros out any obligation on my part. Don't you?"

How could he know? He can't know. He suspects, but he can't know. I was too careful, I left nothing that would—

Forget about that now. Deal with the present problem. He could turn this around. He was, after all, an adept at emotional manipulation and control. Given time, he felt sure he could convince Jos that the man was wrong, that he had made a mistake.

Time, however, was growing short.

"You're under a lot of stress, Jos," Merit said. "I don't know where this delusion is coming from, but I think we should table any further discussion until we're both safely offworld."

Jos laughed, but Merit's empathic abilities sensed no humor. Instead he sensed rage, held in check by cold determination, like an ice cap plugging a volcanic vent.

"Sorry," Jos said. "That just struck me as funny—you thinking you're going anywhere." Thunder rumbled as if echoing his words.

Merit realized two things right then. One, that Jos Vandar wasn't operating on a hunch or suspicion. He *knew.* How didn't matter. And that led to realization number two: if he didn't kill Jos, Jos was going to kill him. He'd played too many card games with the man to believe otherwise.

He sighed. He genuinely liked Jos, liked and admired the man. He had wished to leave Drongar without having to kill again. But wishes seldom came true.

Hidden in his right coat sleeve was a small hold-out blaster.

"Speaking of stress," Jos said, "I have to think you're under a fair amount as well. How could you do it, Klo? What could possibly cause you to betray your friends? Your clients? To kill people you knew, people you worked with, ate with, played *cards* with?"

Shoot him. Shoot him and go. Every second you waste talking with him puts you in greater peril.

"Have you ever heard of the Nharl system?" Merit asked.

"No."

"There were five planets around the local sun. One of them was my homeworld, Equanus. You know why you don't see many Equani in the galaxy, Jos? It's because there are only a handful of us left—a few hundred, maybe a thousand at most—of a species that once numbered almost a billion. And do you know *why* there are so few of us now? It's because only those of us who were offworld two years, six months, and three days ago survived."

Merit had never actually told anybody the story before. He knew he was being foolish, if not downright suicidal. But it was as if a psychic dam had burst. He wasn't sure he could stop the words now, even if he wanted to do so.

"Two years, six months, and three days ago, a solar flare burst from our sun that was over ten light-minutes long. A huge, unheard-of, massive eruption, far greater than any the star had produced in ten million years. A flare that jetted forth with such power and force that Equanus was *cooked*. The atmosphere and oceans boiled away in minutes; the land was turned into a burned-out cinder. Our scientists saw it coming, but too late. It arrived before anybody had the slightest hope of escaping it. They knew it was coming, and they knew there was nothing that could be done. Every comm line on the planet was jammed with people trying to say their final good-byes to each other."

He could sense that Jos was listening; could feel the slightest mitigation of the rage within him, saw that the impact of so many deaths had rocked him. Of course it would—he was a doctor. Merit honestly didn't care, at that moment, just as he didn't care if he was killed by friendly fire in the next minute. All that mattered was the telling.

"All of the Equani, nearly a billion people—our art, our civilization, our hopes, dreams, *everything*—all scorched to ash in a few moments, Jos. Gone. Dead. Forever."

Jos said slowly, "I'm . . . sorry. But what has that got to do with this?" He gestured with the blaster, to encompass the situation, and Merit could have killed him easily right then, could have blown open his chest with the hidden hold-out weapon.

He didn't.

"What has it to do with this? Very simple: that solar flare was not a natural disaster, Doctor. The Republic, the glorious, wonderful, benign Galactic Republic's military leaders were testing a new weapon. A planet buster, a superweapon for some kind of ultimate battle station being developed. They fired it into our sun, and they miscalculated. They had a base on our moon, the scientists and military who'd created this abomination. The flare got them, too. Small comfort to me and the few Equani who were offworld when our planet was murdered."

"I—I never heard about this."

"Of course not. It's not something the Republic's anxious for the galaxy to know. They kept it quiet, but I made it my business to find out.

"The Republic killed my species, Jos. Even if all the

surviving Equani could be gathered together, there's not enough of us left to repopulate another world. Yes, you can say that those who pulled the switch died, too, but what about those who sent them there? What about the bureaucrats who were responsible for allowing it? They continue to laugh, and love, and eat, and sleep—and *live*.

"You wanted to know why? *That's* why, Jos."

The hand holding the blaster lowered slightly, and for one instant Merit thought that maybe, just maybe, his former friend and patient would stand down. But then Jos's expression and stance firmed again. "I can't begin to understand how you must feel," he said. "But I know how I feel. Maybe the death of one being can't really compare with the death of a whole world. But loss is loss. Grief is grief. Do you think Zan's parents feel any less pain than you do?"

"They lost a son! I lost a *world*! Hundreds of millions of sons, daughters, mothers, fathers, Jos! You can't compare the two. It was a crime beyond measure."

Jos shook his head. "Whatever your reasons, whatever your pain—what you did is still wrong."

"Obviously, I see things differently." Merit spread his hands. His right arm was now aimed directly at Jos—all he had to do was flex his wrist. "So. What are you going to do, Jos? Shoot me?"

"I honestly don't want to, Klo, even after what you've done. But I can't let you leave. Barriss went to tell Vaetes. Security will come for you soon."

Merit shook his head. "But I won't be here, Jos."

"Yes, you will."

Only a few moments ago Merit had been sure that Jos would shoot him. But now, after hearing his story, the minder could sense that something had changed. The man's resolve was not quite as adamantine now. "You won't use that blaster, Jos. I know you. You're a doctor, a compassionate man. You save lives, you don't take them. I've seen you during times when you've been on your feet all day, completely exhausted, barely able to stay awake, just to save the life of one single clone. You can't do this. It's against everything you are."

Jos was not a blasterslinger. Merit knew he could kill the man before he realized what was happening. But he didn't need to. Jos wouldn't fire.

Merit started backing up toward the far door.

"Don't do it, Klo!"

Jos aimed the blaster at Klo.

"Don't do it, Klo!"

The big Equani kept going.

Jos remembered looking down at Zan, lying dead on the floor of the transport. Jos had been wounded himself, concussed, barely able to move. It had taken everything he had just to crawl across the deck to his friend's side.

Killing Merit wouldn't bring Zan back. Revenge wouldn't bring any of them back. And Klo was right: Jos was a life giver, not a life taker.

But if Klo got away, he would continue to work for the Separatists, continue to do harm to the Republic. How many others might die as a result of his hatred, of his need for vengeance? And no matter if that number was one or a thousand, if Jos allowed him to escape, those deaths would be his responsibility, too. Because he could have stopped Klo Merit. Right here. Right now.

"*Klo—!*"

Merit backed up another step. The rear door's proximity sensor registered his presence and opened the portal.

Jos took a deep breath, aimed the blaster—

And fired.

There was an explosion, a crushing clap of thunder, a blinding light. Pain seared into him. He cried out, felt himself falling . . .

41

The force-dome blew.

Ironically, it was a lightning bolt, rather than a beam, that finally overloaded the breakers. It was fortunate in a way, Den was to reflect later—though the bolt was powerful enough to stand everyone's hair, cilia, or sensory stalks on end, it wasn't accompanied by the really nasty stuff, like gamma rays. But thanks would have to come later, as well—at the moment Den was too busy cowering under a table in the cantina to think about much of anything except escape. The transports had been ferrying up patients for the past hour, and next in line, he knew, were civilian noncoms like himself. Then came the officers, and finally—assuming there were any left by then—the clone troops.

That order worked just fine for him. He intended to be the first in the noncom line.

I-Five was crouched beside him under the table. The droid's photoreceptors were dark; he'd elected to turn himself off when the play of elemental forces began to crest. While his shielding was usually sufficient to withstand electromagnetic pulses, why take a chance? He'd just gotten his memory back, and he didn't want to lose any of it again.

Den flicked the master switch on the back of I-Five's neck. "Time to go," he said.

"For you, maybe. The droids are scheduled to depart after the troops, if I recall correctly."

Den grabbed I-Five's hand and pulled him along toward the door. The cantina was just about deserted; the staff and tenders were already at the launch pads, waiting to board. He eyed several containers of vintage wines and liquor that he would love to bring along, but somehow he doubted they qualified as essentials.

"You're not a droid," Den said, as the two emerged from the building into the smoke-filled afternoon.

"I'm not?"

"Nope. You're a diplomatic envoy on a mission for the Jedi. Moves you right to the front of the line." A mortar blast less than a klick away showered them with dirt. "Assuming we reach the line," he added.

"Didn't we go through this already, a few months back?"

"Yeah. Except that last time they were just trying to move the front lines back so as to claim more bota. This time they want to wipe us out. They've got little left to lose."

Another explosion, this one entirely too close. There was little attempt being made to dismantle the camp this time, Den noticed; the worker droids were concentrating on saving supplies and whatever viable bota was left.

Den stumbled and nearly fell into a crater. Only I-Five's quick grab for his arm kept him upright.

"The pad's up ahead," the droid said. "Fifteen meters, no more."

Den tried to respond, but suddenly there was acrid smoke everywhere, filling his nostrils. He coughed, struggling for clean air, and finding none.

Abruptly, he felt himself being lifted. I-Five was carrying him, moving rapidly in long strides toward the launch pad. Den kept trying to breathe, and kept failing miserably.

He's carrying me a lot easier than I carried Zan's quetarra case, he thought. It was the last coherent thought he had for a while.

42

Look—he's coming around," Barriss's voice said. It sounded hollow, as if echoing from a well. Jos tried to open his eyes, but white light seared them.

"Zan," he croaked. "Don't do this. Don't die . . ."

But it was too late. Jos knew that, if he opened his eyes, he would see Zan's lifeless body lying there on the deck. He didn't want to see it, not again . . .

"Jos." He felt gentle hands on him. "Jos, it's Barriss. Everything's all right. Come on back to us."

Jos opened his eyes. The light wasn't so bad this time. He blinked and focused on Tolk, who grinned tearfully at him. "Where are we?"

"Sickbay One, on MedStar," she said.

Jos raised himself on one elbow. "Ow!" His head hurt. He touched the synthflesh bandage on his head. Uli pushed him gently back down. "Easy, hotshot. You're lucky to be alive. The roof came down on you. You've got another concussion."

"Merit," Jos whispered. "What happened? Is he—?"

"He's dead, Jos," Barriss said gently.

Jos saw Colonel Vaetes and Admiral Kersos standing behind Tolk and Barriss. He said, "Merit was trying to get away. I shot him."

Vaetes said, "You did the right thing, Jos."

"Yes," Uncle Erel added. "You stopped a dangerous enemy agent from escaping, at the risk of your own life.

"When Uli and Security and I got there, we found you unconscious, and Merit dead. He had a hold-out blaster up his sleeve, but he didn't get the chance to use it. Uli patched you up on the transport." He raised his right hand in a slow salute. "Well done, Captain." He lowered the salute and added, "I'm proud of you, nephew."

"I'm not sure . . ." Jos said.

"About what?"

"Whether I did it because I knew he was going to cause more death and grief, or . . ." He trailed off.

"Because of Zan?" Tolk said.

Jos nodded.

"It doesn't matter. He had to be stopped. You did it. You can work out the rest of it later. We'll have plenty of time."

It was true—he did it. He had killed another sentient being. Never mind why, never mind if there was good and proper reason for doing so. He, a doctor, had destroyed a life. Jos knew there would be some sleepless nights for him as a result of that.

But, as Tolk had pointed out, what else could he have done?

Jos started to shake his head in confusion, then groaned. "Easy," Uli said. "Give the glue a chance to set."

"And the Rimsoo? What happened?"

"Take a look." Den's voice came from nearby. The reporter and I-Five had just entered, and Den was pointing at a viewport. Tolk and Barriss carefully helped Jos to his feet.

The lower quadrant of the southern continent seemed to be on fire—thick clouds of smoke spread in the upper atmosphere, drifting out over the Kondrus Sea.

"Bye-bye, bota," Den murmured.

Vaetes said, "The Separatists are also on the run. We managed to save most of our troops."

"How?" Uli asked. "It looked like they were rolling right over us."

"That's how," Vaetes said, pointing to another port. Uli moved to it and looked out. "Whoa!"

Barriss looked through the port at the gigantic, wedge-shaped ship, bristling with weaponry, cruising slowly toward them. "That's a Republic Star Destroyer," she said. "*Venator*-class."

"The *Resolution*. Sent here to mop up and escort us back to the Core systems," the admiral said. "The Battle of Drongar is over. There's nothing left down there to fight for now. We came out of it with about two metric tons of bota, which our droids are sealing in carbonite as fast as they can. No intel yet on how much the Separatists got."

"Given the intensity of their saturation bombing, I'd be surprised if they got much," Vaetes mused.

"I have to lie down now," Jos said. "I'm a little tired."

Barriss and Tolk eased him back down on the bed. It felt wonderful. He closed his eyes, and the various conversations around him merged into a faraway buzz, like the sounds of wingstingers and fire gnats on a hot Drongaran night . . .

Barriss listened to the various conversations around her with half an ear while she mused on the way things had turned out. Two metric tons of unspoiled bota seemed a small reward for all the coin paid in death and pain. She noticed Den watching her, a slight smile on his face, and smiled back.

I-Five moved over to her. "I assume my mission to Coruscant is no longer the priority it was," he said, "since you're returning there as well."

"True. But keep the vial of extract. It's still a good many parsecs from here to the Core, and much could happen."

I-Five hesitated. "As you can imagine, I'm not usually prone to saying this. But something impels me—"

"Intuition?" she interrupted, with a smile.

"Perhaps. In any case—may the Force be with you, Jedi Offee."

She nodded in acknowledgment, and put a hand on his shoulder. "Good luck in your quest, I-Five. May the Force be with you, as well."

He moved away, and she turned to look through the viewport once more. They were leaving orbit, she saw; already Drongar was receding, as the MedStar frigate, accompanied by the *Resolution,* moved away into interplanetary space.

Her assignment was over. In a couple of standard days, if all went well, she would once again stand before Master Unduli in the Jedi Temple—this time not as a Padawan, but as a full-fledged Jedi Knight. She wondered what new assignments, what new adventures, awaited her after that.

Whatever they might be, Barriss Offee knew that she would face them, secure in the protective embrace of the living Force.

"Well," Den said to I-Five, "looks like your trip to Coruscant won't be costing you that much after all."

"All it took was the destruction of half a planet. Expensive, if you ask me," the droid replied. "And what of you, Den Dhur? What's your destination?"

Den fluttered his dewflaps thoughtfully. "I really ought

to be on my way to Sullust. I have a very attractive fem, and her warren-clan, waiting there, you know. They think highly of me on the homeworld."

"So you've said—several times."

Den sighed. A life of patriarchal reverence and hushed esteem. It had been easy to be nostalgic about his home-world when he was sweating half his body weight away on Drongar. But now he remembered a major reason why he'd left in the first place: Sullust was *boring*.

"Then again, Eyar won't get there for a while yet. No hurry."

"One could make money in the Southern Underground on Coruscant, if one was, say, in need of a dowry," I-Five said. "And I wouldn't mind a partner to keep authorities from worrying over my ownership. Galling as I find such a subterfuge, it's sometimes necessary."

Den nodded. There were always easy marks to be found at the sabacc tables in places like the Outlander Club. No harm in making some creds while he thought about Eyar's offer some more . . .

He looked up at the droid. "I-Five," he said, "I think this could be the beginning of a profitable relationship."

EPILOGUE

Later, after the others had left the room, Jos Vondar and Tolk le Trene held each other and watched the starfield through the viewport as the ship left the Drongan system. "You're sure you want to do this?" she asked.

He nodded. "I'm sure. Are you?"

She grinned. "Where you go, I go. Just promise me that I don't have to be the cook or the maid."

"If it gets too tough, we won't stay," Jos said. "I won't make you live the life of a pariah. But I owe it to my family—and to you—to at least try."

A voice came from behind them. "You'll have one family member on your side, at least." Surprised, Jos turned to see Great-Uncle Erel smiling at them from the doorway.

"I've requested reassignment to Borellos Base on Corellia," he said. "If you can go back there and face this prejudice down, Jos, I can hardly do less."

Jos stared incredulously. "You're serious?"

"Absolutely. I've spent practically my entire life alone. Now that I've finally found some family, I'm not going to give it up."

Tolk hugged him. "Welcome home, then, Uncle Erel."

And, looking at the two of them, his betrothed and his uncle, Jos realized that, in one respect at least, all the fighting and hunting done on Drongar for the miracle drug of the age had been pointless. Because the real panacea for the troubles that plagued humanity or any other sentient species, organic, cybernetic, clone or otherwise, had already been discovered, millennia ago, back when sentients still peered suspiciously up at the stars. Call it the Force, call it love, call it what you will—Jos knew that it could be found, not in the swamps of a distant world, but in the unexplored reaches of the heart.

The comm crackled. A voice warned them to prepare for the jump to hyperspace. Jos took Tolk's hand as the ship's hyperdrive activated, and then they hurtled away from the Rim, toward the bright center of the galaxy.

As a civil war between the Republic and the Separatists rages across the galaxy, nowhere is the fighting more fierce than on the swamp world of Drongar. . . .

Star Wars® MedStar I: Battle Surgeons
A Clone Wars Novel
by Michael Reaves and Steve Perry

A surgeon who covers his despair with wisecracks; another who faces death and misery head on, venting his emotions through beautiful music. . . . A nurse with her heart in her work and her eye on a doctor . . . A Jedi Padawan on a healing mission without her Master. These are the core members of a tiny med unit serving the jungle world of Drongar, where battle rages over the control of a priceless native plant and an endless line of medlifters brings in the wounded and dying— mostly clone troopers, but also soldiers of all species.

While the healers work desperately to save lives, others plot secretly to profit from the war—either by dealing on the black market or by manipulating the events of the war itself. In the end, though, all will face individual tests, and only those of compassionate hearts and staunch spirits can hope to survive to fight another day.

Published by Del Rey Books
Available wherever books are sold

Emerging victorious from this volatile mission
means Anakin Skywalker may become
a full-fledged Jedi Knight.

But if he fails, so will the Republic. . . .

Star Wars®
Jedi Trial

A Clone Wars Novel
by David Sherman and Dan Cragg

Pors Tonith, ruthless minion of Count Dooku,
declares the fate of the Republic sealed. Left
unchallenged, this decisive strike could indeed
pave the way for the toppling of more Republic
worlds . . . and ultimate victory for the
Separatists.

But engaging the enemy throughout the
galaxy has already stretched Supreme
Chancellor Palpatine's armies to the limit.
There is no choice but to move against the
invading battle droids with only a small contingent of clone soldiers. Commanding them
will be Jedi Master Nejaa Halcyon and a skilled
young starfighter pilot Anakin Skywalker, a
promising young Jedi Padawan eager to be be
awarded the title of Jedi Knight.

Published by Del Rey Books
Available wherever books are sold

The original trilogy that started it all—an essential addition to your *Star Wars* library

THE *STAR WARS*® TRILOGY
by George Lucas, Donald F. Glut and James Kahn

More than twenty-five years after the groundbreaking movie *Star Wars: A New Hope* first hit the silver screen, *Star Wars* remains one of the most beloved sagas ever told. Together, the three original *Star Wars* movies—*A New Hope*, *The Empire Strikes Back*, and *Return of the Jedi*—told one epic: a heroic tale of innocence lost and wisdom gained, of downfall and redemption, of the neverending fight between the forces of good and evil. Read the story of the movies—all three in one trade paperback volume—and rediscover the wonder of the *Star Wars* universe.

Published by Del Rey Books
Available wherever books are sold